DEATH MARCH ⑫
TO THE
PARALLEL WORLD RHAPSODY

TAMA
A cat-eared girl.

POCHI
A dog-eared girl.

LIZA
A scalefolk girl.

LULU
Born in the Kuvork
Kingdom. She is Arisa's
older sister.

ARISA
A former princess of the Kuvork
Kingdom. She was Japanese in
her previous life.

NANA

An expressionless homunculus.

MIA

A taciturn elf who loves music.

SATOU

A twenty-nine-year-old programmer who has been transported to a parallel universe.

"Master, would it be all right if I used the Dragon Claw Spear as a backup weapon?"

"That's fine. Was it hard to use?"

"Not at all. It cut right through even the toughest of hides and channeled magic as well as before. It's just…

My weapon of choice is still the Magic Cricket Spear."

DEATH MARCH
TO THE
PARALLEL WORLD
RHAPSODY

12

★ ★ ★

HIRO AINANA
ILLUSTRATION BY SHRI

YEN
ON

NEW YORK

Death March to the Parallel World Rhapsody, Vol. 12
Hiro Ainana

Translation by Jenny McKeon
Cover art by shri

DEATH MARCH KARA HAJIMARU ISEKAI KYOSOKYOKU Vol. 12
© Hiro Ainana, shri 2017
First published in Japan in 2017 by KADOKAWA CORPORATION, Tokyo.
English translation rights arranged with KADOKAWA CORPORATION, Tokyo, through Tuttle-Mori Agency, Inc., Tokyo.

English translation © 2020 by Yen Press, LLC

Yen On
150 West 30th Street, 19th Floor
New York, NY 10001

Visit us at yenpress.com
facebook.com/yenpress
twitter.com/yenpress
yenpress.tumblr.com
instagram.com/yenpress

First Yen On Edition: October 2020

Yen On is an imprint of Yen Press, LLC.
The Yen On name and logo are trademarks of Yen Press, LLC.

Library of Congress Cataloging-in-Publication Data
Names: Ainana, Hiro, author. | Shri, illustrator. | McKeon, Jenny, translator.
Title: Death march to the parallel world rhapsody / Hiro Ainana ; illustrations by shri ; translation by Jenny McKeon.
Other titles: Desu machi kara hajimaru isekai kyosokyoku. English
Description: First Yen On edition. | New York, NY : Yen ON, 2017–
Identifiers: LCCN 2016050512 | ISBN 9780316504638 (v. 1 : pbk.) |
ISBN 9780316507974 (v. 2 : pbk.) | ISBN 9780316556088 (v. 3 : pbk.) |
ISBN 9780316556095 (v. 4 : pbk.) | ISBN 9780316556101 (v. 5 : pbk.) |
ISBN 9780316556125 (v. 6 : pbk.) | ISBN 9781975301552 (v. 7 : pbk.) |
ISBN 9781975301576 (v. 8 : pbk.) | ISBN 9781975301590 (v. 9 : pbk.) |
ISBN 9781975301613 (v. 10 : pbk.) | ISBN 9781975301637 (v. 11 : pbk.) |
ISBN 9781975301651 (v. 12 : pbk.)
Subjects: GSAFD: Fantasy fiction.
Classification: LCC PL867.5.I56 D413 2017 | DDC 895.6/36d—dc23
LC record available at https://lccn.loc.gov/2016050512

ISBNs: 978-1-9753-0165-1 (paperback)
978-1-9753-0166-8 (ebook)

1 3 5 7 9 10 8 6 4 2

LSC-C

Printed in the United States of America

CONTENTS

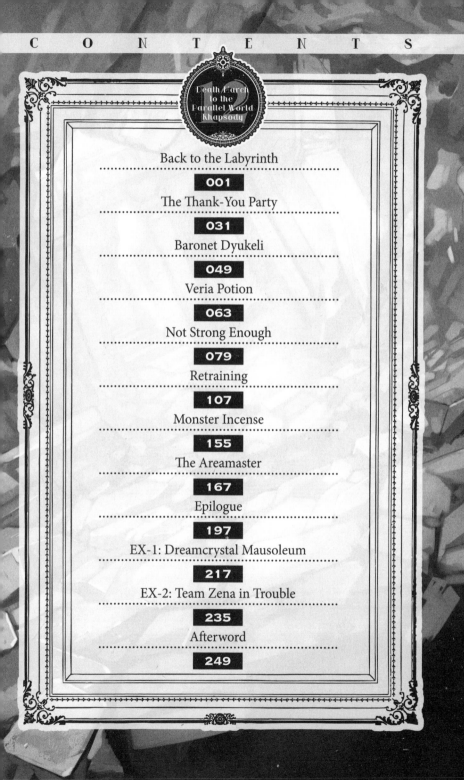

Back to the Labyrinth

001

The Thank-You Party

031

Baronet Dyukeli

049

Veria Potion

063

Not Strong Enough

079

Retraining

107

Monster Incense

155

The Areamaster

167

Epilogue

197

EX-1: Dreamcrystal Mausoleum

217

EX-2: Team Zena in Trouble

235

Afterword

249

Back to the Labyrinth

Satou here. No matter how careful you are about staying out of trouble, sometimes trouble has a way of finding you. It's not just about how you avoid it but how you recover from it with minimal damage, I think.

"Shoot, it's getting away! Lulu! Mia!"

Arisa pointed up at the fleeing moss crab bee, her lilac hair blowing in every direction.

She was wearing adorable equipment that made her look like a magical girl, but thanks to her mannerisms, she seemed more like a valiant little knight.

As the bee flew away, one of its legs suddenly snapped unnaturally and gushed green blood.

Arisa must have used Space Magic without a chant.

"I'll shoot it down!"

Decked out in battle-maid armor, Lulu readied her sniper-rifle-style Fireburst Gun and switched it into rapid-fire mode.

The glowing bullets that shot out of the long muzzle lit up the darkness of the labyrinth, the light reflecting off the crystal pillars that dotted the enormous chamber.

Lulu's long, straight black hair shone against the light, casting a glow on her beautiful features.

"*KWHAAAAAANYWEEEEE!*"

The moss crab bee created a shield with Ice Magic in an attempt to protect itself from the flaming bullets.

The shield managed to deflect a few of the shots, but it finally splintered apart with a light clattering noise, allowing the remaining bullets to rain over the bee's body.

Before long, its wings had suffered so many direct hits that its flight became unstable.

"■ ■ *High Wind* Kyoufuu."

Mia gripped her staff in both hands and held it aloft as she cast Spirit Magic.

A powerful wind similar in strength to the Wind Magic spell Air Hammer sent the struggling moss crab bee hurtling to the ground.

The blast blew Mia's light-green pigtails backward, revealing a glimpse of her slightly pointed ears—the telltale sign of an elf.

…And that wasn't all that the wind sent flying.

The High Wind spell also blew up the girls' skirts, putting their colorful pairs of underwear on full display.

Arisa struck a Marilyn Monroe pose and exclaimed "Oh nooo!" while peeping in my direction, but I decided to ignore her.

"You coward! Decide whether you're a bee or a hornet, I request!"

Shouting with her usual expressionless face was Nana the homunculus, a girl who appeared to be a busty blond beauty but was in reality less than a year old.

Her words were actually part of her "Taunt" skill, which made the moss crab bee spread its tattered wings and attempt to drag itself toward her.

"Wing Slasher…?"

With her short white hair, cat ears, and cat tail, Tama jumped in from the monster's blind spot and sliced up its wings with her twin short swords, both equipped with "Spellblade."

Then she charged the blades with magic to attack again.

"This is our chance, sir."

Pochi, who sported a brown bob, as well as dog ears and a tail, used the "Blink" skill to charge the moss crab bee from the front and attempt to cut off its head.

She was probably hoping to deliver the finishing blow.

Her Magic Sword, also equipped with "Spellblade," left a red line of light in the air as it swung.

"Pochi, watch out!"

My warning came too late. The dying bee flicked its remaining wing to quickly zip to one side and send Pochi flying.

Its charge also sent Tama tumbling to the ground as she attempted to attack it from behind.

From the corner of my eye, I saw Lulu rushing over to save Pochi.

"Let's finish this thing."

"Mm."

Arisa and Mia began chanting attack magic.

Normally they might use paralysis or some kind of binding spell to keep the enemy in place before attacking, but since this one was a lower level, they were planning to simply crush it as quickly as possible instead.

"'Blink'!"

Her crimson hair fluttering through the air, Liza of the orangescale tribe used the "Blink" skill to leap forward with "Spellblade" on her Magic Spear.

She closed in on the moss crab bee at top speed and drove her spear right into the center of its six compound eyes.

The glowing red light drew circles in the air.

"'Triple Helix Spear Attack'!"

The swirling red light around the Magic Spear formed a helix shape as it sliced through the bee's head.

The last remaining third of the monster's HP bar depleted immediately.

"KWHAAANYNYMYNYWE."

Finally, it let out a dying cry before the light left the moss crab bee's eyes, and its part-bee-part-hornet body fell lifelessly to the ground with a loud crash.

"Awww, man. Liza got the finishing blow again."

"Mrrr. Too bad."

Canceling their attack spells, Arisa and Mia shrugged and started using detection spells instead.

They were probably checking to see if any new monsters were approaching.

As Arisa mentioned, Liza's attacks had been standing out among the vanguard lately. Part of it was that she was the only one with anything resembling a finishing move, but I think it was also because her "Spellblade" had become more efficient than the other girls' as of late.

"Pochi seems to be all right."

Lulu, who had rushed over to check on Pochi after the bee's attack sent her flying, reported back with relief.

Pochi's head poked out from behind the wreckage of a broken

crystal. Even though I knew from my menu's information that she was fine, it was still a relief to see her looking safe.

"Don't let your guard dooown?"

Tama appeared at Pochi's side.

"Sorry to worry you, sir."

"You're bleeeeding?"

"This is nothing, sir."

She appeared to have cut herself on a crystal shard.

Tama used a magic potion she had on hand to heal her.

I should probably make them armor that would cover their entire body sometime soon, instead of light armor that left parts exposed.

"Master, should we break down the moss crab bee?"

"This one doesn't have any flowers, and we've got plenty of moss and crab meat, so we'll just store it as is."

"Yes, sir!"

I touched the giant bee monster's corpse to put it away in Storage.

The moss on the backs of moss crab bees was an ingredient commonly used in lesser stamina recovery potions, and the small flowers that occasionally bloomed in the moss could be used to make medicine to treat various illnesses.

The crab meat tended to be a little tough and bland, but it was popular with the kids because of its faint honey-like sweetness.

The monster's carapace was tough and sturdy, so it would likely make decent equipment. It wasn't as strong as the armor my party already had equipped, though; it really could be used only for making crab hot pot.

Incidentally, I'd heard that the wings were useful as a catalyst for Wind Magic.

The wings of the ones that used Ice Magic also possessed ice properties. If infused with magical energy, they would give off a decent bit of coolness, and if I made fans from these wings, they'd probably be ideal for cooling off in the summer.

"Satou."

Abruptly, Mia started clinging to my waist.

I looked down and saw a satisfied smile on her face.

"Went up."

She probably meant that she had leveled up.

Because Mia required about twice as much experience as the other girls to level up, progress took a little longer.

"Praise."

"Congratulations, Mia."

After I responded to her blunt request, the other kids all gathered around to congratulate her, too.

"That means we're all level thirty-eight." Arisa looked at me challengingly. "Perhaps we could finally fight an areamaster now?"

"Not yet. Maybe once you defeat their spawn."

Monsters with the Areamaster title were always at least level 50, so it was still too soon for the rest of my group to face one.

Their spawn tended to be around level 40. It'd be better to start there.

As I patted the impatient Arisa on the head, I looked around at the others.

"This seems like a good place to end this round of labyrinth exploration, I think."

"Awww, already?"

"Yeah, there aren't any enemies left in this area."

There were still some small fries with levels in the single digits, but they were too weak to be effective training fodder.

During this trip into the labyrinth, we had thoroughly overhunted section 6 as planned, so there weren't many powerful monsters left who might be useful experiencewise.

My kids had all worked very hard in this round of labyrinth exploration.

Before this time, we had been busy starting up an orphanage for the homeless kids in Labyrinth City, cleaning up the plunderer problem in the labyrinth, helping young women we had rescued from a fire downtown get back on their feet, and so on. In light of all that, we hadn't been in the labyrinth in quite a while.

I think they might have been motivated by the fact that they hadn't been able to keep up with the yellow intermediate demon we'd fought, as well as the plunderers outside the west guild who had been turned into demons.

Following that incident, we learned that the green-clad noble, Counselor Poputema, had actually been brainwashed by a green greater demon and that the incidents in Labyrinth City were part of this demon's plan to revive a demon lord. Although I guess I'd crushed those plans without even realizing it…

Then I'd destroyed one of the avatars the green greater demon left behind, mostly to vent my anger and to put a marker on the other one before letting him go free.

Prior to this round of labyrinth exploration, I'd noted that the avatar that had been in the northernmost city of the royal territory when I first marked it had passed through Zetts County and was now moving through Lessau County.

Seiryuu County was north of Lessau County, but the avatar's destination seemed to be Vistall Duchy to the northwest, so it looked like Zena and my other friends in Seiryuu City were safe for the time being.

"Okay, let's wrap things up with our usual treasure hunt."

Arisa's words brought me back to the present, and I opened my map.

Previously, we'd entrusted sniffing out treasure to Tama, but this time we had decided to start searching for loot all together after clearing out the monsters.

We learned in the rookie explorers' class that treasure chests were often hidden in the shadows of rocks, under piles of dust, beneath spiderwebs, and so on, so we prioritized those kinds of areas as we searched.

This seemed to do the trick, and we managed to find between one and three treasure chests per area.

None of them had anything too remarkable inside, but we sometimes found magical equipment, cursed armor, expired magic potions, and things like that.

"Sparklyyy…"

"It's a souvenir, sir!"

Tama and Pochi were picking crystals off the ground and putting them into their Fairy Packs.

"Master, I would be happy to collect more crystals if you wish," Liza offered.

"It's okay. I grabbed a really big one earlier."

I had collected around ten tons each of transparent and purple crystals, though the latter wasn't as popular because of its color. I picked up a few tons of the more sought-after aqua- and cyan-colored crystals as well.

None of these crystals was especially valuable, but I thought they could be useful in creating honest work for the people we'd rescued from the plunderers.

My idea was for them to use small fragments of the crystals to make talisman accessories by carving them with runes like Luck, Good Health, Romantic Success, Heroism, and so on. They would probably be popular with the citizens of Labyrinth City.

"Ah! I found one!"

"Nice one, Pochiii?"

I followed the sounds of Pochi's and Tama's voices until I found a huge hornet's nest in a hollow of the rock wall. What she had found wasn't a treasure chest but a moss crab bee nest.

The nest of the local areamaster, the queen forest cancer hornet, was only the size of a fortress, so this must be a relatively young hive.

Many of the queen hornet's body parts were quite valuable as materials, but the best acquisition was the wind pearl crystals I got from her eight pairs of wings.

Those were even better than the huge amounts of honey and wax I got from the colossal nest.

"Sweeeet?"

"So yummy, sir!"

Tama and Pochi scooped up drops of honey from the moss crab bee nest with their fingers and closed their eyes in bliss as they sampled it.

The flavor wasn't as rich as regular honey, but it was just as sweet. It would likely be useful for cooking and making sweet beverages.

"Looks like this batch hasn't fermented into mead."

About a third of the honey I got in the queen's nest was now mead.

We already had more crab-bee honey than we could possibly use up, but since Pochi seemed so proud of her find, I decided we could take this batch with us as well.

"L-look!"

"It's a treasure chest."

Once I stored away the hive, we found a golden treasure chest sitting in its place.

The bees must have built their home right on top of it.

"No traaaps?"

"That's unusual."

When my "Trap Detection" skill didn't find anything, either, I used "Spellblade" on my fingertip to sever the lock and open the chest.

"Looks like a booklet, a scroll, and a vial."

According to my AR, the vial contained a **Cure-All Potion**, and the recipe for it was on the scroll.

The booklet contained Earth Magic spells related to making golems.

I relayed this information to my party.

"Ooooh, that's a pretty good find, huh?"

"Yeah…"

…*Wait, huh?*

"What is it?"

"Looks like this cure-all recipe is missing half."

Maybe the other half was hidden in a different treasure chest. Either way, that was a pretty mean trick.

I already knew the elves' recipe, so I thought I would be able to fill in the blanks from there, but this recipe half wouldn't be much help on its own.

Maybe this was the beginning of a recipe-fragment-gathering quest or something.

"Too baaad?"

"So sad, sir."

"These things happen."

The golem-making spell collection and the vial of cure-all were treasures enough in their own right.

We continued our treasure hunt, stored the excess cores in the warehouse of our vacation home, and headed out to find maze frogs in section 8 to acquire some meat for the orphanage kids.

◆

"Is it very far?"

"It's around a two-hour walk."

"Geh!"

"Geeeh?"

"Geh-geh, sir."

Tama and Pochi imitated Arisa's groan.

"Arisa, don't make such strange noises," Lulu scolded her.

"Sowwyyyy."

"Sowwy…"

"Sorry, sir."

Tama and Pochi mimicked Arisa's apologetic pose, too. I guess they were just at the age of liking to play copycat.

"Mew?"

Just then, the pair's ears twitched.

"I hear fightiiing?"

"Lots of fighty noises, sir."

About five minutes after Tama and Pochi gave this warning, we arrived in a vast cavern where several large groups of explorers were locked in combat with monsters.

Despite the size of the cavern, it was tough to see what was in the distance thanks to a sea of weeds that grew to chest height and a curtain that hung from the cavern ceiling. The latter was made up of the dusty remains of the kind of spiderwebs we'd seen in various other caves and corridors.

"Hmm? They're fighting mantises, not frogs."

"This area is primarily bug-type monsters. The frogs only live in one corner."

The explorers were doing battle with mantis- and grasshopper-like monsters and had cut away patches of weeds to set up encampments.

There were several large groups of them, ranging from ten to twenty people, and all were led by garnet-badge explorers; the majority of the groups consisted of a few main members above level 20 and supporting members closer to level 10.

Most of them were warriors, but each group had a few healers or mages.

Mantis monster parts were worth a lot of money, which meant the bigger groups with better equipment were battling them.

We didn't want to get in the way, so we took a roundabout route that skirted the edges of the cavern.

"Sparklyyy?"

"It's shiny, sir."

Tama and Pochi pointed at a group of people wearing shiny silver armor.

According to my AR display, they were a party called **Silverlight**, which consisted solely of noblewomen.

Four heavily armored warriors served as the tanks, while the mid-guards in chain mail attacked from behind the tanks with spears and polearms.

"Master, aren't those girls the ones we rescued from the rampaging maze ants before?"

Two familiar-looking women were breaking down a previously defeated mantis behind the armored group.

"Oh yeah. The Lovely Wings."

Evidently, the garnet-badge expedition party they had mentioned joining last time I saw them in Labyrinth City was this Silverlight party.

As they were working, a level-5 maze hopper flew toward their group. "Danger."

"No need to worry, I declare," Nana reassured Mia, who'd turned around.

Two shield-bearing women who were guarding the group turned to fight the creature.

Seeing this, the girls who were breaking down the dead mantis reached for their weapons, too, but their armored supervisor stopped them and had them get back to work.

The disassembly team looked a little frustrated.

"That one shield girl kinda seems like a scrub, though."

One of the shield-bearing women was a veteran, but the one Arisa was pointing at was awkward and clumsy.

"I believe that is the same young woman we saw at the rookie explorers' class. It appears she has yet to grow used to battle in the labyrinth," Liza said, prompting me to remember her.

She was Sir Darrel's daughter. Gina, I think her name was.

"Hey, you lot! Unless you have business with Silverlight, keep moving!"

An armored lookout brandished her halberd at us and shouted threateningly.

Oh right. In the labyrinth, you had to be cautious, even of other explorer parties. I thought we'd be all right, since we were so far away from them, but I guess we put them on guard because we were just standing there and staring.

After apologizing, we left the cavern.

From what I could tell as we left, it seemed like all the parties kept some of their people on reserve instead of having their entire forces fight at once.

This was probably a measure against monsters or plunderers who might try to attack while the group was exhausted or any ill-mannered explorer parties who could try to steal their weakened prey.

Of course, I guess it might have just been in case of emergency or the appearance of more monsters, too.

◆

"I smell blood, sir!"

When we were about halfway through the main passage between

the site of Silverlight's fight and the next major cavern, we came upon a few corpses being eaten by monsters.

The monsters were flat, bug-like black creatures.

"Wait!"

As the rest of the group started to run over, Tama called out sharply.

She pointed at the archway, which was dripping with a dark-red liquid.

Blood.

A centipede-like monster dropped down from the shadows of the arch.

It was only level 15, but its head was the size of a pillow, and its body must have been fifteen feet long.

"I'll use Space Magic to check our surroundings... Be careful. There are still two more maze centipedes up on the ceiling."

As Arisa was using chant-less magic to investigate, the monster that had already dropped to the floor charged at us to attack.

"Centipede! Do not think that having more legs makes you more important, I declare!"

...I don't think the centipede actually thinks that.

Nana blocked the charging centipede with her shield.

The creature used its momentum to climb over the shield and try to attack Nana, but she pierced its head with her Magic Sword.

Then, as the creature stopped moving, Pochi's sword quickly cut through its joints.

"The monsters around here sure are weak," Arisa remarked.

As we watched, the electricity from Lulu's Thunder Rod rifle dropped the other two centipedes to the floor, and Liza quickly finished them off with her spear.

"Guard's dooown?"

Tama, the only one who hadn't joined the fight with the centipedes, struck down a demi-goblin assassin that was sneaking up on Arisa from behind.

"Geh! Th-thanks, Tama."

"Don't worry, be happy..."

Demi-goblin assassins use narrow passages to approach their targets from the shadows and often attack explorers from behind if they let their guard down.

With our random encounters taken care of, we went to deal with the monsters gathered around the corpses.

...*Ew.*

I knew that shape looked a little too familiar—it was a giant cockroach.

I definitely didn't want to battle that thing up close.

"Master, if you lure it away from the bodies, I can light it up."

"All right."

I used Remote Stun to catch the maze cockroach's attention and draw it toward us, and Arisa's Fire Ball burned it to a crisp.

I guess they were particularly weak to fire.

"Maybe these poor souls were fighting the cockroach when the centipedes dropped down on them?"

Arisa cast a mournful glance at the half-eaten remains while Liza recovered bronze badges and identifying locks of hair from the deceased.

"Affirmative. The children should look away, I advise."

The centipedes had dragged the wounded into hollows in the arch, so I went up with "Skyrunning" and brought the remaining bodies down to the ground. It looked like they had been a five-person party.

"I'll cremate the remains."

"Thanks."

Arisa used the Fire Magic spell Flamethrower to cremate the bodies.

If bodies were left alone in the labyrinth, they could become coreless or cursed undead monsters. The proper course of action was to recover identification from and then burn any corpses one came across.

"I don't suppose there were any survivors?"

"I'll check..."

I opened my map, but I didn't see any explorers moving in small groups around here.

If we turned left at the four-way crossroads up ahead, we'd find a large group of twenty or so on standby in a large cavern, and there were a few other explorers farther down that passageway acting on their own, but they were probably scouts for the big party, not survivors of this one.

"Doesn't look like it."

Just as I was about to close the map, I noticed something unusual.

The scouting group in question had apparently failed at drawing away a lone monster or two, and now they were running back toward the large cavern with several dozen monsters chasing them.

As I watched, the number of monsters increased, and soon it grew into a horde of fifty or sixty.

"Uh-oh. Looks like a chain rampage."

"Oh my. Haven't seen one of those in a while."

Like Arisa said, we hadn't seen a monster chain rampage since the plunderers led one, kamikaze-style, toward the labyrinth army encampment.

I guess we'd run into one the first time we entered the Celivera Labyrinth, too.

"Think it'll be okay?"

"Well, *we're* safe…"

The problem was the big party in the cavern.

They were outnumbered, and worse, their levels weren't terribly high overall.

There were about five core members who were above level 20, but the other fifteen or so were only in the levels 5 to 10 range, so they weren't likely to fare well against the monsters around here. To put it bluntly, they were screwed.

Even the maze cockroach and maze centipedes my party had just easily defeated against ranged from levels 9 to 15.

Regardless of whether the party got completely wiped out, there would likely be huge casualties among all the non-core members.

We weren't obligated to help them, of course, but I would feel guilty if I left them be.

My girls could probably win without getting hurt; perhaps we should go poke our heads in.

"Mind if we take a little detour?"

The rest of my party enthusiastically agreed.

◆

"Outta the waaay!"

"If you block our path, we'll cut you down!"

Just as we arrived at the crossroads, two men with unsheathed swords came running from the direction of the large cavern.

Both of them were covered in sweat and blood, and their panicked expressions suggested that they really would attack us if we weren't careful.

I prefer to avoid danger if I can help it, so we stepped aside and let them pass.

"Besso! Troy and the newbies aren't following us!"

"Bah, leave those idiots! If they're getting eaten, that oughtta slow the monsters down enough for us to get outta here."

"R-right. You got it, Besso!"

I heard the men's voices as they ran the other way.

I guess they'd abandoned their comrades.

There was quite a long distance from here to the labyrinth exit. I wasn't sure if they'd make it there on their own, but that wasn't really my problem, and I swiftly erased them from my mind.

"Those were the same guys we saw in that other chain rampage."

"Were they?"

"Yes, master. No doubt about it."

Arisa and Liza recognized the men from the maze ant chain rampage.

"Master, enemies approaching from ahead, I report."

I didn't really want to save those jerks, but they were heading in the direction of the bee chamber, so I decided to defeat the monsters chasing them for the safety of our hunting grounds.

On my command, Lulu's Fireburst Gun, Mia's Spirit Magic spell Sharp Wind, and Arisa's Fire Magic spell Chain Fire Shot blasted the approaching monsters to bits in seconds.

"…Well, this doesn't look great."

While the explorers were at a clear disadvantage, their front lines hadn't fallen apart yet.

Their leader must be an exceptional commander.

That said, they were being driven into a corner of the cavern. As soon as one part of their ranks broke down, they could all get wiped out at any moment.

The explorers were surrounded by cockroach monsters.

We were coming in to attack from the opposite side.

"Mia, when I give the signal, light up the room with Spirit Magic. As soon as she does that, Arisa, you send a chant-less Fire Ball into the middle of the monsters. When it hits, I'll draw them away from the explorers so the vanguard can attack and destroy the cockroaches. Lulu, you protect Arisa and Mia, please."

As I relayed the battle plan, I cast Enchant: Physical Protection on the group.

Incidentally, since Lulu's Fireburst Gun was too strong, I told her not to use it.

I also had the vanguard refrain from using "Spellblade" and Foundation techniques and Arisa from using other chant-less magic or Space Magic. These restrictions weren't some kind of gamelike handicap—they were for the sake of secrecy.

"All right, here comes the cavalry!"

"Wait a second, Arisa." I grabbed her by the collar before she could rush ahead. "Let's greet them before we charge in to save them."

"Oh, good point. I'd hate for them to think we were plunderers and attack us."

The Silverlight group seemed wary of other explorers, and since these ones were already in a panic, they might assume we were here to take advantage of their plight.

"This is the explorer party Pendragon! We're here to help!"

"Thank ya kindly! If we get out of here alive, we'll treat ya to all the beer you can drink!"

I had been braced for hostility, but the group's leader accepted our help immediately. I guess they really were in a tight spot.

"Mia, now!"

"■■ *Sun Light* Youkou."

First, Mia's Spirit Magic lit up the battlefield from the area of the ceiling.

Immediately, Arisa's Fire Ball exploded into the center of the group of cockroaches.

The monsters it hit burst into flames, and the fire spread to those around it as well.

Slipping in amid the dust and flames, I used my go-to Practical Magic spell Magic Hand—basically a kind of magical psychokinesis—to toss the cockroaches away from the group of cornered explorers.

"Ew, gross!"

"Mrrr."

I understood Arisa's and Mia's disgust all too well. I felt the same way. Leave it to the worst insects ever to be able to adjust themselves in midair and take flight.

"Let's go."

"Tallyhooo?"

"Chaaarge, sir."

"Commence extermination. No mercy, I declare."

The four vanguard fighters charged into battle with their Magic Swords and Spears aglow.

…It was an absolute slaughter.

Pochi drove her sword into a cockroach up to the hilt, depleting its health in a flash.

Tama's twin blades danced, slicing away the cockroaches' health without leaving them a window to counterattack.

Nana cut down the cockroaches on the ground with her Magic Sword and crushed the ones that flew down to attack her with a Shield Bash. It was a very dynamic fighting style.

And Liza darted among the cockroaches, her spear piercing them one after the other with attacks faster than the eye could follow.

Talk about an overwhelming victory.

"Damn…they're slicin' through those tough shells like nothin'."

"Tch, I could do that, too, if I had magic weapons."

"Nooo, I don't think sooo. My Mantis Sword's a Magic Sword too, y'know, but, well, you've seen what it can dooo…"

My "Keen Hearing" skill picked up the explorer party's voices.

I was using Magic Hand to control the paths of the cockroaches so that the explorers didn't get attacked by more than they could handle at once, so I guess they had enough energy to spare now for a conversation.

I'd made Mantis Swords before, but I didn't think simply using parts from a soldier mantis was enough to call it a Magic Sword. It took a lot of extra work to turn monster parts into a true magical weapon, after all.

Besides, unlike Liza's Magic Cricket Spear, that guy's sword wasn't glowing red.

Of course, it wasn't only the vanguard who were bringing the heat. The rear guard was hard at work, too.

"Bwa-ha-ha! The cockroaches are like garbage…" Arisa was getting a little carried away. "Boy, they sure burn easily. I think I'll try out Fire Circle next!"

Still, at least she was using the chants each time and being careful to aim away from the vanguard or members of the other party.

"Master, above you!"

Lulu pointed up at a maze centipede crawling along the ceiling.

I had covertly tossed it away with Magic Hand, but I guess it had come back.

"Go ahead and shoot it, Lulu."

"Yes, sir!"

A fireball from Lulu's Fire Rod Gun brought the centipede down.

Unlike the rifle-style Fireburst Gun, this was a kind of rod with a rifle-like silhouette. When the trigger was pulled, it absorbed some of the wielder's magic and shot a small fireball out of the fire stone at the tip of the "muzzle."

Lulu didn't have as much magic power as Arisa or Mia, but now that she was level 38, she had more than enough to use the Fire Rod Gun for a while without running out.

As the centipede tumbled to the ground, I finished it off with my fairy sword.

Then I left Lulu to guard Arisa and went over to the explorers with Mia, who was now wearing a red nurse's armband. It should go without saying that Arisa was the one who had made this cosplay accessory.

"We'll heal you! Please gather the wounded here."

Arisa and the others cleared a space for me to make my way over to the explorers.

"Go ahead, Mia."

"Mm. Okay."

Mia used Water Magic spells like Water Heal and Remove Poison to cure the explorers' injuries and afflictions, while I took the role of her guardian and manager.

"The pain's wearing off."

"Ooh, my wounds are healing! I feel like I can keep fightin' now."

"Whoa, the feeling came back to my arms and legs."

"Me too."

"Thanks, little mage girl!"

Because Mia was wearing a hood, the explorers didn't notice that she was an elf, but they must have assumed she was a young girl from her petite figure.

"Mm."

Mia nodded shyly.

Thanks to her healing, the explorers who had been down for the count were gradually able to return to battle. Soon, their front lines restabilized. Even the low-level explorers teamed up to take down cockroaches one at a time.

As the battle turned overwhelmingly in their favor, the explorers started chatting among themselves.

"That bastard Besso. *Prime hunting spot*, my ass."

"He told us that stray maze cockroaches would wander in here alone, so we could safely hunt as much as we wanted."

"Yeah, he claimed he was an expert at luring monsters, and look how that turned out."

Apparently, the pair we had seen running away had suggested this hunting spot.

"Where are those two anyway?"

"Maybe they got eaten by monsters?"

"Serves 'em right."

They didn't seem to be very well-liked.

"Satou."

Finished with her healing, Mia tugged on my sleeve for instruction.

"Looks like the battle will be over soon. Let's just keep an eye on things from here."

"Mm. Together."

We sat down on a craggy rock and watched the fight, supporting them with the occasional tossed stone or healing spell.

Within less than an hour, the fight was finished.

"Thanks for saving us, Sir Noble."

"Not at all. I'm just glad we made it in time."

Mr. Koshin, the garnet-badge explorer who seemed to be in charge of the large party, had come over to thank me.

His party, Ivory Mane, had only four veterans. The rest were trial members he had recruited.

"So about your reward—"

Koshin looked hesitant, but I interrupted him.

"That won't be necessary."

"But…"

"If you happen to run into any explorers in trouble in the future, please lend them a hand."

"Uhhh…you sure that's enough? Doesn't seem like much…"

"Koshin, you don't know much outside of exploring, do you?" the man in glasses standing next to Koshin interrupted. "He means 'passing on a favor,' right, Sir Noble?"

"Passing on a favor"? I guess the Shiga Kingdom has a concept like "paying it forward," too.

I nodded at the man, who explained the concept in detail to Koshin. As he did so, some other explorers came over to give their report.

"Koshin! That bastard Besso is nowhere to be seen."

"We found the two newbies he brought with him dead in the corridor near the nest."

There must have been some casualties before we got here.

"We found that Troy guy! He was sleeping behind a rock!"

Judging by what I'd heard, this Troy person was a member of Besso's party.

The person who had shouted dragged Troy over to be interrogated by Koshin.

According to him, they had attempted to gather a rare ingredient called "bewitching slime" from the maze cockroach nest and failed, causing a chain rampage of monsters.

"Master, I've collected the cores from the monsters we defeated. Would you like us to start gathering the other materials as well?"

"No, it's all right. They're too bulky."

Centipede meat was poisonous, and maze cockroaches were probably riddled with germs, so I didn't want anything to do with that.

"…What?" Overhearing this, Koshin stopped mid-interrogation and spun around to stare at me. "Are you serious, Sir Noble?"

He explained that centipede shells were a popular material for shields and armor, and the wings and carapaces of the cockroaches were valuable for making light armor for scouts.

Even the centipedes' poison sacs and the cockroaches' stink glands could be sold to alchemy guilds or on the black market.

"Please feel free to sell them yourselves, then."

We already had more labyrinth materials than we knew what to do with.

Taking all that as a reward for rescuing them seemed silly to me.

"Mr. Koshin, we collected all the cores. 'Cept the ones that belong to Mr. Noble's little ladies, of course. Should we start breaking down the materials?"

"Uh…yeah. Go ahead."

Mr. Koshin accepted a sack of cores from the blood-drenched man, then turned to me.

"Mr. Noble, we'll gratefully accept those materials. So at least take the cores with ya."

It would be awkward to keep declining all his offers. I relented, accepting the bag of cores from him.

"Well, we'll be on our way now."

"Sir Noble! Once we get back aboveground, let us treat ya to some drinks like we promised!"

"Of course. I'm looking forward to it."

Waving to Koshin and company, we left the cockroach disassembly site.

◆

"No frooogs?"

"Lots of explorers and Mr. Flies, sir."

When we finally arrived at the frog area, which was about the size of a school ground, there were hardly any maze frogs. The few that remained were already fighting other explorers.

There were a couple rotten-smelling pits in the uneven ground of the area, full of discarded maze-frog innards and such.

The puppy-size maze corpse flies Pochi had pointed out seemed to be feeding on them.

Since they appeared to have plenty to eat, they didn't attack people as long as you didn't interfere with their meal.

"There really are quite a few people here," Liza observed.

There were nearly ten different parties in the area, including some I recognized. Among them was a group of about eight of the female explorers I had rescued from the plunderers, led by their big-sister figure, Sumina.

Normally they hunted in the areas appropriate for lower-level explorers, with the potatoes and beans and so on, but today it looked like they were on an expedition here with just their higher-level members.

"Master, aren't there any frogs anywhere?"

"Yes, in there."

I pointed at a muddy pond in the center of the large area.

Explorers with long-range attacks or the "Taunt" skill were gathered around its banks, waiting for frogs to emerge from the water. Some had even tied ropes around maze corpse flies and tossed them into the lake in an attempt to lure the frogs out.

"This reminds me of camping a rare-monster spawn point in an MMORPG."

"Yeah, it's pretty brutal," I agreed.

I took my group over to an area with less people.

"Fishing."

"Master, there are fishermen, I report."

Riding on Nana's shoulders, Mia pointed at some fishermen on the bank.

They were probably explorers, but they looked like fishermen to me.

I went a little closer and spoke to them. "Any bites?"

"Nothin' but eyeless fish today. Can't even fish up a single rock cray."

The friendly fisherman explained that rock crays were lobster-size crayfish that disguised themselves as rocks.

"Yummyyy?"

"Rock crays and eyeless fish both sell for a lot, but they taste a little too muddy in my opinion, bein' from a port town and all."

So they cook them without even washing out the mud?

Though he said they sold for a lot, the postings I saw at the labyrinth gate later said eyeless fish were worth two copper coins each, and rock crays were worth one large copper coin.

"What're you guys here to fish?"

"We're frog fishing, sir."

"Huh?"

At Pochi's response, the fisherman looked up from the water's surface to stare at us in disbelief. After a moment, he sighed and explained.

"The frogs don't come over here. See those red flowers there? They hate the smell, so they stay away from 'em."

He nodded toward the red lotus-like flowers floating on the water's surface.

What a nice person.

"If you wanna wait for frogs on the edge of the lake, you're better off going over there, past those rocks."

"Just don't space out at the water's edge. Otherwise…"

As another fisherman started to warn us, we saw one of the explorers near the rocks in question get dragged into the water with a splash.

The rest of his group panicked and hurriedly pulled him back up with a rope he appeared to be using as a lifeline.

I was going to go over to help, but I guess that wouldn't be necessary.

I thanked the fishermen, and we headed over to the rocks in question.

"All right, shall we fish up some frogs?"

"I'll tryyy?"

"I'll open my *saucers like eyes*, sir."

Other way around, Pochi.

"This could be tough…"

"It'll be fine."

I used my radar to locate the area with the most maze frogs, then the See Through spell to pinpoint their location.

Then I produced a harpoon from my Garage Bag, tied a rope to it, and threw it at one of the frogs underwater.

"*GWELOROOOON.*"

The harpoon pierced the flesh of a maze frog, which bellowed in rage and came up to the surface.

Although the frog was probably over six hundred pounds, it was only level 13, so we finished it off easily. The frogs in this area seemed to be a little smaller than the ones we'd fought before.

"Hey there, youngster. Can ya spare some bones and cartilage? I'll throw out the innards for ye."

"Give us the skin, too, if'n you don't need it. We can even break it down, quick as ye like."

As I watched Liza and the others breaking down the frog, a couple of explorers came up behind me with large baskets on their backs. I noted that both of them had the title Looter.

"No need for that. I'm happy to give you the bones and skin in exchange for disposing of the garbage, but we're keeping the cartilage."

Fried maze frog cartilage was one of the guildmaster's favorite foods.

"Say, what do you use the skin for anyway?" Arisa asked curiously.

"We sell it to workshops."

They told us that maze frog skin was used for waterproof bags, rain gear for watery areas, and so on.

I had recipes for some of those things in my documents, but they didn't seem terribly effective, so I didn't intend to make them.

Saving time by letting the looters dispose of the garbage for us, we fished up two more frogs and defeated them easily, acquiring enough frog meat to feed the orphanage kids.

Sumina and some of the other explorers asked about my trick for finding frogs underwater, but I couldn't very well tell them the truth. I used my "Fabrication" skill to make up an arbitrary answer. "Just trusting my gut and keeping an eye out for bubbles on the water's surface, I guess."

◆

"There is a group in red up ahead, I report."

"Mrrr. In the way."

Once we finished our frog hunt, we returned to the first room in section 1.

All we had to do now was ascend the long staircase and return to Labyrinth City, but there was a problem: A group of explorers in matching red armor had formed a line in front of the staircase.

They were apparently heading to the middle stratum.

"Hmm? If it isn't Sir Pendragon."

"Hello, Mr. Kinkuri."

The foxfolk general from the labyrinth army greeted me.

I didn't see the captain who was usually with him. Instead, someone else was at his side.

"Good to see you again, Sir Jelil. Are you on your way to defeat the floormaster?"

"That's right. I intend to bring it down with this flaming Magic Sword you lent me."

Mr. Jelil, a garnet-badge explorer, hefted a bronze sword.

It was one of the prototypes for a third-generation Magic Sword I had created. I'd wound up lending it to him at the viceroy's wife's tea party.

I could easily mass-produce them with help from Arisa and Mia, but since they were chock-full of secret technology, I was reluctant to hand them out freely.

"But we have to dispose of the monsters in the Chamber of Trials before we can summon the floormaster, so it'll probably be half a month before we can actually fight the damn thing."

"Well, I have no doubt you'll succeed, Sir Jelil."

It sounded pretty tough, but at least they weren't on a ridiculously tight schedule or anything.

I learned later from the guildmaster that the floormaster appeared only if you placed the core of an areamaster on an altar in the Chamber of Trials.

"Jelil!"

"If you'll excuse me, one of my comrades is calling."

"Of course. May fortune be with you."

"Good luck…"

As the foxfolk man and I encouraged him, Jelil turned and left, his red cape flowing behind him.

I bid the foxfolk officer farewell, and we headed back aboveground.

"Looks like the recovery efforts are almost finished."

As we passed the west gate of Labyrinth City and cut across the plaza, Arisa looked around.

It felt rather warm, maybe because we'd been in the cool underground for so long. The rest of my group looked sweaty, too.

"Yeah. Seems like all that's left now is rebuilding the tower of the west guild."

It had been less than half a month since the Plunderer King Ludaman had turned into an intermediate demon and rampaged in front of the west guild.

The speediness of the repairs was likely thanks to the machinelike golems and the architectural magic of the earth mages.

"Hey, young master! Wanna try some of our new *takoyaki*?"

Neru, a high school–age girl with red hair, called out to us from one of the stalls. She was wearing a tank top and no bra, likely due to the heat of the flat-top grill she was working with. I wasn't sure where to look.

She was one of the girls I'd rescued from burning to death in the fire downtown.

These girls, as well as the girls we'd saved from the plunderers, now worked at food stalls and similar places to eke out a livelihood, all under the protection of my alias Kuro.

"Sure, thanks. What'll it cost to get enough for the whole group?"

"Oh, we can't take money from you, young master."

Neru tried to decline, but I insisted on paying her.

Watching fondly as the girls blew on their piping-hot *takoyaki*, I took a bite of my own.

"Delicious. Is this maze octopus?"

"Heh-heh, not quite." Neru grinned proudly. "It's octopus kraken meat that Lord Kuro acquired for us."

While my group was staying in the labyrinth, I had gone back aboveground as Kuro and brought some of my excess stock of octopus kraken and sea serpent to the tenement houses where Neru and the others were staying. I'd also sold some wholesale to a few big companies.

"Wow, that's impressive."

"Aw, man. That's not the reaction I was hoping for."

Neru pouted. I guess my surprised expression wasn't convincing enough.

"How are sales going?"

"So-so… Oh, Miss Tama! Can you draw a *takoyaki* signboard for us like the other stalls?"

"Okey-dokeyyy?"

Tama agreed without a fuss. She had already drawn similar boards for the girls' other stalls: DANCING CROQUETTES, WINNING SKEWERS, and FLYING FRIED POTATOES.

All of them were amazingly lifelike for pictures of food and easily stimulated the appetites of anyone who saw them.

"Want some croquettes, young master?"

"These skewers are freshly made, too."

"How about some salted fried potatoes for a snack?"

The salesgirls at the other three stalls, who had been serving customers, joined in on our conversation. They were all dressed as lightly as Neru.

Though the stalls were successful enough that others had started selling imitations of their products, they still weren't popular enough to have long lines of customers.

"Ahem, ahem."

Hearing a very deliberate throat-clearing, I turned around to see a familiar noble boy.

If I remembered correctly, this kid was Luram, the second son of Baron Tokey. He was one of the boys who usually followed around Gerits, the third son of Labyrinth City's viceroy.

"Hello, Sir Luram."

"I-indeed, Sir Pendragon. I am glad to see you in good health."

I understood that kids his age sometimes tried to seem mature, but the croquettes and skewers he clutched in both hands dampened the effect somewhat.

The girls who ran the stalls said he was a regular customer.

"Are you doing market research today?"

It would probably hurt the young boy's pride if I asked if he was snacking, so I decided to make it sound more professional.

"Market…? Erm, yes. Yes, indeed. Market research, no doubt about it. Research is very important. My pa— I mean, my esteemed father, Baron Tokey, is in charge of supervising the market stalls, you see. So I'm market researching whether the food is still good quality and keeping an eye out for changes in the cost—er, market price."

It confused him at first, but Luram seemed to quickly take a liking to the phrase.

He always seemed timid when he was with Gerits, but today he was making a show of using difficult words. Maybe he was just trying to show off and seem more grown-up.

"…Oh, it's Mary-Ann."

Immediately, Luram went back to his usual sheepish tone.

Following his gaze, I saw another of Gerits's crew: Mary-Ann, the daughter of Baronet Dyukeli. She was talking to some explorers admiringly.

"Her father forbade her from exploring the labyrinth, but I guess she still hasn't given up…," Luram murmured to no one in particular.

From the sound of things, her parents had probably banned her from entering the labyrinth after she, Gerits, and their friends all went exploring and had their lives endangered by the former acting viceroy Sokell and his schemes.

I wasn't particularly close with these kids, and I worried that they'd ask me to take them into the labyrinth if I talked to them too much. I made sure we left at the first opportunity.

"Welcome home, young master."

""""Welcome home!"""""

After taking a horse-drawn carriage back to the mansion, we were greeted by the head maid, Miss Miteruna; the senior maids, Rosie and Annie; and the young maids-in-training.

"Thank you. Miteruna, did anything happen while we were gone?"

I handed my coat to a maid as I spoke.

"Just after you left for the labyrinth, a messenger came from Viscount Siemmen."

Miss Miteruna handed me a package.

They must have finished the scrolls I ordered.

My requests this time:

Pixie Light, which I thought might be profitable for the viscount like the Fireworks spells.

Mist Control and Paralyze Water Hold, which I had made during our seafaring journey on the sugar route.

And Flash Grenade, Stun Grenade, and Dimension Cutter, which seemed useful for labyrinth exploring.

Of these, Mist Control and Flash Grenade were for obscuring enemies' fields of vision, Paralyze Water Hold and Stun Grenade were for suppressing enemies without killing them, and Dimension Cutter was for defeating monsters without damaging the meat.

"I also passed along your additional requests for Viscount Siemmen."

"Great. Thank you very much."

The additional scrolls I had ordered were original spells of mine to work with magic tools and my Menu ability.

They were an intermediary for output from technological spells I'd made previously, like Picture Recorder, Sound Recorder, Standard Out, and Graphic View, and even included the ability to input data on an imaginary keyboard.

The scrolls' names were Virtual Keyboard, Data Input, and Data Output.

They were all lesser Practical Magic spells, so they should be completed within ten days or so.

"I sorted any other letters you received by the sender."

"Thanks, Miteruna."

The letters were arranged in a box on the desk in my study.

I sat down on the hard chair and sifted through it, looking at the wax seals of the senders.

Most of them were from Labyrinth City nobles like the viceroy's wife, but there were a few belonging to noble acquaintances of mine from the Ougoch Duchy.

According to Miss Miteruna, I had also received letters and parcels from merchants, craftsmen, temples, and so on.

The letters from the director of the private orphanage contained the résumés of newly hired personnel.

"Do you have a lot of work to do, master?"

"No, none of it seems too urgent."

"Then can we deliver the meat to the orphanage now?"

I nodded at Arisa and the others, closed my letter box, and stood up.

"You must put strength into your little finger when you form a fist, young one."

"Like this?"

"Yes, now there's a good lad."

In the open field by the mansion, the Saga Empire samurai Mr. Kajiro was teaching some kids how to swing a sword.

The other samurai, Miss Ayaume, was patrolling the grounds. She was probably doing it alone because it would be difficult for Mr. Kajiro, who had lost a leg in the labyrinth.

"So can we be explorers now, mister?"

"You have a long way to go yet, you young fools."

Mr. Kajiro ruffled the impatient child's hair and grinned.

"Dang it, but I wanna eat meat every day like Pochi and Tama…"

Oh, I remember this now.

These were the kids who had vowed, back at the hamburg steak party we threw at the orphanage, to become explorers when they grew up.

I guess they were actually working toward that goal.

"Good evening, Sir Kajiro."

"I am glad to see you safely returned, Sir Knight."

"Thank you."

As we spoke, I saw Tama and Pochi come running over from the back door of the mansion.

Excusing myself, I headed to the orphanage with them.

"Meeeat?"

"We brought gifts, sir!"

Hefting the hundred-plus pounds of meat, Tama and Pochi charged through the gates to the orphanage. Liza and Nana were carrying the rest with carts.

I had already requested that Miss Miteruna distribute some to the neighbors.

"Hooraaaay!"

"It's meat!"

"Oh, it's been so long!"

"Welcome home, Miss Tama."

"Are you hurt at all, Miss Pochi?"

"Not at aaaall?"

"Pochi is amazingly unbeatable, so we're fine, sir."

"Larvae, please surround me and praise my efforts as well, I request."

"Ha-ha, Nana, you're so weird…"

"Nana! Pick me up!"

There were smiles all around as kids ran over to welcome us back with open arms.

"Allow me to offer my congratulations on your safe return, Sir Knight."

"Thank you."

I greeted the director and the staff members who came to welcome me.

The newly hired personnel all seemed like good people who would do well with kids, to my relief.

"We're having a grilling party today! Eat till your bellies are full to bursting, everyone!"

""""Yaaaay!"""""

That evening, we enjoyed a meat-grilling party with the orphanage kids.

Partway through, we ran out of meat, and I produced more from Storage while no one was looking.

Growing kids sure have impressive appetites.

Or so I thought…

"Yummyyyy?"

"Pochi can still eat lots of meat, sir!"

"You children took such small helpings. You must eat more to grow big and strong, you know."

…but I guess it was my kids who had the biggest appetites of all.

Pochi's and Tama's bellies swelled up visibly, but the real question was where Liza was packing away all that meat on her slender frame.

The world is truly full of mysteries.

The Thank-You Party

Satou here. I was always fond of the biergarten that my coworkers would frequent after work. If all you needed was to cool off, you could always go to a regular bar with an air conditioner, but I liked the festive nighttime atmosphere of the biergarten.

"There sure are a lot of food stalls."

"Master, I believe it's that group over there."

One evening, a few days after we returned from the labyrinth, we were invited to an explorers' banquet.

It was being held in a vacant lot in a certain corner of the downtown area, somewhere between the west gate and the labyrinth army base, where there were plenty of cheap lodging houses and tenements for explorers.

The normally empty lot was lined to the edges with stands selling food and drink.

It looked like most people were buying things at the stalls, then eating and drinking in the center.

There was no bonfire or anything, but the majority of the stalls had lit-up signs that brightened the area. An Everyday Magic user must have cast some kind of lighting spell.

"It's like a nighttime festival or a flower viewing."

I nodded in agreement with Arisa.

"Thank you very much for inviting us today."

"Sir Knight! Come, take the seat of honor!"

Mr. Koshin, the organizer of the night, beckoned us over. Upon greeting him, I gave him the small casks of wine and liquor I'd brought as a thank-you.

Instead of chairs and tables, people were simply sitting on the ground in a circle. Lulu and Liza had already secured an area for us to sit.

There were many other people enjoying the food and drink stalls, too: explorers, sailors, day laborers, and so on. I also caught colorful glances of scantily clad ladies and oddly alluring young men, all of whom seemed like sex workers.

I rather enjoyed the bawdy atmosphere myself, although I wasn't sure if it was entirely appropriate to have brought the young ones.

"Now, a toast to the Pendragon party for rescuing us! Let's drink till dawn to celebrate our safe return!"

""""Woooo!"""""

We must have been the last to arrive. With Mr. Koshin's toast, the party began.

The main menu for the evening included baskets of rye bread, some kind of grilled meat, boiled beans, and boiled potatoes. There were mountains of all of these.

Several barrels of ale were set up in the center of the circle, although the only nonalcoholic beverage around was water.

A few of the men teased Koshin for "going all out" before the party started, so this must have been a particularly lavish spread by their standards.

At the encouragement of Koshin and the other explorers, my group started to dig in as well.

No alcohol for the kids, of course.

"Tooough…"

"Mr. Meat is pretty chewy, sir."

"Ha-ha, you'll never bite through it that way, kids. Cut it up with a knife before you eat."

SNAP! Just as a young explorer was admonishing her, Pochi bit right through the meat. The young man's eyes widened.

"Maybe it's tendon meat?"

Lulu gave me a plate of meat cut into small pieces.

It certainly was tough when I chewed it. Cooking it in a pressure cooker might soften it up a bit. The taste was a bit too strong to call delicious, but not quite gross enough to spit out.

"It's cheap monster meat. It might not suit your tastes, Mr. Noble."

"Although bug meat does grow on ya if ya eat it every day."

Some female explorers noticed my expression and spoke to me about the meat, which apparently came from an insectoid monster. It was very dark before being cooked and tasted like a tougher version of animal tendon.

The specific kind of insect varied depending on the day, so the explorers called it bug meat or even just meat. It was incredibly cheap. Only a copper coin for a skewer.

The black color reminded me a bit of the grasshopper monster meat I'd eaten in the Muno Barony, though the taste and texture were a little different.

They were both gross, for sure, but at least this kind wasn't as harsh on the palate.

Although they were also similar in that I never wanted to eat either of them again.

"When we first became explorers, we used to follow stronger parties around and harvest the leftover meat from monsters after they killed and stripped them."

"It paid the bills, but we sure got made fun of a lot."

This anecdote came from the same female explorers who had identified the meat for me.

Evidently, many explorers took only the most valuable parts like shells and fangs from insect monsters. As a result, there were other explorers who specialized in retrieving meat from these discarded monsters. These explorers were known as Looters and had a bad reputation.

Come to think of it, I remembered hearing something similar from the young explorers we saw gathering goblin meat in the labyrinth.

It seemed strange to me that they would be looked down upon when their work supported the livelihood of others.

"We'll pour you a drink, young master."

A few young explorer women, probably in their twenties, crossed the center of the circle to pour liquor into my cup.

"Thank you."

I nodded and took a sip of the ale.

Ewww, that's sour.

It tasted like flat, watered-down beer mixed with vinegar. But everyone around me was savoring it like it was a rare delicacy.

"Ale is so good! It's nothing like goblin liquor!"

Goblin liquor, one of them explained, was a fermented beverage acquired from monsters in the labyrinth called "demi-goblin drunkards."

"Have you had much to eat, young master?"

"The bug meat's tough, but these beans and potatoes are nice and soft."

More explorer girls appeared from behind the ones with the ale, offering me and the rest of my group more food.

The beans and potatoes were made from walking beans and hopping potatoes, so if you ate them carelessly, you could end up with paralysis or an upset stomach.

Since they were so cheap and filling, though, they were popular calorie sources for poor newbie explorers, sailors, and the like.

"Here you are, young master."

"Thank you."

A kindly young woman offered me some beans from a plate.

In the face of her guileless smile, I couldn't bring myself to say *No thanks—they're gross.*

Because the dark-red veins in the potatoes and beans were the source of most of the bitterness, it probably wouldn't be too bad as long as I avoided those.

I reached into my breast pocket and produced a slim spoon from Storage to remove the veins, then scoop out and eat the rest.

I couldn't do much about the smaller veins, so it still maintained a bit of the bitterness, but it was fairly edible.

"Wow, nobles eat so fancy…"

"Maybe I'll try using a spoon, too?"

…*Oops.*

I wasn't trying to put on airs, but for some reason it seemed to catch the attention of some of the explorers around me.

The word *fancy* must have struck a chord with Mia and Arisa, who produced their own spoons from their Fairy Packs and started eating the same way.

They even stuck out their pinkies on the hands holding the spoons, looking rather pleased with themselves.

At least until Arisa started choking on her fancily eaten potato.

"W-water!"

Lulu passed a cup of water to Arisa.

"Geh, yuck!"

"Oh dear, is the river water too nasty for the young lady?"

"They sell well water at the stand over there."

The female explorers laughed at Arisa, who had spit out the water as soon as it touched her lips.

I remembered the garbage-filled state of the aqueducts.

Yeah, I wouldn't want to drink that, either.

"Master! Our next renovation project is the filtration system! I can't bear the thought of all that unsanitary drinking water."

At least Arisa was processing her anger in a productive way.

The cleanup we did in the plaza after our soup kitchens was already well on its way to eliminating all the garbage from the streets, so it shouldn't be too hard to assign our volunteers to clean the aqueducts next.

Realizing we might need permission to do it, I told Arisa we would have to inquire at the government office about it first.

Mr. Koshin came over to give Arisa a pitcher of water. "Here, missy, drink from this pitcher." He held out a bottle of wine in his other hand. "Let me pour you a drink, too, Sir Knight."

Behind him were some scantily clad women carrying plates full of meat skewers, fried vegetables, a dish of appetizers like spring rolls, roasted tree nuts, and so on.

They appeared to be not explorers but companions Mr. Koshin had hired. Specifically of the nighttime variety.

"Hey, Koshin! What about us, huh?"

"You guys eat your potatoes and meat! This food's made special for the folks who saved our lives."

When Koshin shouted at a rowdy explorer, the others around them guffawed heartily.

I guess they had kindly saved some slightly fancier food for us.

"Sorry, Sir Knight. These guys are all about quantity over quality. You might find this stuff a bit more to your liking."

"I'm sorry. You didn't have to get anything special for us."

"Nah, no big deal. 'S the least we could do." Sitting down across from me, Koshin smiled humbly and bowed his head. "We really do owe you a huge debt of gratitude, Sir Knight. If you all hadn't come along, I don't think most of these guys woulda made it back."

He had already thanked me countless times, but it still didn't seem to be enough for him.

As we drank together, I asked him to tell me some of his exploring stories. According to him, this most recent venture wasn't his first time heading deep into the labyrinth with multiple parties.

"'S not that unusual for someone to mess up and get hurt or worse, but..."

Most of these expeditions were made with all-male or all-female parties, but since Koshin accepted anyone, they sometimes ran into trouble.

"The last time we were in that much danger was when we got caught in a chain rampage caused by plunderers."

"A man-made chain rampage?"

Now that he mentioned it, I did remember that incident when plunderers created a chain rampage and nearly wiped out the labyrinth army.

"Yeah. Plunderers sacrifice slaves or new recruits to run ahead and bait monsters into a chain rampage. The ones who don't run fast enough get eaten by the monsters."

That level of cruelty was typical of plunderers.

"Wooow, sir."

"Whoa, Nellyyy?"

I was starting to get angry, but the cheers of Pochi, Tama, and some other explorers successfully distracted me.

In the center of the circle, a big bearfolk man was hoisting a green fairyfolk man over his head and spinning him around like a ball.

What's so impressive about that?

As I looked on in confusion, the fairyfolk man suddenly jumped nearly ten feet in the air, eliciting another chorus of cheers.

It wasn't just the bearfolk man's "Super Strength" skill. The fairyfolk man had jumped up in perfect time with the bearfolk man's toss to achieve that kind of height.

"Those guys are explorers who used to be traveling performers," Koshin explained.

"What an interesting career path."

"Let's tryyy?"

"I want to try, too, sir."

Tama and Pochi looked to me for permission.

"Just be careful and don't hurt yourselves."

"Aye-aye!"

"Yes, sir."

Tama and Pochi saluted, then ran into the middle of the circle.

I signaled to Liza and Nana to be on alert in case of an emergency.

Of course, I also had my Magic Hand on standby, but that was a last resort.

"Pochiii!"

"Tamaaa, sir!"

Tama was the base, while Pochi was to be the ball.

They were spinning a little too fast, though.

"Ready, seeet…?"

"Go, sir!"

Pochi's eyes spun as she went sailing into next week.

"Watch out!"

Pochi nearly went flying out of the circle, but Liza jumped up to catch her.

Since she caught her by the ankle, though, Pochi smacked face-first into the ground as soon as Liza landed.

"Ouchie, sir."

"I'm sorry, Pochi. That was my mistake."

"It's no big deal, sir."

Brushing away the dirt on her face, Pochi grinned broadly.

"Okaaay?"

"Nosebleed."

Mia used lesser Healing Magic on Pochi.

"Must be nice having a mage around."

"It takes a hell of a donation to get a priest who can use Holy Magic into your party, though, right?"

"Yeah, I hear it'll cost ya an arm and a leg."

The explorers chatted enviously among themselves.

"Whaaat? Why not use potions, then?"

"Sure, if you could afford to buy cheap ones at the guild all the time."

"The potion shops are crazy expensive, and the ones you can buy on the street don't really work."

"Yeah, 'cause most of them are expired or made by untrained alchemists."

"But it's stressful not having one on you at all, y'know?"

"Right. You'd be in real trouble if a strong monster showed up in your hunting grounds, then."

Magic potions tended to be expensive and didn't last long, so they were an expensive emergency item for newbie adventurers.

"Y'know how the garnet-badge explorer Kumuli and the Beetle Breaker Margill both retired 'cause of injuries? Well, I heard it happened 'cause they ran outta potions and weren't able to heal up in time."

"Oh geez. Even a garnet?"

"But wasn't it 'cause they kept hunting even though they used up all their potions?"

"Guess they reaped what they sowed, then."

From the sound of things, explorers who didn't take safety precautions risked losing their reputations.

Many retired explorers seemed to end up out on the streets, too.

"So you should always save the last one just in case, huh?" I commented.

"Oh, I wish. But I never have any potions on me in the first place!"

"I know, right? They're way too expensive."

The newbie explorers sighed in response.

"Rumor has it that the potion shops get away with overcharging because they've got some nasty noble behind them."

"Yeah, some bastard named Dyukeli, right?"

"Ugh, I hope that guy drops dead, y'know?"

"Yeah right. Even if he did, someone else would just take his place."

The explorers grumbled about Baronet Dyukeli.

I'd once heard similar rumors from some explorers at a bar. Baronet Dyukeli did have a vested interest in the fields of potions and magic tools, so maybe there was some truth to it.

"Y'know, weapons and armor have been going up in price lately. Think it's the same kind of thing?"

"Have they?"

"The cheap stuff's still the same, but now there's pricy stuff like Antwing Silver Swords and Mantis Swords out there, too."

"For real? Man, my goal just keeps getting further away…"

"You can't say that when you haven't even bought a real weapon yet, idiot."

The explorers stopped their complaining to tease a youngster, then burst out laughing.

They were probably so drunk that everything seemed funny to them.

"Ohhhh damn!"

"Whoa, you for real?"

In the middle of the circle, Tama and Pochi had succeeded at their performance this time.

And since leveling up had made them that much stronger, they got twice the height of the previous performers, even without using "Body Strengthening."

"It's exactly like the twins' finishing move from *Wing Captain*."

"What was it, Love-Love Tornado?"

"Bzzzt! Nope, it was Sky-Sky Typhoon."

I did vaguely remember the soccer manga Arisa was referring to, but it had been so long since I'd read it that I got the moves mixed up.

"…A finishing move, you say?"

"A cooperative move might be a wise idea, I propose."

Liza and Nana took things in a different direction.

But in a world with a level system, maybe re-creating manga and anime moves might actually be pretty doable.

"Sir Koshin, care for a song?"

"Ooh, a minstrel, are ya? Give us a lively one, please."

Holding a lute in one hand, the minstrel accepted a large copper coin from Koshin and went into the center of the circle.

"Now, if you'll lend me your ear…"

Removing his wide-rimmed cap and bowing, the minstrel strummed the lute.

"*'Twas a pale moon that rose that night…*"

His song was about our battle with the demon Ludaman from a few days prior.

It focused mostly on General Erthal, the guildmaster, and Miss Sebelkeya, but it did mention me in phrases like *a youthful noble* and *young man with the beautiful mithril sword*.

In the end, of course, *the Hero's disciple Kuro* appeared, brought lightning down from the sky, and defeated the demon Ludaman after he'd merged with the pink slime, ending the tale.

I had to say, listening to a dramatized version of my own battle was pretty embarrassing.

At least the song didn't mention the names *Satou* or *Pendragon*.

◆

"My, how refreshing. Thank you, Sir Pendragon; this will make things far more comfortable."

Today I was visiting the home of Baron Moffo, a noble who had always hated me. Miss Miteruna told me that the temperature in Labyrinth City was rising, so I made a fan from a moss crab bee wing to bring as a gift, but it got an even better reception than I'd expected.

Next thing I knew, he was treating me like an old friend.

Never underestimate the power of an electric-fan-style magic tool, I guess…

Since it was hastily made, it didn't have a magic-power storage vessel. Thanks to that, it had to be constantly supplied with magic to work, which one of the maids of the baron's house was currently doing. This flaw didn't seem to bother them, though.

I noticed that at some point I had acquired the title **Bribe Master**.

"Did you make this fan yourself, good sir?"

The baron looked like he wanted to acquire more.

"A traveling merchant from Lalagi, the Kingdom of Sorcery, supplied us with the materials, so unfortunately, I'm not sure when I'll be able to purchase more."

"I see. That's a shame."

I didn't actually say that it came from Lalagi or that we bought it, and I didn't plan to buy them; therefore, I wasn't lying.

Because an old butler in the room had **Eyes of Truth**, a gift from the Urion faith, I decided to give a roundabout answer. The gift couldn't actually detect lies, to my knowledge, but I didn't have all the details about it, so I was trying to be careful.

"Still, it seems unfair to keep an item like this all to myself..."

"Don't worry. I have some to offer His Excellency the viceroy as well."

I had already made enough for the viceroy, the guildmaster, General Erthal, and so on. The wings of a single moss crab bee could make around twenty fans. I still had plenty of materials left.

I had also installed three cooling fans in the orphanage.

The fans required a regular supply of magic, which the kids took turns doing. Perhaps some of them might gain the "Magic Manipulation" skill.

"Good, good."

The baron tapped his chin thoughtfully.

His attempt at seriousness was somewhat ruined by his relaxed expression as he enjoyed the breeze from the fan, but obviously I wouldn't be so rude as to point that out.

"As thanks for this splendid gift, let me offer you two pieces of information."

He went on to share some intel with me, acting self-important all the while...

"...A war?"

"Indeed. I heard this information from a merchant who had just returned from the west part of the continent. He said the prices of food and iron ore had risen in that area and that the export of Magic

Swords—as well as mithril, monster parts, and anything else that could be used to make them—was being restricted."

According to him, the actual fighting was still a long way away, but I wasn't sure how information about some far-off corner of the continent could pertain to me. It was a conversation starter at best.

"You don't seem to understand." The baron looked at me like a teacher judging a slow-witted pupil. "This means that merchants will be trying to buy up monster parts before our own land starts restricting exports as well."

In other words, he was telling me that if I hunted monsters for weapon parts, I could sell them at high prices and turn a big profit.

"The other piece is about magic potions."

"Are they about to jump in value, too?"

"No, Sir Dyukeli controls those prices within Labyrinth City, so that won't change."

My prediction was wrong.

"But the price of potion ingredients will probably rise in the king's territories and coastal areas. The potion prices at the guild might go up, or their supply might go down, I suppose."

That seemed like it would cause problems for a lot of explorers.

If their stock was to get that low, I might have to disguise myself as Kuro and bring some watered-down potions to the guild myself.

"But I digress..." The baron took a bite of sorbet, which I'd brought as a gift along with the fan, then sighed. "What I was trying to speak of is the demonic potion that the viceroy's flunky was making in secret."

I remembered the flunky in question: the former acting viceroy Sokell.

He was now confined in a prison in the viceroy's castle, albeit one for aristocrats.

"They uncovered a large-scale demonic-potion smuggling operation in Tartumina Bay."

I had been to the trade city Tartumina before, too.

Come to think of it, I had seen an illegal drug deal go down when I was there.

Fortunately, they'd managed to put a stop to the smuggling itself, but the smugglers got away.

Based on the build of their ship, it was suspected to be a weaselfolk merchant ship, but the situation was further complicated because a Parion Province warship also disappeared.

I'm no detective, so I personally wasn't that interested in the business of a faraway city.

So why did he make a show of giving me such irrelevant information...?

"Patience, friend. I wasn't finished yet."

Taking the final bite of his sorbet, the baron gestured to a maid for seconds, then waved his spoon.

"The crime-syndicate members who were captured swore that Marquis Kelten was the one who provided them with the demonic potions."

Marquis Kelten... If I remembered correctly, he was an important noble of the royal capital, with strong influence in the military.

"Of course, no one is going to take some criminals at their word, but the subject of demonic potions is no laughing matter."

"Right," I agreed absently, since it felt rude to sit there in silence.

"So the kingdom secretly put their intelligence unit on the matter... and they found a huge amount of demonic potions in the storehouse of one of Marquis Kelten's armies."

On top of that, he added, there were Fire Rods and monster-part weapons hidden in the warehouse that weren't in the army's records. They even had a big anti-fortress Magic Cannon.

As such, the other nobles started raising a fuss about Marquis Kelten potentially plotting an uprising, throwing the royal capital into chaos.

"You still don't get it? For someone the viceroy's wife values so highly, you have a long way to go in terms of finesse."

Sighing, the baron explained that if Marquis Kelten was to lose his title, it would present the opportunity to snag a military position in the royal capital with the support of the viceroy's wife.

I appreciated his thoughtful suggestion, but I wasn't interested in climbing the ranks any more than I already had.

I thanked him for the information but conveyed, in a roundabout way, that I had no intention of advancing my station in that manner.

"Hmph. Then you'll never become a permanent noble."

"That's quite all right. An honorary title is more than enough for me."

Once that conversation ended and the baron finished the sorbet I'd brought, I excused myself.

Then I went around visiting other noble families.

The rest of them weren't as high-ranking as Baron Moffo, so instead of cooling fans, I brought them sorbet and five ice pillars for cooling down a room.

I had been told at the viceroy's wife's tea party that both were highly prized, and sure enough, all the families were delighted to receive them.

It didn't earn me the same bosom-buddy treatment as it did with the baron, but it seemed like they at least stopped viewing me with hostility.

It's important to get along with your neighbors, after all.

◆

"Oh my. You certainly catch wind of things quickly, don't you, Sir Pendragon?"

Once I finished making the rounds to the noble families, I visited the viceroy's wife to verify the truth of the rumors of war I'd heard from Baron Moffo.

"The western part of the continent is always having skirmishes," the viceroy's wife said as she savored the breeze from the cooling fan. "There have been rumors of impending war among a few nations there for around half a year now. I heard recently from Dyukeli that more foreign merchants have been coming to Labyrinth City to buy weapons and supplies lately."

As it turned out, the discussions I'd heard the night before at the explorers' banquet, about magic weapons getting more expensive, were directly related. Baronet Dyukeli was deliberately raising those prices to minimize the exporting of Magic Swords.

"Is there some problem with Magic Swords being exported?"

"Well, yes. The loss of Magic Swords, mithril weapons, and so on reduces the defensive capabilities of our land and raises the incentive of other nations, after all."

The viceroy's wife added that it wasn't too big of a problem if it was only a few being exported.

Personally, I thought it would be better to amass lots of Magic Guns and large golems if you were planning to go to war, but in a world with a level system, high-level soldiers with powerful weapons were certainly nothing to sneeze at.

In spite of the unpleasant rumors, I guess Baronet Dyukeli was more than just a simple miser.

"Many monster-part weapons can't be repaired if they're damaged, so Shiga Kingdom knights and soldiers generally don't like to use them… But I'm told that in the west of the continent, they have a secret technique for repairing them."

The viceroy whispered this last part of the rumor to me.

Oh, wait. I wonder if Liza's Magic Spear is like that, too?

I was pretty sure I remembered it getting small cracks or chips before, but I couldn't actually recall seeing them on the spear.

Maybe it fixed itself or something.

I decided to ask Liza when I got back.

"Baron Moffo is right about the effects of war. You're certainly free to capitalize on this opportunity, but please do be careful about whom you sell materials to. Said materials possess the potential to become powerful weapons, after all."

"I will. Thank you very much."

I wasn't planning on selling rare materials like those from areamasters and their spawn in the first place, but I would have to be careful about selling other materials, too.

But enough about the war situation.

"I also heard that a demonic-potion-smuggling operation was uncovered in the trade city Tartumina. Do you think they were the same goods that were being sold in Labyrinth City?"

"I imagine the materials came from the same place. Only a labyrinth can produce enough materials to make such a massive amount of demonic potion." Sadness crept into the round face of the viceroy's wife. "We know how they were smuggling it into Labyrinth City, too."

She explained that they had found an underground tunnel leading out of the city in the basement of a house that had been Sokell's love nest, at the outskirts of the pleasure quarters near the outer walls.

"Creating a tunnel like that in secret must have required several talented earth mages, but Sokell didn't have any such connections. Poputema said he wasn't involved in that when he was brainwashed by the demon, either. The only organizations with earth mages like that would be the Shiga Thirty Staffs of the royal court or the kingdom army."

In other words, there was a good chance that the person who was pulling the strings behind Sokell had influence with either the royal court mages or the kingdom army.

"Did you know they found demonic potions in the royal capital, as well?"

"Something about finding them in an army warehouse, wasn't it?"

"That's right. There's quite a fuss in the royal capital that the man in charge of that army may have been planning a revolt."

The viceroy's wife quietly told me the man's name, which was, of course, Marquis Kelten.

"So now we won't be able to send Sokell to the royal capital for a while yet."

The information about this incident had come on the very airship that was supposed to escort him there. If they sent Sokell to the royal capital now, he might be used as a tool in the political uproar around Marquis Kelten, so he was being confined to the tower in the viceroy's castle instead.

Oh right…

"That reminds me. Was Sokell being brainwashed by a demon, too? He certainly seemed deranged when he was arrested."

I had been wondering about this for a while.

Since it seemed like demons and even demon lord worshippers had been involved in the incident in Labyrinth City, it occurred to me that they might be connected to Sokell's case, too.

"Hmm? I thought you weren't interested in Sokell, Sir Pendragon." The viceroy's wife's eyes flashed. "After we put Poputema in suspended animation, we had the head priestess of Heraluon, who discovered his brainwashing, examine Sokell as well, but she said there were no signs of brainwashing there."

Sokell's derangement was apparently a side effect of a magic potion he'd been using, the equivalent of what we on Earth would call a semi-legal drug. This potion was a by-product of demonic-potion creation.

Honestly. Why does something like that even exist in a fantasy world?

The conversation threatened to take a dark turn, but fortunately a maid brought out some tasty-looking sorbet just in time to lighten the mood.

"Sorbet is particularly delicious on a hot day like today."

The sorbet, which seemed to have been made by freezing a citrus-like fruit, had an invigorating scent and a deliciously light aftertaste.

"Celivera is close to an enormous desert, so it can get quite hot without proper climate regulation."

"…Climate regulation?"

"Oh, yes. Normally, my husband uses his power as the viceroy to regulate the climate, but since he had to use it to sweep the area for demons, I'm afraid it will be hot until enough magic power has been saved up."

So using the City Core to search takes so much magic that they can't even adjust the climate...? No wonder they don't do it regularly, even if it means demons have a much easier time getting in.

It must be very different from my "Search Entire Map" skill, which uses almost no magic at all.

"The entire Shiga Kingdom received an imperial command from His Majesty, not just his directly controlled territories. The royal capital and duchies have enough magic to spare, but in counties and smaller cities, the lack of magic power means a poorer climate."

As an example, she mentioned Seiryuu County in the north, where she said it had become considerably colder.

I worried about crop failure and famine, but she said the magic power needed to adjust the climate should be back up within a month or so, so it shouldn't lead to anything too dire.

"But following the order was worth it. Three demons were discovered in the kingdom and some of the neighboring territories."

There were lesser demons found in the neighboring Zetts County and Kiriku County, one in Vistall Duchy in the north of the Shiga Kingdom, and even an intermediate demon found in Lessau County.

Still, I was curious why they didn't find any demons in the royal capital, which seemed like the most likely target. Was it because the Eight Swordsmen of Shiga—said to be the strongest band of fighters in the kingdom—were there?

Oh, that's right.

I opened my map and checked the marker I'd put on the avatar of the green greater demon that had caused the demon incident in Labyrinth City a few days ago.

He had been wandering around near the border of Vistall Duchy and Lessau County, but now the marker was gone.

They probably found him with the demon search and dispatched an army to destroy him.

I had let it go in the hopes of finding out where the demons planned to cause trouble next, but I guess that wasn't going to happen now.

I'll just have to put another marker on the next one I find.

"Was there a lot of damage in the process?"

"I'm told the capital of Lessau County was greatly damaged, and Count Lessau was killed in battle."

Count Lessau was the depraved lord who had sexually harassed Tifaleeza and Neru and made them into criminal slaves.

I wouldn't say I felt good about news of his death, but I wasn't exactly troubled by it, either.

"Count Lessau's son led the city's army to destroy the demon, so now they're focused on rebuilding. He intends to make his fiancée, Lady Sistina, his first wife at the next kingdom meeting. He must be in a hurry to get his land back on its feet."

I hope the son is a little better than his father.

But since the demon was defeated, I guess I had nothing to worry about.

"I haven't heard the damage reports from the other cities, but there's bound to have been damage and casualties until the emergency armies arrived on the scene to dispatch them. It's nothing short of a miracle that powerful fighters like General Erthal and the Crimson Devil Lady Zona happened to be on the scene when those demons showed up here a few days ago. Most cases aren't so lucky.

"And brave youngsters like you, too," she added with a smile.

Crimson Devil was apparently a nickname for the guildmaster.

"So we don't need any special permission to clean the aqueducts?"

"Not really, but please do let the government offices know that you plan to do so in advance. They hate things being done without their knowledge."

"Understood. Thank you."

Since Arisa was raring to clean up the city aqueducts, I checked with the viceroy's wife to see if we could start clearing the garbage from them as part of our volunteer efforts. She said it wouldn't be a problem.

The government did clean them twice a year, she added, but people threw trash in them so frequently that they quickly grew dirty again.

There was a knock at the door, and a lady-in-waiting peered inside.

"Lady Reythel, he's arrived."

"Send him in, please."

With her permission, a cruel-looking government official entered the room.

As it turned out, he was a royal capital official sent to make a record of the demon-attack incident that happened a few days prior.

Normally he would question me alone, but the viceroy's wife was concerned for me, so she had the questioning take place in the viceroy's castle and even sat in on it herself.

It may have been thanks to her presence that the questioning was simply a cursory summary of the events.

Except at the end…

"Did the intermediate demon say anything else?"

"Like what?"

"I'll ask the questions here."

"Erm, okay. But I don't think he said anything noteworthy?"

I played the memory back in my mind, but I couldn't recall anything special that was said.

At any rate, it was the green demon's avatar who said things like that.

"Nothing about the Rite of the Second Coming or a False King?"

"No, not that I recall."

So don't raise flags with important-sounding key words like that, please.

"Are you quite finished with your interrogation? I do have other business with Sir Pendragon. If you're done, I would appreciate it if you left, please."

Recognizing that the viceroy's wife's request was in fact an order, the official withdrew.

Those words sure hinted at a demon-lord revival to me, but he had nothing to worry about. I had already crushed the green demon's plot to revive one in Labyrinth City.

As long as there weren't other plans to revive any more demon lords anyway.

◆

"S-S-S-Sir Pendragon!"

After my meeting with the viceroy's wife, I got permission from the government office to clean the aqueducts. I was headed to the guild-master's office in the west to relay information about the potential war. However, along the way, a plump young noble boy called out to me.

"Hello, Sir Luram."

The boy came running up to me in such a panic, he nearly tripped and fell. "H-help!"

There must've been some kind of emergency. He looked like he was at his wit's end.

"What's the matter?"

"I-it's Mary-Ann!" Luram cried as he grabbed my arm. "Sh-she went into the labyrinth!"

I guess a new round of trouble was already beginning.

Baronet Dyukeli

Satou here. I think that as long as society persists, conflicts of interest will occur one way or another. Even if it's impossible to please everyone, I think it's important to try and reach a compromise so that we can get closer to our ideals, one step at a time.

"Calm down, Sir Luram."

The boy was flying into a panic, repeating the phrases "help!" and "Mary-Ann's in the labyrinth!" over and over without giving me any details.

Once I got him to take a few deep breaths and calm down, he explained that he had been walking around eating when he saw Mary-Ann, Baronet Dyukeli's daughter, get invited into the labyrinth by a rogue party of explorers.

"Have you contacted the baronet's family?"

"Uh-huh. Th-the old man sent me."

Luram said it had been less than half an hour since Miss Mary-Ann had gone into the labyrinth.

"I shall go into the labyrinth to find her, then."

"L-let me—"

"You must stay here and inform Baronet Dyukeli of the situation when he arrives, Sir Luram."

I stopped him before he could say he wanted to come with me.

"A-all right."

Leaving the young man there, I headed for the labyrinth.

As I went through the gates and dashed down the uneven steps, I used my map search to ascertain Miss Mary-Ann's current location.

She was in a narrow passage not far from the main hallway of section 1, hunting demi-goblins with three female explorers.

Silencing my footsteps, I snuck toward the spot where they were fighting.

"Come on, little lady! If you're too focused on one, another monster'll getcha!"

"Gah-ha-ha! Guess even little noble brats bleed red!"

"Uh-oh, there's a maze moth above you! Watch out for its paralysis, girlie!"

I could hear the women jeering unpleasantly up ahead.

"P-please assist me. I can't do this on my own."

Judging by the position of the dots on my radar, the explorer women were just standing around watching Mary-Ann struggle, ignoring her requests for help.

As I reached the end of the passage, I could see them down below. This passage seemed to come out right above where they were fighting.

"Oh dear, I thought you said you could take a goblin no problem?"

"Why, you've even fought a soldier mantis, haven't you?"

"If you can handle that, you don't need armor to fight a goblin, right, girlie?"

This last speaker was holding a metal breastplate and smirking.

So they were forcing Mary-Ann to fight demi-goblins without her armor.

"What do you think you're doing?"

I felt like I was witnessing a particularly nasty form of bullying.

Jumping to the ground about ten feet below, I cut down the demi-goblins with my fairy sword, then stood between Miss Mary-Ann and the female explorers to protect her.

> Title Acquired: Savior of Maidens

"We were just training the kid, that's all…"

"And you had to take away her armor to do that?"

The demi-goblins' claws had torn up Mary-Ann's shirt, and her health bar was down by nearly half.

"Th-this is how we train, that's all!"

"Ugh. Let's get out of here, ladies."

"Have fun with your man, little girl!"

The women started to flee, but I grabbed one by her leg with Magic

Hand to send her tumbling to the ground, and the other two tripped over her and fell.

As they tried to scramble to their feet, I quickly tied them up with rope from my Garage Bag.

"Wh-what the hell're you doing?"

"Untie us!"

"You perv!"

"You didn't seem to have the best intentions. I'm taking you to the guild."

If I hadn't gotten there in time, there was a good chance they would have watched Miss Mary-Ann die.

These women had gone a little too far for me to let them off with merely a warning.

"Why would you rescue some bastard noble's daughter?"

"Yeah, everyone hates Dyukeli. We just wanted to cheer up our pals."

"How many explorers d'you think died 'cause of Dyukeli's money-making schemes?!"

"If we made him regret it, magic potions would be cheaper!"

As the tied-up female explorers flailed and raged, Mary-Ann looked away sadly.

These women must have lured her into the labyrinth to get their revenge on Baronet Dyukeli.

"No, you only wanted to take out your own frustration on her. Don't claim to speak for other explorers."

"But it's true! Everyone says so!"

"And who is 'everyone,' exactly?" I shot a cold glare at the women. My gaze must have been affected by the "Intimidation" skill, because they started to cower immediately.

I didn't doubt that some explorers had likely died because they couldn't afford magic potions, but that was no excuse to blame everything on Baronet Dyukeli, in my opinion.

If they didn't have magic potions, they should take safety precautions accordingly.

And picking on his young daughter in retaliation certainly wasn't the answer.

"Lady Mary-Ann, those wounds might leave a scar. Drink this magic potion to help with that."

I handed Mary-Ann a lesser magic potion.

Her wounds seemed shallow enough, but since they were caused by demi-goblins' undoubtedly filthy claws, they would probably get infected if left untreated.

Mary-Ann looked at the potion but made no move to drink it.

She must have felt self-conscious about it after what the women said.

"If you're covered in blood, His Excellency will surely be worried."

I pulled out a fake scroll and pretended to use it while I healed her wounds with Healing Magic and cleaned away the dried blood from her clothes with Everyday Magic.

"Here's a change of clothes, Lady Mary-Ann."

Even with the blood removed, her shirt was still torn in all sorts of places, so I carefully averted my eyes while handing her one of Lulu's spare shirts. The fabric was ordinary cotton, but since it was made by brownie house fairies, it was exceptionally comfortable.

"Thank you, Sir Knight."

Mary-Ann bowed her head quietly. I had her put her armor back on before we headed to the exit.

Since I was dragging the tied-up women along, we got some strange looks from explorers on the way, but they were quick to avert their eyes when they noticed my noble clothing.

At the gate, I explained the situation and turned the women in to the guild employee. Then Mary-Ann and I left the labyrinth.

While we were walking toward the west guild, I saw a stylish black carriage speeding into the square. Not far behind it were some armored men riding in a cart.

The carriage screeched to a halt, the door burst open, and an older gentleman—Baronet Dyukeli—came flying out.

From a distance, I saw the baronet speak with little Luram, then come running toward us with the men in tow. He looked extremely distressed.

"Your ride is here, Lady Mary-Ann," I commented.

"Father…"

Mary-Ann looked up with a mixture of relief and discomfort.

"Mary-Ann!"

Noticing us, Baronet Dyukeli flashed a look of relief, but it was quickly replaced by anger as he charged over.

I thought he was going to scoop her up in a hug, but instead he slapped her harshly across the cheek.

"You foolish child!"

"Father, I was—"

"You can give your excuses at home."

Baronet Dyukeli grabbed his daughter's slender arm, ignoring her protests. Then his sharp gaze fell on me.

"I deeply appreciate your assistance. Allow me to thank you someday soon."

With that, he dragged Mary-Ann away.

For a moment there, I had been bracing myself for him to assume that I was the one who had taken his daughter into the labyrinth, but fortunately it seemed that Luram had told him that I went to rescue her.

As Baronet Dyukeli stormed back into the carriage with his daughter in tow, Luram came up to me instead.

"I'm glad Mary-Ann is okay." Luram's stomach grumbled. "All this relief is making me hungry."

"Here. A little reward for my helper behind the scenes."

I produced some handmade fried-whale skewers from Storage and handed them to the boy.

He was today's MVP for alerting me to Mary-Ann's plight, after all.

"Wow, it's even yummier than usual!"

Thanking Luram as he delightedly gobbled up the whale meat, I bought some veria water from a passing peddler to quench my thirst.

I guess that takes care of things for now.

"Welcome, Sir Pendragon. Glad you could make it to our banquet."

"Thank you for inviting me."

A few days after I rescued Miss Mary-Ann, I was invited to Baronet Dyukeli's place for dinner.

Seated at the long table in the dining room was the baronet, his wife, Mary-Ann, and her older brother, the baronet's eldest son.

According to the information I'd gathered beforehand, the baronet had no concubines or lovers, which was rare for a noble of the Shiga Kingdom.

Mary-Ann's cheek had been healed with a magic potion, so there was no trace of the spot where her father had slapped her, but her makeup couldn't quite hide the reddening around her eyes that suggested she'd been crying.

This was the second time I'd seen her in a dress, the first time being at the viceroy's wife's tea party. Personally, I thought it suited her better than her usual boyish attire with a rapier at her waist.

"S-so you're Sir Pendragon? Thank you for rescuing my sister."

The pale eldest son smiled at me weakly.

He seemed sort of wispy, and not in a good way. My AR display showed his status as **Goblin Disease: Chronic.**

He was sixteen, two years older than Miss Mary-Ann, but he looked younger than her.

Seeing them all lined up like this, the large gap between Baronet Dyukeli's age and that of his children was very clear.

"Since you're known as a gourmet, I outdid myself with the food today."

"I'm looking forward to it."

Should you really be tooting your own horn like that?

The way he said that bothered me a little, but the meal itself really was delicious and consisted of ingredients that were very rare in Labyrinth City.

Someone with the "Item Box" skill had probably transported the ingredients here in a refrigerating magic tool over a long distance.

"Joss, eat your vegetables."

"But I hate vegetables."

With my "Keen Hearing" skill, I heard the baronet's wife scolding her son, who was eating only meat and bread.

Noticing this, Baronet Dyukeli scowled. "Quiet, Hoshess. Not in front of our guest."

His wife stiffened and apologized to her husband and me. She looked back at her son as if she wanted to say something else, but he continued to ignore his vegetables and happily scarfed down a filet of Ohmi beef with sweet-and-sour sauce.

The uncomfortable atmosphere made it difficult to enjoy the delicious food, but I did my best to keep up polite conversation until the dinner finally ended with a pear compote that I forced down so quickly, I couldn't remember the taste.

"You're an explorer, right, Sir Pendragon? Tell us some stories."

"Joss, I have to talk business with Sir Pendragon. You can ask to hear his stories another time."

"Hmph."

The boy pouted childishly, and his father smacked him upside the head.

"Honestly, will you ever grow up?"

My "Keen Hearing" skill picked up on his muttered remark.

"That seems about right for his age," I volunteered.

"Can you really say that when you're younger than he is?"

Baronet Dyukeli smiled wryly as he led me into the parlor.

Oh right. I guess I look only fifteen or so.

"I wish my son could be more like you in... No, I suppose I shouldn't make that sort of complaint to a guest."

I sat down on the sofa in the understated parlor. It wasn't terribly soft, but it had a nice antiquated aesthetic.

"Thank you for saving Mary-Ann twice now." Baronet Dyukeli placed two old scrolls on the table. "Consider these a token of my appreciation."

"Magic Scrolls?"

"I heard that you collect them."

"Do you mind if I take a look?"

He shook his head, so I carefully opened the scrolls. One was for the Stone Object spell, and the other was Create Earth Servant.

They both sounded so enticing that I wanted to teleport to the labyrinth and test them out right away.

Delicately, I placed them back on the table so I wouldn't damage them.

"These seem very rare."

"I originally collected them for Count Fudai and Viscount Gohato, but because I didn't have anything else that seemed likely to excite you, I decided they should go to you instead."

"I'll have to thank Count Fudai and Viscount Gohato, too, then."

"Neither of them is terribly practical, so don't expect too much."

The baronet seemed to have sensed my excitement.

"I'm only interested in collecting them, simply happy to own such rare scrolls."

"Very well, then."

"By the way, these look different from the scrolls Viscount Siemmen's workshop produces. Were they found in treasure chests in the Celi-vera Labyrinth?"

I could tell from my AR that they were from a place called the **Sand-storm Labyrinth**, but I decided to ask in a roundabout way.

"No, I'm told they came from a labyrinth that has long since perished."

He went on to explain that they were sold to him by a foreign merchant who came looking to buy magic weapons.

When I collected the scrolls, maids came over to place beautiful drinking glasses on the table and filled them with a whiskey that smelled powerfully of barley.

"Incidentally, Sir Pendragon..." Baronet Dyukeli took a long drink of whiskey before he spoke. "I have a request to ask of you. It's about my son."

"What can I help you with?"

"Do you know about his illness?"

"I'm not aware of the name of the illness, but I have heard that he fell victim to an incurable disease of some kind, yes."

After requesting that I not speak a word of this to anyone, the baronet told me that his son had the serious Goblin Disease, which he had been treating with ogredrink potion provided by Sokell.

Of course, I already knew all this from my map, but obviously I couldn't reveal that.

"So are you asking me to make an ogredrink potion?"

Maybe he knew that "Transmutation" was among my publicly viewable skills.

"No, I have plenty of alchemists I could go to for that. I want to ask you to procure ingredients."

"Ingredients, is it...?"

The ogredrink potion contained ingredients also found in illegal drugs like demonic potion and corpse potion, so they would be difficult to acquire while there was such a fuss about illicit demonic-potion production going on.

I could find the ingredients easily enough with my map, but that would probably make people suspect me of producing illegal drugs.

"I know they are difficult to obtain. And I've been told that the guildmaster and a so-called follower of the Hero burned the plunder-ers' hideouts. But the explorers who can go deep into the labyrinth are too obsessed with defeating floormasters to listen to me. I've asked Silverlight and some of the mid-ranking explorers as well, but none of them responded favorably."

That made sense to me. Mid-ranking explorers could earn a steady living easily enough, so I didn't think they would accept a risky request to wander the labyrinth in search of rare ingredients.

"Is there no other cure but ogredrink potion?"

"Of course there is. Bloodstone powder and cure-all would both be more effective than ogredrink potion. I have ordered them, but they are too expensive to use so readily."

More expensive than sending garnet-badge-explorer parties into the labyrinth?

Come to think of it, he hadn't mentioned bloodpearl powder, which should also cure Goblin Disease. The imperial family of the Saga Empire had a monopoly on bloodpearls. Maybe he thought it wasn't worth mentioning?

"I was hoping that Princess Meetia's Breath of Purification might be of help, but judging by Miss Shina's condition, it seems I can't expect too much."

My mind ran to the young Princess Meetia from the Nolork Kingdom.

Her gift from the Heraluon faith, Breath of Purification, had healed the Miasma Poisoning of the viceroy's fourth daughter, Shina, but it had had no effect on her Goblin Disease.

According to my documents, because this illness was essentially a lifestyle disease brought on by vitamin deficiency, purifying it wouldn't do much.

If anything, drinking vegetable juice would probably be more helpful.

At any rate, I hadn't cured the viceroy's daughter myself because I didn't want to cause any trouble for Princess Meetia, who was friends with Arisa and the others.

It was becoming clear over time that her Breath of Purification didn't work on Goblin Disease. I suspected they would seek another cure soon.

So I was copying down all the documents I had about the disease for just such an occasion.

"Would a cure-all work?"

"We tried it once when my son was younger. It seemed to have cured him at first, but the disease returned within less than a year."

My guess was that the cure-all had fixed it, but it came back because he didn't improve his eating habits.

"I researched this when I learned of Lady Shina's illness…"

With that, I gave him the information in question and recommended improving his son's diet.

I even showed him the original documents to make it more convincing.

"Hmm. Vitamin deficiency, you say? I do believe I've read about this in the great ancestral king's writings."

Ooh, nice one, Ancestral King. That's helpful information to leave for future generations.

"It refers to good spirits that hide in vegetables and livestock entrails and the like, yes?"

…Not even close.

Where did the "spirits" part come from?

Oh well. At least the important information was in there somewhere.

"Yes, that's right. The ones that hide in entrails are tricky, however, so I'm told you have to cook them over flame first to burn away their tendency toward trickery."

Using my "Fabrication" skill, I came up with an arbitrary reason to warn him against eating liver and similar foods raw.

"But my son despises vegetables, I'm afraid…"

Yeah, I noticed.

"Have you considered trying vegetable juice?"

"I have heard of such things for fruit, but vegetables?"

It occurred to me that I had never seen a magic tool resembling a juicer before.

"Yes, an alchemist friend of mine had a magic tool that could turn vegetable ingredients into liquid. If you give me some time, I can ask whether we'd be able to acquire one."

Baronet Dyukeli frowned in thought.

I'd expected him to agree right away, but apparently, something was making him hesitate.

"Turning vegetables into liquid… And you're certain there are no negative side effects?"

Ah, I see. A very parental concern.

"It's just like regular cooking. The only difference is that it uses a magic tool instead of cooking implements."

It would be dangerous if he had some kind of vegetable allergy. I called on his wet nurse and asked her, but she said he had never shown such symptoms on the rare occasion he did eat vegetables.

When I said there should be no problem, then, the baronet asked me to acquire one for him.

"All right. I'll send a letter requesting to purchase the magic tool, then. Since this friend of mine lives far away, I may need a little time… How much ogredrink potion do you have in stock?"

"About a month's worth. That's how long it stays effective, so His Excellency the viceroy is probably in the same state."

That's not much.

I felt confident that the vegetable juice could cure his condition, but probably not in one month.

"Then it might be best to submit a request for potion ingredients to the explorers' guild."

"You cannot take the request on yourself?"

"I'm afraid we specialize in defeating monsters, not gathering ingredients. We'll search any likely areas along the way, but I do not know whether we'll be able to harvest them while preserving the active ingredient."

I gave a distant response, not wanting him to depend on me too much.

Although of course I would collect enough ingredients just in case, with the viceroy's daughter's condition and all.

"If you put out the request, explorers are likely to search for them, and other experts might come to Labyrinth City if they hear that there's a potential for profit."

Most of the garnet-badge explorers might not be available, but harvesting specialists probably wouldn't be too eager to fight floormasters, so they were probably just collecting magic potion ingredients due to the high demand.

"No, I won't be submitting a request. If I do, it might have the opposite effect."

The baronet appeared to be aware that he was hated by explorers.

"Could you perhaps ask a doctor or alchemist friend to submit it in your place?"

"The result would be the same. Explorers dislike anyone in my employ as well."

They must think of them as his cohorts.

"About the magic potions...," I began.

"Yes, I know. If I was to lower the price, the explorers would doubt-less change their tune, but I cannot do that. Do you know why?"

Sure. It's a major source of income for you.

I couldn't very well say that, so I just shook my head.

"Compared with the royal capital area, Labyrinth City has far less areas where one can find magic potion ingredients. I keep the price stable because if it was any lower, the alchemists would have a hard time eking out a living due to the rising costs of ingredients. Some of them can barely afford to eat as is."

I see. So it was actually a case of extreme deflation.

"The situation even led some to quit alchemy or leave Labyrinth City altogether."

He explained that he took the lead for the waning alchemists' and doctors' guilds and accepted the role of being hated for raising the prices.

Incidentally, he added that the guilds were obligated to sell magic potions at the same price as they went for in the royal capital area.

This is a problem.

If the potions were too expensive, the explorers would be in trouble, but if they were too low, the alchemists would struggle.

For explorers, magic potions were a life-saving last resort in the case of unforeseen danger. Ideally, they should be affordable even for newbie explorers.

But it wasn't right for alchemists and doctors to not be able to eat, either. I sorted through the information in my mind, trying to find a solution that would satisfy both sides.

High costs of ingredients. Shortages. Not enough areas to find the necessary materials.

So if the ingredients were cheaply and widely available, would that solve the problem?

There were plenty of them deep in the upper stratum of the labyrinth, but going that far to get them wasn't profitable for explorers.

Determined, I searched through the documents left behind by Trazayuya, the elf sage who had once worked in the Celivera Labyrinth.

"…Veria potion?"

Veria was a kind of succulent that grew plentifully outside Labyrinth City and could apparently be used to make a health recovery potion.

"Hmph. An oft-used lie of swindlers."

"Swindlers?"

"That's right. If someone tried to sell such a thing to you, you should report them to the police immediately. That's a swindler, without a doubt." Baronet Dyukeli's voice was hard. "They use the so-called legend that an elf sage once made magic potions from veria and try to sell fakes from an incomplete recipe at high prices."

The baronet added that nobles and merchants who were new to Labyrinth City often fell for such schemes.

"An incomplete recipe?"

"Indeed. Two hundred years ago, an apprentice of the sage was able to reproduce it using transmutation equipment the sage left behind, but ever since that equipment broke, veria potions have been the stuff of legend."

I looked at the recipe in my documents.

True enough, it wouldn't be possible to make it in this state without an elf Transmutation Tablet.

If I wanted to popularize the use of these potions in Labyrinth City, I would have to adapt the recipe for human Transmutation Tablets.

Deciding to research this later, I went back to the topic of ogredrink-potion ingredients for now.

"As for the ingredients we discussed before, would it be all right if I submit the request to the guildmaster and have her put it out as a formal request from the guild itself?"

"I suppose those damn explorers might accept it then…"

Damn explorers?

Couldn't you be a little more respectful?

"These are the ingredients we're missing."

I looked at the list of ingredients and their requisite amounts listed on the paper he handed me, then wrote down the reward amount he was offering.

I was willing to just put out the ingredient-gathering request as a favor, but he gave me a rare magic spell book as thanks.

The book was written by an Earth Magic user who had dedicated his life to the labyrinth, including his studies about golems.

He had probably prepared this to go with the scrolls he gave me earlier.

"By the by, Sir Pendragon, do you know of a magic potion called Monster Incense?"

"No, I've never heard of it."

It wasn't anywhere in my recipes, either.

"It's a forbidden potion that attracts nearby monsters," Baronet Dyukeli explained. "I'm told that someone has been bringing bewitching slime to unlicensed alchemists and demanding that they make Monster Incense."

He didn't know who the culprit was.

I tried searching my map for Monster Incense but didn't find anything. Unfortunately, the contents of an Item Box wouldn't show up on my map search, so I couldn't say for sure that it didn't exist within the city.

"That's troubling news. I'll have to be careful when next I enter the labyrinth."

With our discussion at an end, I decided to take my leave.

"Thank you for your help."

"Not at all. I'll handle it."

Baronet Dyukeli saw me to the entryway, then bowed deeply.

I guess he cared more about his son than he let on.

Miss Mary-Ann was watching from the window. She seemed like she wanted to say something, but, worried about raising weird flags for future events, I ignored her.

I would just have to find an explorer school that she could attend with the viceroy's son Gerits to keep them both happy.

Veria Potion

Satou here. With the advent of middleware, it became standard to release games on multiple platforms. But before that, it was very difficult to downsize from desktop gaming computers to handheld consoles.

"Lord Kuro!"

"Sorry to show up in the middle of the night, Lelillil."

After I returned to our house, I changed into my Kuro disguise and used the Space Magic spell Return to go to the Ivy Manor.

I wanted to research whether it was possible to adapt the veria potion recipe I'd learned about at Baronet Dyukeli's place so that it could be made with humans' Transmutation Tablets.

The youthful house fairy Lelillil came to greet me, so I told her I would be using the laboratory in the basement.

"I'll get it ready right away!"

Lelillil scurried off briskly. She seemed to be in an energetic mood.

As Lelillil left, another girl appeared in her place.

"Lord Kuro! You're back!"

Miss Eluterina, the blond noblewoman, wore a look of evident delight on her lovely features.

She'd been staying in the Ivy Manor since I'd rescued her from the plunderers.

Since she was from a noble family, any rumors that her purity had been compromised by plunderers would bring disgrace to her and her family; I was waiting for things to blow over before releasing her and her fellow nobles from the manor.

Oh right.

"I have a question for you."

I didn't want to make her stand around and talk to me, so we sat down in the reception area of the study. Since she was the grand-daughter of Marquis Kelten, I asked her about the rumors I'd heard in the baron's house the day before.

"Lord Kuro! My grandfather would never commit such treason!"

"Are you sure about that?"

"Grandfather worships the royal family, since they are descended directly from the great ancestral king Yamato."

So he's not just loyal—he worships *them?*

Doesn't sound like the type of person I'd like to be friends with.

"Is it possible that he was forced to obey some villains because they'd taken you hostage?"

"…Not at all." Eluterina's voice was faint. "Grandfather would side with the royal family even over his own children or grandchildren."

"That's pretty extreme."

"Such is the way of the Kelten family."

The blond noblewoman was from an offshoot of this family, but she still seemed to take pride in their nature.

"As a result, our family has earned a great amount of trust from the royal family, and we have commanded the king's army for generations."

Eluterina was a good judge of character. There must be more than just personal bias in play for her to declare this so confidently.

"If you're worried about them, would you like to return to the royal capital?"

"N-no, thank you. Someone like myself wouldn't be of much use anyway."

She shook her head, but she did look worried.

"Why don't you go—?"

I was going to suggest that she check in on her family, but I was interrupted by a knock at the door.

"Lord Kuro? It's Tifaleeza."

"Come in."

Tifaleeza entered the room, her silver hair swaying barely above her shoulders, framing her lovely face and sharp eyes.

The light in the room seemed to flow across her soft curls.

Though not quite on the level of Lulu, her beauty was still incredibly captivating.

"Here are the account books for the food stalls and other side jobs."

She handed me a register tracking the numbers for the work of the rescued girls who were currently living in tenement houses in the downtown area.

There was dust in her hair. She must have just come through the secret underground passage that connected the downtown tenements to a place near the Ivy Manor.

The passage was made with Pitfall and strengthened with Wall and Hard Clay, so I wasn't surprised that people would get a little dirty passing through it.

If my new Stone Object spell turned out to be useful, maybe I could reinforce it with stone.

As I thought about all this, I brushed the dirt from Tifaleeza's hair.

"L-Lord Kuro?"

She turned bright red and squirmed. Maybe she didn't like having her hair touched so suddenly.

"My apologies."

With that, I quickly skimmed the books.

"Hmm. We're in the red."

The food stalls were fairly profitable, but thanks to lots of household expenses, the total was in the negative.

Even the earnings from Miss Elder Sister and her explorer group were lower than those of the frog-hunting group.

"Yes. So Elder Sister and the others proposed an expedition to the mantis area."

"Put a stop to that. They could be hurt or worse."

They might have decent armor, but their levels weren't very high, so they would undoubtedly have a difficult time against soldier mantises or war mantises.

"But there aren't many day-labor jobs that will hire women, and the pay for the other side jobs is quite low…"

We might have to come up with some kind of marketable product for the girls to sell.

"Lord Kuro, perhaps we could sell the magic tools made in Labyrinth City to people in the royal capital, plus sell accessories from the latter to explorers in the former?"

This was Eluterina's suggestion.

"Commerce, eh? Do any of you have experience in that area?"

"Yes, Neru and three of the other girls who manage the stalls."

She explained that two of the girls had parents who were merchants, and one had actually been a peddler herself.

As long as some of them had experience, they would probably be fine.

"All right. I'm putting you and the peddler girl in charge of investigating the market."

"It would be my pleasure!"

This would allow the blond noblewoman to check in on her grandfather, too, so it would be killing two birds with one stone.

"Bring the other noblewomen from the mansion, as well. Market research will be easier with more people."

I figured this would let some of the other girls go back to visit their families, but Eluterina's expression darkened.

Maybe she thought I was fishing for an excuse to kick them out for good?

"I'll give you a month for the investigation. Don't forget to account for travel time both there and back."

And with that, the blonde broke into a relieved smile.

I guess she understood what I was getting at when I mentioned the trip back here.

"While you're at it, see if you can find an estate in the royal capital that we can use as a base, too."

This was mostly so I could place a Return seal slate there.

"Lord Kuro, I've heard that you need a trade license to deal in magic tools in the royal capital."

"Oh dear, you're right. I had completely forgotten."

The blond noblewoman agreed with Tifaleeza's observation.

"We'll have to get ahold of one before we start trading, then."

If I asked the king as Nanashi the Hero, I could probably get any number of licenses, but negotiating with him directly sounded stressful.

"I'm terribly sorry."

"It's fine. My master will get the trade license for us."

While I was there, I would be able to sell first-generation handmade Magic Swords to my heart's content.

They were the same kind as the Magic Sword Akatsuki, which Viscount Siemmen had shown off to General Erthal after buying it at the dark auction in the old capital.

After the demonified-Ludaman incident, General Erthal had told me that there were few people with valuable mithril or mithril-alloy swords even in the royal army, let alone wielders of Magic Swords.

I wasn't interested in becoming an arms dealer, but I figured I could sell them some Magic Swords to protect the land from monsters.

So I was just going to sell them my handmade Magic Swords, keeping my salvaged weapons of war, like large Magic Guns and Magic Cannons, hidden away in Storage.

I had plenty of fins from monster fish and giant monster fish, which were used to make skypower engines for aircrafts and such, so I could probably sell some airships and engines, too.

If air transport became more common, then I could comfortably travel the skies in my regular Satou form.

And even if that didn't happen, I'd be more than happy if the distribution of rare ingredients became more widespread.

But I could deal with all that after Eluterina and the other ladies concluded their research.

"I'll put Polina and Sumina in charge of researching goods in Labyrinth City. As I said before, I'll allocate a month for research. Two days from now, I'll bring you to the city with my Teleportation Magic. Be ready by then."

When the conversation concluded, I headed into the basement laboratory.

◆

"Let's start with the basics."

Dressed as Satou again, I put on a white lab coat, enjoying the scientific atmosphere as I attempted making magic potions from veria plants by following Mr. Trazayuya's recipe.

"All right, that seems to work."

Even the best veria potions were only around as effective as a decent lesser recovery potion and about 10 or 20 percent less effective than one of the same quality.

But that wasn't a big enough difference to be a problem, since the real issue was the cost and availability of ingredients.

If it was possible to make potions using evil veria, the giant veria-like plant that grew in abundance to the west of Labyrinth City, it would be possible to make a near-infinite supply of magic potions. But that was nowhere to be found in Trazayuya's recipes.

I would have to experiment with that later.

Noticing the tablet I was using, Lelillil slipped into her habitually rude tone. "What in the hell are you using a human Transmutation Tablet for, erm...Lord Satou?"

"I'm trying to adapt this recipe so that humans can make it with this kind of tablet."

"You're changing the recipe?!" Her eyes practically bugged out of their sockets.

Brushing her off with a smile, I started going over the adaptation process in my mind.

Ugh. I shouldn't have bothered.

It was such an undertaking that I almost started to regret it.

I was taking a transmutation process that was already difficult with high-performance equipment and trying to reproduce it on far inferior equipment, so I knew it wasn't going to be easy, but this was much more difficult than I'd expected.

Once I finished running simulations in my head, I started working for real with the Transmutation Tablet.

Sometimes the components refused to mix, sometimes they blew up with a puff of poisonous smoke, and at one point my concoction emitted a foul odor that nearly knocked out Lelillil and myself.

I was more or less fine, but I still had to use an Antidote: All-Purpose for the first time in a while.

This grim battle continued for another two hours.

Finally, I managed to make a relatively successful batch.

> **Title Acquired: Porting Master**
> **Title Acquired: Reorganizer**
> **Title Acquired: Finder of New Paths**

Now that I had a new recipe figured out, I wanted to make sure that people besides me would be able to transmute and alchemize it, so I transformed into Kuro and went to fetch the alchemists and doctors among the girls.

"Incredible! To think that making magic potions from veria is actually possible!"

The lone alchemist in the Ivy Manor exclaimed in surprise.

""""You're amazing, Lord Kuro!"""""

The doctors and Lelillil all praised me in unison.

"The formulation stages are similar to that of veria salve."

The doctors agreed that this recipe would be doable.

Incidentally, veria salve is an ointment used to disinfect wounds and stop bleeding, popularly used by everyone from the poorest to the most experienced explorers.

I had never heard of it until now, since it wasn't mentioned in the rookie explorers' class.

"The transmutation stage is a little too difficult for me at my current skill level."

After a few attempts, the alchemist girl called me over.

Sure enough, most of her attempts were failures, and the ones that succeeded were of the lowest possible quality.

"Lord Kuro…"

I thought she was going to give up, but instead she clenched her fists.

"Please give me a little more time! I'll master it in a month—no, half a month!"

"All right. We've got plenty of veria, so practice as much as you need."

I gave the alchemist girl a Magic Bag containing many cores that were grade 3 or above to use for transmutation. I also gave her some watered-down magic recovery potions.

"As for the rest of you, please make enough veria salve for Sumina and the other explorers."

""""Yes, Lord Kuro!""""

The doctors seemed to have time on their hands. Best put them to work.

Since their names might have been spread as the creators of demonic potions, I had Tifaleeza give them new names just to be safe.

Since they would be returning to their real names eventually, I gave them names in alphabetical order: Ann, Beth, Chris, Debbie, and Emily.

"Oh right. Do you know about a potion called Monster Incense?"

My casual question made the girls all stiffen.

"I…I do."

"You don't have to talk about it if you don't want to."

"No, no. We will! This sin is ours to bear."

According to the alchemist girl, the plunderers had used this item to cause chain rampages.

The recipe had been disseminated in the underworld of Labyrinth City, spread by cohorts of Yellow Robes—the same yellow-skinned demon who had taught the plunderers how to cultivate ingredients for demonic potion.

Those plunderers and demons were both always up to no good.

"You were just forced to make it. I won't say to forget about it, but don't let it keep weighing on you. All the blame lies with the plunderers, not you."

I comforted the girls, who were painfully holding back tears, leaving the Ivy Manor only after they had calmed down.

My revised veria potion was likely to have a huge impact on Labyrinth City, so I was planning to wait for the right time to release it.

I had Tifaleeza use "Name Order" to give me the fake name Tsarayuya, an imitation of Trazayuya the Sage, for when I released the recipe.

◆

"For today's volunteer work, we're cleaning up the aqueducts!"

""""Yes, ma'am!""""

The kids all waved their cleaning implements and cheered enthusiastically in response to Arisa's rallying cry.

Since we'd gotten permission to clean the aqueducts, we decided to get started right away.

It would be dangerous to have only the kids and old folks who came to the soup kitchen do the cleaning on their own, so I hired the girls from the downtown tenements as backup.

I had just mentioned it to Neru this morning, but there was a bigger turnout than I'd expected.

Despite the low pay of a copper coin per person, they all seemed eager to help.

"This is a strange tool, young master."

The redheaded Neru was gazing curiously at one of the trash-picker tools I had hastily constructed.

"Will the stalls be all right without you, Miss Neru?"

"Just 'Neru' is fine, mister. The other gals are there, too. It'll be okay! Figured I'd come help out here, since I can use Everyday Magic and all!"

My title had slipped from "young master" to "mister," but I decided not to comment.

"How convenient, eh?"

"I wanna pick stuff up, too."

"Wait your turn!"

The old folks and kids alike seemed to be impressed with the trash pickers. It sounded like they were having fun as they set about clearing the garbage from the aqueducts.

I would have to make more trash pickers for the next day, since they were more helpful than I anticipated.

"Mister, I mean, young master! This tool is from a foreign land, isn't it?"

"Is it?"

"Yeah, I ain't... Erm, I've never seen one."

The girls from the tenement houses came up to me, struggling to keep their language polite as they spoke.

"If you pull this string, the thingies on the end close! That's so cool!"

"Erm, excuse me, young master. Would it be all right if we made something similar to these trash pickers and sold them?"

While Neru continued to gawk at the trash picker in admiration, another girl, wearing a serious expression, approached me with a proposal.

"Sure, that's fine. If you can find some branches that are hollow like this, it should be pretty easy to make."

However, because the handle of this trash picker was made thin but sturdy with Treespirit Pearls, they would have to use different components.

"That should be fine! I know a lumber dealer who sells thin bamboo."

If the girls had a new product to sell, that would certainly be a good thing.

They might even level up in the process of developing the product and gain some creation-related skills.

With only a few minor incidents, the aqueduct cleaning was proceeding smoothly.

"This is quite a lot of garbage."

"What are we going to do with it? Burn it?"

"There's a dump site outside the city, so we've been told to throw it away there."

A government official had told me this when I went to get permission the day before.

We used a human-wave tactic to carry the garbage out of the city.

"What an enormous pit."

About a hundred and fifty feet away from the south gate, the hole was nearly thirty feet around and ten feet deep.

"The viceroy hires Earth Magic users to remake this hole once a year."

"Wow, that's interesting."

This piece of knowledge came from one of the old folks who had helped transport the garbage.

"No one tries to go through the garbage?"

"No, sir. There are slimes at the bottom."

Sure enough, I could see some gray slimes wriggling around at the bottom of the pit.

Slimes had to be used to dispose of food waste, scraps, and so on, the old man explained, or the pit would overflow right away.

I'd been under the impression that everyone just threw their waste in the aqueducts, but apparently, that wasn't the case.

Once we finished throwing out the garbage, we distributed rewards some distance away from the garbage dump site.

"Wow! These fish-oil drops are delicious!"

I distributed the treats to the tenement girls as well as the volunteers.

"Yeah, but I dunno. I'm so hungry, I could eat a horse."

"We have biscuits, too."

A hungry girl voiced her complaints with an old-fashioned phrase, so I offered the ladies some biscuits and dried meat.

"Neru, the aqueduct cleanup is going to be a several-week project. Can I hire all of you to keep helping us?"

"Sure, but…you gonna be all right, mister?"

Neru looked hesitant. She was probably concerned about whether I could afford to pay everyone, since it would add up to about one gold coin for every three days.

"Sure. Don't worry about the expense."

I smiled at Neru to show my gratitude for her concern.

Paying around ten gold coins for a month was no big deal. We couldn't cover much ground in a single day of cleaning, but if we kept it up for a month, the city's water quality would drastically improve.

You've got to take your time with things like this.

◆

"Here I thought there were less morons bringing gabo fruit into the labyrinth, but now the bastards are using Monster Incense. I guess we've got no shortage of idiots."

After the aqueduct cleaning session, I went to the guildmaster to tell her the rumors I'd heard about Monster Incense, war, and so on.

She already knew about the latter and actually seemed to be better-informed than I was about the effects of war, even going so far as to warn me not to get caught up in any get-rich-quick schemes.

As it happens, feckless explorers sometimes illegally brought gabo fruit into the labyrinth in order to incite demi-goblins to multiply. But in most cases, this ended with the explorer parties being wiped out by a tidal wave of demi-goblins multiplying out of control.

"Is that all you needed to talk about?"

It appeared that the guildmaster had caught on to the fact that I was leading up to making a collection request.

"Actually, I want to put out a request for ogredrink-potion ingredients. Would it be possible to share it as a request from the guild?"

"For the viceroy's daughter? …No, this is because of that Dyukeli bastard, isn't it? You should choose your friends more carefully, Satou."

The guildmaster seemed to dislike Baronet Dyukeli as well.

"It's mainly for the viceroy's daughter."

I made this excuse with the help of my "Fabrication" skill.

The guildmaster sighed. "You're too damn nice," she grumbled. "You'll be providing the money, I take it?"

"Of course. I'll submit the fee in advance." I gave her a bag containing the request payment as well as the retaining fee. "Actually, I'd like to make one other request as well…"

"You want to buy up any Magic Scrolls from the labyrinth?"

Since I'd received some labyrinth scrolls from Baronet Dyukeli yesterday, I was hoping to get lucky again.

"And you're offering ten gold coins for each, no matter what kind of magic it is?" The guildmaster stared at my personal request with widening eyes.

It was certainly a high amount compared with the market rate for most scrolls being sold, but intermediate Magic Scrolls could be worth five gold coins or more, so I didn't think it was too outrageous.

Besides, a mere ten coins was a small price to pay for expanding my arsenal of spells.

Still, since Magic Scrolls were one-use-only for the average person, it probably seemed like a ridiculous pastime.

"I'm paying one silver coin for used scrolls, however. And I won't be buying duplicates or market goods."

"Boy, you're a strange one, all right."

You're one to talk, guildmaster.

"When are you going back into the labyrinth?"

"Tomorrow."

"Tch, guess I can't invite you to go out drinking tonight, then. Let's get drinks as soon as you come back, y'hear?"

The guildmaster looked grumpy, so I responded "yes, of course" with a smile and excused myself from her office.

"Please! Just give us three more days!"

"We'll pay the interest, I swear!"

As I passed the reception desk on the first floor, I heard two women's frantic voices.

"Sorry, but I just work here. I have to follow the rules."

It was the Lovely Wings pair who was pleading with the guild employee, and it sounded like they were trying to get more time to pay something back.

"I can cover for them for now, if that's all right," I offered. These two were familiar faces, and they didn't seem like the type to shirk a debt; I figured I'd intervene on their behalf.

"M-mister!"

"We can't cause trouble for you like that…"

"The interest for one trimoon is two silver coins total for the pair."

The guild employee told me the price, completely ignoring their protests.

He was a regular at my drinking parties with the guildmaster. He must have known that I often purchased expensive drinks and snacks.

He probably figured that I could spare two silver coins easily.

As soon as I paid the money…

"Th-thank you, mister."

"Oh, mister, we really owe you big-time…"

…the two women clung to me and wailed in gratitude, making things pretty awkward.

Even with my "Poker Face" skill, I was painfully aware of the curious looks from the other explorers and employees.

I couldn't bear all the attention much longer, so I offered to listen to their troubles at a nearby bar.

"Really, we can't thank you enough, mister."

"You saved us from becoming slaves, you know. We're so grateful, we'd happily give you Jena's purity if you want."

"Why me? What about yours, Iruna?"

"Yeah right. Why would he want *mine*?"

The two women finally calmed down and started joking around.

My AR display reminded me that the charming one was named **Iruna**, while the beauty was named **Jena**.

"Here's the chef's special today and some ale…," the friendly waitress said, dropping off our food.

I gave her a big tip and ordered another round of food.

"Wow, boiled rock cray! I've never had this before!"

"Y-you sure you wanna treat us to such a classy meal?"

"It's no problem."

I quenched my thirst with some ale, then dug into the boiled rock cray, which looked like a giant spiny lobster.

It was a little salty but tasty. The chef here seemed to be pretty skilled.

"It's so delicious, I can't believe it…"

"Yeah, this is a far cry from the hard biscuits and dried meat we always eat in the labyrinth."

The pair nearly started crying again as they gobbled up the rock cray meat.

They didn't eat it, shell and all, like the beastfolk girls, though.

"You're not supposed to drink ale so daintily, mister!" Jena of the Lovely wings scolded me as I took a small sip of the unpleasantly sour ale and tried not to scrunch up my face. "You gotta chug it all at once and feel that tingly sensation as it travels down your throat!"

She appeared to be quite the impassioned ale enthusiast.

"Mister, you can ignore Jena's so-called wisdom."

"Oh, come on, Iruna. You're the one who never shuts up about the right way to grill meat!"

As they exchanged friendly banter, we enjoyed the other dishes.

When I noticed them looking sadly at their empty ale glasses, I told them they could have unlimited refills of whatever they wanted. But that might have been a mistake...

"You won't believe it, mister! Those Silverlight jerks are sooo mean!"

With a drunken beauty on my right and a foggy-eyed charmer on my left, I was subjected to complaints about the Silverlight party.

"We finally went on an expedition, but we got stuck with breaking down monster parts, throwing out garbage, and odd jobs like that—they didn't let us hunt a single maze locust!"

"Yeah, they just treated us like lowly carriers."

"I mean, technically we *were* invited along as carriers, but still! We were told that even carriers got to hunt straggler prey sometimes."

"Nothing we can do, though. They told us they wanted to train their newbies instead, y'know?"

I briefly recalled the scene between the Silverlight party and the Lovely Wings that I had happened across back in the labyrinth.

They must have been pretty miserable throughout the expedition. Their complaints washed over me like a waterfall.

Still, as a programmer in Japan, I'd often listened to the complaints of Mr. Tubs and my other seniors. This was no big deal by comparison.

"This is all because that greedy moron Besso had to try and steal the royal-jelly ball, y'know?"

"Yeah, if it weren't for that idiot, we wouldn't be stuck paying off a fine for the stupid chain rampage!"

Ah, the target of their complaints shifted from Silverlight to Besso.

If I remembered correctly, he was the same guy who'd been causing yet another chain rampage for Mr. Koshin's party the other day.

Some people never learn.

"He'll get what's coming to him sooner or later, I'm sure."

"Yeah, you said it!"

"Let the bastard screw up and get eaten by monsters!"

Thus, I ended up drinking along with them as they complained into the night, until eventually the alcohol carried them into slumber.

The looks from nearby explorers seemed to beg the question *Which one's he gonna take home?* so I contacted Arisa and the others with the Space Magic spell Telephone to come get us.

"Guilty."

"You've got some nerve, calling your wives to the scene of your cheating."

Wives? Since when?

Mia and Arisa narrowed their eyes at the drunken Lovely Wings pair.

"Liza, Nana, can you help me out?"

"Understood."

"Yes, master."

I didn't know where they lived, so we ended up loading them into a carriage to bring them back to the mansion with us.

We had open guest rooms; they could sleep there.

"Both of them? Really?"

"Good going, kid."

Dismissing the comments from drunken explorers with a wave of my hand, I climbed into the carriage.

Then I reassured the infuriated Arisa and Mia on the way home, letting the evening breeze disperse my tipsiness.

Looking out at the street, where there were no longer any kids sleeping in alleys, I felt a little accomplished as we returned to the mansion.

I think I'll be able to sleep well tonight.

Not Strong Enough

Satou here. Everyone makes mistakes. However, I think it's a waste to live your life in fear of making them. In my opinion, mistakes are the fertilizer that fuels personal growth.

"Seems like we caused you some trouble yesterday…"

"We're so sorry."

The two Lovely Wings winced through the pain of their hangovers as they apologized for their behavior the previous night.

They said they normally didn't drink to the point of blacking out in bars, but between me paying for their drinks and their pent-up frustration over Silverlight and Besso, they weren't quite able to restrain themselves.

I gave them some potions that would help with the hangovers and invited them to breakfast.

"L-look, Iruna, white bread!"

"Jena, this is a noble's breakfast. Of course they have wh-white bread."

Today we were having bread with breakfast instead of the usual rice, which seemed to impress the pair.

"This yellow stuff must be eggs, right? …Holy smokes, it's so good!"

"I guess you just drink this amber soup from the bowl… W-wow, it's way too good!"

After Iruna tasted the cheese omelet and Jena drank some of the consommé soup, they smacked each other on the shoulders to express their joy.

We get it already. Calm down and eat, please.

They continued singing the food's praises as they tried all the available dishes.

Lulu and the others who had made breakfast looked sheepish but proud of themselves.

Once the meal concluded…

"We swear we'll repay you once we're back on our feet, mister."

"Yeah, we're good for it, I promise."

"I trust you. Just don't push yourselves too hard, please. I don't want you getting hurt."

With that, the pair headed off to the labyrinth.

"You're sure giving those two an awful lot of help. Are they your type?" Arisa accused.

"No, not particularly," I answered honestly. "I just can't help wanting to support someone when I see them working hard."

"If you say so."

I'll take your word for it, her expression seemed to say. I ruffled her hair.

"H-hey! What if my wig falls off?!"

"Relax, it's fine."

Laughing among ourselves, our group headed for the labyrinth gate as well.

"Huh? Is that Zakorin? He's with a pretty big group—I wonder if they're going after the floormaster."

Arisa pointed at a party of nearly seventy explorers, with an equally large pile of supplies next to them.

Zarigon's party, the Hellfire Fangs, was leading them.

I listened in on their conversation with my "Keen Hearing" skill.

"Sounds like they're taking on an areamaster first."

Not only that, but they had already failed once, so this was their second attempt.

"Wow. I didn't realize that normally took so many people."

"That's quite a lot of baggage, too."

Arisa and Lulu seemed impressed.

"Master, over there…"

Liza pointed out Besso, the man we'd encountered right before rescuing Mr. Koshin's crew.

Since he was standing next to Zarigon's group's bags, it looked like he was participating in the areamaster challenge, too.

"I hope he's not planning to cause another chain rampage…"

Arisa seemed to remember him, too.

"Don't worry. Rumors about him have spread among explorers. I'm sure Mr. Zarigon knows to be on the lookout."

This information came from little Luram, who was holding a plate of *takoyaki* in one hand.

Is he trying to become an information broker or something?

"I'm impressed you know all that."

"Well, you hear a lot of things when you're doing market research."

I guess his hobby of wandering around buying and eating food had its benefits.

"Take this as thanks for the information."

"Oh-ho, I like the way you think."

I handed Luram a little bag of handmade *konpeito*, a star-shaped candy.

Zarigon and the others didn't seem to be going into the labyrinth yet, so we parted ways with the smug-looking Luram in order to enter before their giant party blocked our path.

"Wow. That's the labyrinth village?"

"Looks that way."

We were paying a visit to the labyrinth village, a place explorers used as a stopping point during expeditions.

We didn't really have any business there; I was just curious to see it.

"In the aaaair?"

"Rope bridges, sir."

As Tama and Pochi observed, the village appeared to be made with the remnants of spider monsters' giant webs. It was supported by long, narrow stone pillars that extended to the floor and ceiling and connected by a series of suspension bridges to form a circle.

The size of the rope bridges ranged from wide enough for a carriage to so small that one person would barely be able to go across.

"There are lights up there, too."

"Looks like spiderfolk live in the area."

As Lulu pointed up at the top of the village, which looked like a fragmented spiderweb, I relayed some information from my map.

Since their eyes saw well in the dark, there were spiderfolk soldiers patrolling above the rope bridges.

"Did those people make the village, then?"

"Apparently not. From what I've been told…"

I repeated what I'd heard from Polina and Sumina, two of the tenement girls, to Arisa and the others.

According to them, the village had been built during the demi-human war sparked by King Gartapht. The ones who built it had been trying to avoid the persecution aboveground. These people included fairy races, such as rockfolk and mudfolk, and a group of human monster tamers called "bee tamers."

"Dark."

"I cannot see the bottom, I report."

Mia and Nana gazed down into the moatlike pit that surrounded the village.

According to my map, the donut-shaped hole was a hundred feet deep and about a hundred and fifty feet across.

Though I couldn't see them from above, mudfolk doing some kind of work at the bottom showed up on my map.

"There don't appear to be any monsters."

Liza's observation was right.

Much like the area with our labyrinth vacation home, there weren't any spawnholes here, so in order to make this a safe area, they had probably sealed up any passages monsters might take.

"It seems very close to the entrance to the labyrinth, though."

"That's only because we took a shortcut."

We had climbed over a sheer cliff, fought our way through a colony of monsters with special abilities, and finally made our way through a spawnhole to get here.

It took about three hours in total. In comparison, it would take half a day for garnet-badge explorers to follow the dangerous route here, while people carrying baggage on the safe route would need about three days.

"Give up your weapons and show us your explorer badges!"

The men standing in front of the first rope bridge crossed their spears and shouted at us.

They wore unusual tasseled clothing beneath their scale armor and had oddly pale skin, perhaps from living underground for a long time.

"Will this do?"

"Never seen you around before… A garnet badge? What are you, some noble's brat?"

"Bought this with gold, I bet."

The men checked our garnet-explorer badges, then tossed them back at me.

One of them was looking us up and down in great detail; he had the Urion-faith gift called the Eye of Judgment.

"Go on in. Just don't cause any trouble up there."

"The village chief's word is law around here. He'll tear you apart, noble or not."

Sounds like a dangerous village.

For some reason, they gave me a puzzled look when I thanked them for the warning.

"Weird smellll?" As we crossed the bridge, Tama pinched her nose.

"Yeah, really. What is that?" I asked.

"It smells like monster repellent powder, sir," Pochi said, pleased with herself for knowing the answer.

"Good job. You two have sharp noses."

"Hee-hee..."

"Aw shucks, sir."

I patted Pochi's head as a reward for her identifying the smell, and I patted Tama's head for being the one who noticed it first.

Finally, we crossed the bridge and arrived at the gate to the labyrinth village.

A small window opened in the side door, and a man poked out his head.

Like the men who had been guarding the bridge, he was wearing clothing with distinctive tassels. It was probably the native garb around here.

"If you wanna come into the village, you gotta pay the fee."

The thuggish declaration made Liza narrow her eyes sharply.

According to my AR, he was the **Village Tax Collector**.

I motioned to Liza to stand down and addressed him myself.

"How much is the fee?"

"One silver coin for nobles, one copper coin for explorers. If you've got outside food, we can take that instead."

It was unusual to hear nobles getting this kind of treatment in this world.

"Would liquor do?"

"That'd be more than welcome, for sure. One cask of ale or a bottle of red wine would do nicely."

I produced a bottle of cheap wine from my Garage Bag.

I couldn't remember when I bought it, but it was unopened, so it should be fine.

"Ooh, this is Lessau's Lifeblood, ain't it?!" The collector exclaimed in delight. "If you got any more, sell it to the drink vendor outside the pillar, will ya? It's in high demand. They'll buy it for a good price."

Thanking the suddenly kindly tax collector, we entered the labyrinth village.

"Monsterrrs?"

"It's Mr. Meat, sir."

Seeing the barn on the other side of the gate, Tama's and Pochi's eyes sparkled.

It was a place called a "monster mount shop," which couldn't operate outside the labyrinth.

"No, those are mounts, so you can't eat them."

Most of the mounts were for battle, but they still had some for carrying bags and such, like go-cart-size bug monsters and four-legged beasts with suction pads on their feet, reminiscent of geckos.

The former were being stabled there by monster tamers, while the latter were for sale.

Using my "Estimation" skill, I found that the battle monsters were around ten gold coins, and even the pack monster prices started at three gold coins or more.

"You there, young man! How would you like to try some monster-meat skewers? They're a labyrinth village specialty!"

"We've got mystery-meat stew over here, too!"

"Goblin liquor, two penny coins a cup!"

At the food stalls near the barn, some bearded men were loudly hawking their wares.

I didn't really want the goblin liquor or the self-proclaimed mystery stew, but the skewers looked tasty, and I bought enough for the group.

As we munched on the skewers, we wandered the narrow passageways of the labyrinth village in a single-file line.

There were lots of suspicious characters around with crimes in their bounty columns, so I kept a close eye on our walking order.

Of course, there was no one in the village who could take my party head-on. We were able to keep out of trouble without difficulty.

Before we had even walked thirty feet, we saw two fights break out.

"Blocking the waaay?"

"He's sitting in the middle of the path, sir."

Tama and Pochi tilted their heads at a man who was sitting right in the center of a narrow passageway.

"Only villagers are allowed beyond this point," he informed us gruffly when he noticed our expressions, and he shooed us away like someone warding off stray cats.

According to my map, this path led to an underground area where the villagers lived.

I couldn't blame the man for sending us away, then. Giving him a cordial wave, I ushered my group off.

"There are all kinds of stores here."

"Yeah, no kidding."

Some ladies waved from a brothel down a side street, and I waved back.

They seemed wilder and more vulgar than the ones in Labyrinth City aboveground.

"Mrrr."

"No sneaking peeks!"

I think brothels are pretty useful for information-gathering, but I decided not to say that out loud.

"Ah-ha-ha. Sorry, sorry."

Apologizing, I continued down the path, peering at the shops along the way.

Most of them were street stalls, with the occasional storefront. Aside from food, there were mostly weapon and armor shops, as well as repair places.

The occasional general stores primarily sold flash bombs, smoke bombs, monster repellent powder, and other such consumable goods. There was an apothecary, too, but rather than potions they carried more bandages, veria salves, and other such first aid items. Surprisingly, there were a lot of stalls that sold clothes, underwear, and other essentials.

All the prices were relatively high—anywhere from two to five times more than what you would pay in Labyrinth City.

"Golemmm?"

"It's a kind of mount, apparently."

Unlike the magic tool–like golems the elves made, this golem was made on the spot by an Earth Magic user.

The name of the golem creator and the person using it were different, which was why I concluded that it was a kind of mount.

"Everyone's sorta dirty."

"Well, there probably aren't any baths or showers in the labyrinth."

I searched the labyrinth village, but the only watering hole was near the pillar that supported the structure.

The pit that surrounded the village contained a few bogs, which seemed to be where the village drew its water from.

"You got some kinda problem with us?!"

I heard a familiar voice from the direction of the pillar.

On the other side of a crowd, I found Mr. Dozon and a scantily clad beauty arguing. Both of them seemed to be drunk.

"It's Sir Dozon and Mahiruna from the Owlbeard party."

"Those two again…"

While Dozon looked infuriated, Miss Mahiruna wore a very amused expression.

Her party, Owlbeard, consisted entirely of female explorers.

"Of course not. The prey we were hunting just happened to line up with yours a few times, that's all."

Her clearly insincere tone only enraged Dozon further.

"'Just happened'? But it happens practically every other time!"

I think 50 percent of the time could still be a coincidence.

"Look, Dozon. You seem to think we go around snatching requests from you, but you've stolen more than a few requests from us, too, you know."

Miss Mahiruna seemed to enjoy toying with Dozon so much that she couldn't help herself.

"Mahiruna! We've got all the supplies we need, plus a few hard newts from the monster mount shop."

"Excellent! Well done. See you next time, then, Dozon. The golden scarab is ours!"

"Tch, so you're after it, too…"

Miss Mahiruna walked away with the female explorer who'd come to get her.

"Don't screw up and get eaten by a wanderin' elder lance beetle!" Dozon yelled after her.

"As if! Thanks, though, Dozon! Let's settle this in bed another time, eh?"

Mahiruna smirked over her shoulder as she fired a parting shot.

"Guess you can't beat your ex-wife, either, huh, Lord Dozon?"

"Shut it!"

The friend who teased Mr. Dozon was rewarded with a fist.

Ah, so those two used to be married.

"...Hmm? Hey, it's my old pal Pendragon!"

Noticing me, Mr. Dozon waved us over with a yell.

The last time I saw him was when we'd fought alongside each other against the Plunderer King Ludaman near the west guild.

"If you're here, are you beetle huntin', too?"

"No, we just wanted to see the labyrinth village."

"What a strange lad!" Dozon chuckled.

He told me more about the labyrinth village over some spring water, which was a copper coin per glass.

Evidently, some particularly tough explorers used this place as a base to hunt beetle monsters for months at a time.

There were necromancers living here in secret, too; they sold skeletons for breaking curses or creating monster mounts.

Finally, I learned that there were branch offices of a few religions in the village chief's house, like the Zaicuon and Karion faiths.

"Dozon! We finally got ahold of a guide who knows the beetle area inside and out."

"Great! Then let's get goin'!"

Mr. Dozon's comrade came over with a young spriggan guide in tow. Before he left, Dozon gave me one last piece of advice.

"One more thing, friend. The plunderers might not have been completely wiped out after all. Be careful, y'hear?"

Wondering if a new group had cropped up, I searched the nearby area on my map, but there didn't appear to be any plunderers in the labyrinth at present.

"I thought the guildmaster and the Hero's follower purged all of them."

"Maybe some new baddies came outta the woodwork."

According to Mr. Dozon, his group had been attacked a few days ago at the first area boundary by an unusually large swarm of monsters, hence his suspicion.

He said the monsters had gathered in a different way from a normal chain rampage.

"I wonder..."

"What, ya know somethin'?"

With the disclaimer that I couldn't say for sure, I told him the rumor that someone had been getting unlicensed alchemists to make Monster Incense.

"Tch. There's always some damn idiots up to no good, huh?"

Dozon's grumbled remark reminded me of the guildmaster's similar complaint.

To be safe, I checked the nearby areas on the map, but I didn't find any Monster Incense.

"I'll get the village guards and gossips to spread the word about this Monster Incense stuff. Be careful out there, Pendragon. If ya think ya sense a chain rampage, don't question your gut—just get outta there."

With that, Mr. Dozon left the bar.

"Let's continue our sightseeing, shall we?"

We went to look at the giant pillar in the center of the labyrinth village and the village chief's house, which enclosed the pillar.

"Bonesss?"

"So big, sir."

The village chief's roof was decorated rather nastily with some giant monster bones, which seemed to impress Tama and Pochi.

I guess that sort of thing is cool to them.

"Are they giving out rations over there?"

"Drinking water, it looks like."

Some villagers were lined up at a spring in the village chief's garden, showing wooden tags and getting big jugs filled with water.

"Master, I have located the drink vendor, I report."

Nana pointed at a bell-shaped shop next to the village chief's house. Inside, it was packed with barrels, bottles, and so on.

I hadn't particularly been looking for it, but since it was right there, I figured we might as well take a peek.

"Buying some water, Sir Noble?"

"No, we have enough. The tax collector told me that if I had extra wine, I could sell it at the drink vendor..."

"Selling, are we? We don't want just any wine, you know. It's gotta be red wine from Lessau County—Lessau's Lifeblood, to be precise."

That was the only kind of red wine I had from Lessau County, so I nodded, produced five bottles from my Garage Bag, and handed them to the shopkeeper.

"Ah, that's it—Lessau's Lifeblood, the genuine article! Now, we'll be fine anytime the Blue People come through."

"...Blue People?"

I had heard this phrase before.

They were a mysterious race said to appear to people who got lost deep in monster territory. We'd used their existence as a cover story for the people I rescued from the plunderers, to explain where they had been when they returned to society.

"Do they come often?"

"Heavens, no. A few times a year at most."

That rarely, huh...?

I was interested in meeting them, but it sounded unlikely unless I got extremely lucky.

I couldn't find them on my map search, either.

"So do they come to sell things or what?"

"Yeah. Unusual produce, rare monster parts, that kinda thing."

The shopkeeper answered Arisa's question easily, but he wouldn't specify the type of produce.

The monster parts, he said, differed every time.

We thanked the shopkeeper and took our leave, walked around the rest of the labyrinth village, then left through a different way from where we'd come in.

Once we left the village, we found an empty area and used Return to teleport to the hunting ground.

Today, we were hunting in the rodent area.

Looking around the cavern, I could see all kinds of plump monsters.

"Squishyyy?"

"Lots of meat, sir."

"These will certainly be worth hunting."

There were maze rabbits and flame rabbits, poison mice and flame mice, though sadly no electric mice to be found.

Aside from the monsters, even the vegetation was largely flame-themed: fire grass, flame flowers, sulfur seeds, and other valuable alchemy ingredients grew scattered throughout the area.

One small room full of ice rabbits contained plants like freezing flowers and snow grass, which were effective for burns.

Once we were done hunting in this room, we could all go harvest some together.

"Master, we wish to challenge the areamaster, I report."

None of the other kids had objections to Nana's proposal.

The areamaster here was called the "king burning bunny," while its spawn were called "prince flame bunnies."

Because both were covered in flames, breathed fire, and had flame resistance, Arisa's Fire Magic and Lulu's Fireburst Gun probably wouldn't have much effect. Only the king burning bunny could actually use Fire Magic, however.

It didn't seem like the best type matchup, but they were close to my party in level. I wasn't worried.

"We can try it once we clear out this big cavern and make a place to fight, then."

Everyone nodded, so once I used my Earth Magic to create trenches and a simple encampment, the battle began.

As I watched over everyone from behind, I tested out the scrolls I'd acquired the day before.

First, Stone Object.

My creations were pretty shabby when I used it with the scroll, but with the magic menu, the stone statues and temples I made were so impressive that the girls turned to look at them mid-battle.

The amount of magic and effort required seemed to vary based on the size and complexity of the creation.

It was a bit of a pain, but adding detailed carvings definitely made them look nicer.

This spell seemed like it would be useful for a lot of things: making targets for shooting practice, decoys to confuse opponents, constructing concealed structures to put Return seal slates outdoors, and so on.

I was even able to use it on stones from my inventory or use glass and crystals to make cut glass and things like that.

It was even possible to use it on jewels, although it took a lot of magic power. For some reason, even diamonds worked. Carbon, huh?

The spell also worked for making weapons, so I played around with creating glass swords, sapphire daggers, and things like that. Testing out all the different functions was a lot of fun.

I'll have to be sure to thank Baronet Dyukeli for giving me this scroll.

I was so grateful that I would even be willing to give him blood-pearls or elixirs next time I found some.

The second scroll was for the spell Create Earth Servant.

According to one of my spell books, it was an intermediate Earth Magic spell, the least powerful of the golem-creating magics.

The book also said its creations could follow only simple orders, like Ghost Magic skeletons, with no ability to think for themselves.

On top of that, it said they were so fragile that they could barely serve as shields, never mind fight in battle.

So I wasn't expecting much as I used the scroll and added the spell to my magic menu.

The small golem I made with the scroll was about four heads tall, similar in stature to Pochi and Tama, with a simple, rounded body. Its face was very simple, too, essentially just two dots and a line.

This must be the most basic model.

According to my AR, it was **level 1**.

Even making this weak golem still took a relatively high amount of magic. An ordinary mage would probably have to be at least level 20 to have enough MP for it.

Next, I tried using Create Earth Servant from the magic menu instead.

When I activated the spell, the ground suddenly rose at an alarming rate and started constructing a human form.

It's huge.

The form was the same, but it was almost twenty feet tall.

My AR told me that this golem was **level 30**.

"MVA."

The golem's mouth produced a strange sound somewhere between "MA" and "VA."

"What is *that*?"

"A golem I made with magic."

I had made only one this time, but it looked like I could make several at once if I wanted, just like my Magic Arrows.

"Golemmm?"

"It's very big, sir."

"And it looks quite strong, too."

The rest of my group, having finished up their battle moments before, gathered around with interest.

"Master, this small one is cute, I report."

"Mm. Simple."

Nana and Mia seemed to prefer the golem I'd made with the scroll.

"I want to see how it fights a little, so I'll be taking one of these monsters."

Without further ado, I chose a level-30 flame rabbit.

"Golem! Attack that flame rabbit!"

"*MVA.*"

"*A.*"

Both golems turned toward the rabbit.

I guess I have to give them names, otherwise all the golems I've made will respond to my orders.

"I will protect the golem larvae, I report."

The small golem started to totter toward the monster, but Nana lifted it up from behind. It flailed its short limbs but couldn't escape her grasp.

While I was watching this charming scene unfold, the large golem began to battle the flame rabbit.

"Fire doesn't seem to work on it much."

"Well, it is an earth golem, after all."

"It appears to attack rather slowly, though."

"Yesss…"

"Yeah, you're supposed to move splickity-lick when you fight, sir."

Pochi probably meant to say *lickety-split.*

The beastfolk girls watching must have thought the giant golem's fighting style was considerably clumsy.

That went without saying, though, since the spell was meant to create only noncombat servants.

"Master, can't you synchronize your vision and movements with the golem like in a manga?"

"Hmm, I'm not sure."

The golems made in the elf village didn't have features like that, but…

"Oh, hey, I did it."

"For real?!"

"For real."

I tested a few things out of curiosity and found that if I used magic and mana as an intermediary, I could see through the golem's eyes or display its vision in a window on my menu.

> Title Acquired: Golem User

And as for movements…

"Ooh, niiice?"

"It started moving a lot better, sir!"

There was a bit of time lag before it obeyed commands, and it didn't move very well, but I managed to control the golem.

> Title Acquired: Golem Operator

However, the golem possessed only vision and hearing. There was no way for me to sync up with its other senses.

I figured that out through the small golem, which Nana was holding tightly.

…Putting that aside, the default-mode golem could hardly defeat a monster weaker than itself, but if I was synced with it, it could just barely beat a monster around the same level. Since its body was brittle, it probably wouldn't be able to deal with anything stronger.

Once the golem was no longer needed, releasing the spell would turn it back into clumps of earth.

According to the spell book, they would fall apart on their own once the magic that was put into them ran out. In a labyrinth or near a source, though, they could draw on outside magic and continue to move without running out of power.

If the creator was nearby and had the "Magic Manipulation" skill, it was also possible to give the golem a continuous supply of magic.

The book further stated that when the golem was first created, it could also be equipped with a magic-power supply like a magic-filled core.

"Hey, master. Is that round shape the only kind you can make?"

"There are form parameters, so I think I can change it."

Aside from adjusting the parameters, it turned out that the spell could also be used on preexisting targets.

So I tried using Create Earth Servant on a stone statue I'd made with Stone Object earlier.

"Ooh, wow!"

"How does it walk when it doesn't have joints?" I wondered aloud.

"Are you serious? The round ones don't have joints, either."

Arisa rolled her eyes at me.

Oh, I guess not.

"Looks like using a preexisting statue costs less magic."

"And as a bonus, they're pretty strong."

When I sent the statue golem to attack a new flame rabbit, it proved to be much stronger than the previous giant golem.

It fought relatively well even without me controlling it.

I went on to make more statues and use Create Earth Servant on them, and I found that they could be preinstalled with a few basic movements when they were made into golems.

I was able to make other shapes besides humans, too, like stone wolves and horses.

"Birds don't work, huh?"

"Yeah, since they're made of stone."

The stone and earth were too heavy to create any flying golems.

"No more monsterrrs!"

"Guess we're finally done cleaning up."

Arisa stretched in response to Tama's report.

My golem experiments had gotten in the way, taking all my time until evening to clear the cavern of monsters. I regretted that, to be honest.

"Want to fight the spawn tomorrow instead?"

"No, no! Let's do it before dinner! Right, guys?"

The rest of the group cheered in response.

I put a seal slate in the center of this cavern, and we headed for the large expanse where the areamaster waited.

Sure enough, the king burning bunny was sitting imposingly on a boulder in the center of the uneven, grassy field.

There were five of its spawn, the prince flame bunnies, all of whom were lined up in a circle below the areamaster. Protecting the king, they seemed more like knights than princes.

There didn't seem to be any queens or princesses, as I'd noted with curiosity on the map.

Noticing me, the bunnies all let out a howl of warning.

"That one should do."

I set my sights on one of the prince flame bunnies and used "Flashrunning" to get close to it instantly.

As soon as I had grabbed the bunny monster, I used Return to teleport back with it to the room where my party was waiting.

Then I used Magic Hand to fling it across the room and switched out with the girls for combat.

"Lulu! This guy's strong against fire! The Fireburst Gun might not do much, but aim at its face to distract it! No living thing likes that! Liza! I think those bumps on its head are for attacking. They look extra tough. Be careful!"

"Got it, Arisa!"

"Understood!"

Investigating the prince flame bunny's abilities, Arisa shouted warnings at the rest of the group.

"*GRAAAAH!*"

Its fur standing on end, the prince howled with rage, and a flaming aura formed around its body.

According to my AR, it was a barrier that reduced flame damage taken and weakened other physical attacks as well.

Getting anywhere near that thing would probably result in some painful burns.

"Gather round, everyone! I'll cast Enchant: Resist Fire on all of you! Help me out, please, Mia!"

"Mm. ■■■■ ■■ *Aqua Protection Ryuusui no Mori.*"

Once they had finished setting up various resistance and protection buffs, the group went into battle against the monster.

I was pleased to see them being so careful.

"Flame rabbit! Come back when you have become a grilled hare, I declare!"

Protected by Flexible Shield, Nana shouted with the "Taunt" skill from the shadow of her giant buckler.

That dish name sounded a little familiar, but I couldn't quite put my finger on it.

"It's about to breathe fire!"

"Scatterrr?"

"Roger that, sir!"

As soon as Liza sensed the oncoming attack and shouted a warning, all the vanguard except for Nana dodged to the left and right. Nana used "Blink" to charge forward.

The prince flame bunny was nearly as big as a house, and its size was all the more apparent up close.

"Shield Bash, I declare!"

Shouting an attack name for some reason, Nana attacked the rabbit with her shield.

Hit square in the chest with the giant shield, the bunny monster flinched back a little, but it didn't stop charging its breath attack.

"Bwah-ha-ha! Your own fire breath shall be the cause of your defeeeeat!"

Judging by Arisa's weird shout, she must have used some kind of magic.

Ignoring her, the prince flame bunny opened its mouth—or at least tried to.

But its mouth wouldn't open, so it spurted flames from its nose and ears, roasting itself from the inside.

That didn't seem to cause much damage, though; the rabbit monster's HP gauge barely went down in my AR display.

Arisa must have used Space Magic to keep the prince flame bunny's mouth closed.

"...■ ■ ■ *Paralyze Water Hold Mahi Mizu Shibaru!*"

Mia's Water Magic wrapped around the rabbit's back legs. It seemed to be too big for her spell to restrain its entire body.

With the enemy's movements slowed, the vanguard team went on the attack.

On top of being huge and covered in a fiery aura, it also had a tough hide. Slashing attacks slid right off its fur, making it difficult to do much damage.

"Switch to thrusting attacks, you two!"

"Aye-aye?"

"Roger, sir."

On Liza's command, the pair used "Blink" to charge in with jabbing attacks.

Tama's twin blades didn't pierce very far, but Pochi's Magic Sword went in about halfway.

However, as she was stuck there, the rabbit's paw smacked her away.

"Waaah, sirrr!"

Pochi didn't sound too upset as she tumbled into a corner of the room thanks to her armor protecting her from its slashing claws.

"Take this!"

The prince flame bunny was about to go after Pochi, but Lulu interrupted it with a barrage from her Fireburst Gun.

The glowing red bullets hit the bunny head-on, sending its flames scattering, but all it did was dye things red, failing to burn the fur at all.

Instead, the monster angrily turned toward Lulu.

Since elemental rods and guns weren't usually affected much by the difference in level between the user and the target, I had expected the Fireburst Gun, an advanced version of the Fire Rod, to have more of an impact.

Still, it at least bought enough time for Pochi to pull out her spare Magic Sword and return to the front lines.

"Mia, time to rain on its parade!"

"Mm. ■ ■ ■…■ *Intense Cold Stream Gokkan Ryuusui.*"

Just as Mia completed the spell, the vanguard jumped aside to give her a clear shot.

Pale-blue water gushed out of the end of Mia's staff, connecting with the prince flame bunny and turning its glowing red fur a deep blue.

"*GRAAAABBBUH!*"

The bunny's muffled roar echoed through the room, and steam rose off its body.

Its health bar in my AR display had been depleted by half. That attack seemed to have worked well.

Lulu's attacks stood out all the more since most of the vanguard except Liza weren't having much luck dealing damage.

"Again."

Puffing determinedly, Mia started to chant another Intense Cold Stream.

"Mia, the paralysis is wearing off."

"Mrrr."

At Arisa's warning, Mia dropped that chant and switched to the Paralyze Water Hold chant instead.

In the meantime, though, the bunny recovered from paralysis and regained its speed, leaving Nana and the rest of the vanguard in the dust.

Even with their speed, further enhanced with "Body Strengthening," they couldn't keep up with the speedy prince flame bunny.

"*GRAAAAH.*"

Once it put some distance between itself and my group, the rabbit monster howled, bringing back the flame aura around it.

"Deracinator!"

"...■ ■ ■ *Paralyze Water Hold Mahi Mizu Shibaru.*"

Arisa's Space Magic wall helped hold the monster in place so that Mia could aim more easily.

Her spell activated and surrounded the prince flame bunny's lower half with blue water, but then it quickly dispersed.

The bunny must have resisted Mia's spell.

"Mrrr. Again. ■ ■..."

"Nana! Stop that bunny, at least for a second! I'll hit it with a Dimension Pile."

"Understood, I reply."

Undaunted by the mishap, my group moved on to their next strategy.

Lulu and the beastfolk girls threw in attacks to distract it, and after a few more failed attempts, they finally managed to land some de-buffing magic.

Spawn enemies like these seemed to have a high resistance to de-buffs.

The back-and-forth battle continued for a while, and though the girls took damage a few times, they finally started to wear down the prince flame bunny, which had no way of healing.

"■ ■ ■...■ *Intense Cold Stream Gokkan Ryuusui.*"

Mia's second Intense Cold Stream spell hit, dispelling the monster's flame aura.

"Dimension Pile!"

Arisa's Space Magic attack quickly followed, pinning the rabbit's forelegs to the ground.

They were almost there. The prince flame bunny's remaining HP was less than 20 percent.

"I'm going on the attack, too. Liza, lead the charge, please!"

Arisa focused on preparing an advanced Space Magic attack spell.

"Right!"

Liza's Magic Spear pierced the bunny's hide, cutting into its flesh.

Without the flame aura, attacks seemed to hit more effectively.

"Nana!"

"Your flame has been put out! Hurry up and get on our dinner table, I declare."

"*GRABBBAAAARGH.*"

The monster roared at Nana with fury in its eyes, but the flame aura didn't reappear.

It must not have enough magic to produce it anymore.

"Tama, Pochi! Let's finish this!"

"Aye-aye, sirrr!"

"Roger, sir!"

The beastfolk girls charged at the prince flame bunny from either side.

"Dimension Cutter, cross-style!"

As Arisa shouted, a cross shape cut deeply into the rabbit's forehead, and its HP dipped below 10 percent in my AR display.

"Brain Crusherrr?"

"Gotcha, sir!"

Tama's and Pochi's Magic Swords jabbed into the cross-shaped wound.

But it wasn't quite enough to bring it down.

Flames coalesced in the monster's mouth to burn the pair away.

"I won't let you, I declare."

Just as it was about to breath fire, Nana used "Blink" to jump in with a Shield Bash, striking the prince flame bunny on the nose.

The cracked shield broke in two, and the halves clattered across the floor.

Flames still escaping its mouth, the bunny pulled its head back.

But then—

"'Blink'! 'Triple Helix Spear Attack'!"

A trail of red light followed close behind Liza as she sped forward, stabbing the monster in its unguarded throat with her Magic Spear.

The spiral blade whirled around, piercing deep into the prince flame bunny's head and destroying its brain.

"GRAHHH...BUH."

The light faded from the monster's eyes, and it collapsed to the ground with a loud *thud*.

It took quite a while, but they managed to win without sustaining any serious injuries, so I was glad for that.

"Looks like we won."

"Victoryyyy?"

"Let's all strike a victory pose, sir!"

The group posed in front of the prince flame bunny.

That encounter was a lot more challenging that I thought it would be.

Maybe it was time to remodel all the vanguard's armor. But if she got stronger armor, the gap between Liza's strength and the rest of the vanguard would probably get even bigger.

Maybe I should go back to Bolenan Forest and get some advice from the elf teachers.

"Master, now that we've learned the fire bunnies' attack patterns, let's fight the areamaster next!"

Arisa came running over excitedly.

But after spectating that narrow victory, I wasn't about to give them permission to fight an enemy ten levels higher than they were.

"Maybe after you've leveled up a bit more. You have to be able to beat the spawn easily before you can take on the areamaster."

"Awww, all right. You're so overprotective, master."

This isn't a game. It's important to value everyone's lives.

◆

"Yesss, that was perfect! Spawn have nothing on us anymore!"

One morning, three days after the initial fight and after a lot of training in four different areas nearby, I let the girls fight more spawn to celebrate reaching level 42.

They had become considerably stronger, but the difference in skill between Liza and the rest of the vanguard was getting that much clearer.

The rear guard had started focusing more on attack magic than de-buffing magic, since the latter was easily resisted.

Part of the reason was that Tama's and Pochi's attack powers were particularly insufficient, so if the magic users focused on de-buffs, the battle would get drawn out and lead them to run out of MP.

"Finally! Let's take on the areamaster next!"

"Mm. Let's."

"I will exhibit my best skills for master, I declare."

"Tama's gonna wiiin?"

"Pochi wants to get praised by master, too, sir."

"We mustn't let our guards down, everyone. Just take it slow and steady."

"Hee-hee. You say that, Miss Liza, but you're the one who does most of the winning."

I was a little bit concerned by how excited the group was.

Since fighting the areamaster had been their goal for a while, I understood that they would be looking forward to it, but it might be best to get them to calm down a little first.

"Everyone, the areamaster is a notch above the spawn, so make sure you take it seriously. And you've been putting a bit too much focus on offense lately. Please be extra careful. Your safety is the top priority."

Just to be safe, I put Enchant: Magic Protection on them as well as the usual Enchant: Physical Protection and even the rarely used Enchant: Shield.

"We know, we know. Ohhh, master, you're such a worrywart..."

Arisa's lighthearted response only made me even more worried.

If it looks like someone's about to get hurt, I'll step in right away.

"Okay, want to try it once everyone's ready? I'm going to beat it myself if it gets too dangerous, though."

Once the group was prepared, I went to the king burning bunny, which was the size of a hill, and brought it into the room with Return.

It was far larger than the prince flame bunnies, which were the size of a house. The distinctive bumps spread from its head to its shoulders. Some of them even sprouted into gray spikes with reddened ends.

According to my AR, it was **level 50**—eight levels higher than my group.

Maybe I should have waited another five levels or so before letting them try this...

"MRRRABBBAAAARRRH."

The king burning bunny howled, and like the prince flame bunnies, a fiery aura appeared around its body. This aura was more violent and a deeper red.

"Begin."

Mia started a chant.

The vanguard had already scattered, wary of a charge from the rabbit.

Naturally, they had already applied support magic and used magic recovery potions to fully restore their MP.

"*MRRRABBBAAARGH.*"

The areamaster howled again.

"...■ *Intense Cold Stream Gokkan Ryuusui.*"

Mia's spell activated, and bluish-white water burst from her staff.

I'm sure everyone was expecting its fur to turn blue, just like the prince flame bunnies' had.

"...It didn't work?" Lulu murmured.

The king burning bunny's fur was still covered in the flame aura.

Looking closely, it was evident that the flames had died down, but my panicked party members didn't seem to notice.

The giant rabbit gathered its strength in its rear legs.

"Dimension Cutter, slash-style!"

But Arisa's Space Magic attack only cut through the king burning bunny's afterimage.

The ground behind the giant rabbit burst open, sending up clouds of dust and dirt.

That second howl appeared to have been a Fire Magic strengthening spell to enhance its charge.

"Tallyhooo?"

"Hi-ya, sir!"

Tama and Pochi used "Blink" to leap into the dusty battlefield, catching the rabbit as it landed, but their strikes couldn't pierce its defenses.

The king burning bunny ignored their attacks and took another leap.

No, it might have been dodging Liza, who was charging in with her spear at the ready.

"Ouchiiie?"

"Owie, sir."

Tama and Pochi were sent tumbling across the ground.

Liza's Magic Spear skimmed against the rabbit's back leg but didn't quite reach it.

Then the monster used its third jump to spring toward Mia.

Shocked by the speed and suddenness of the attack, Mia and Arisa were rooted to the spot.

They were in the area with the trenches, but just to be safe, I teleported over to their side with "Warp."

"I will protect Mia, I dec—"

Nana jumped in front of Mia and tried to use "Taunt" but was struck squarely by the king burning bunny's head-butt.

The Flexible Shield protecting her shattered in an instant, and Nana was sent flying, shield and all.

This areamaster was considerably more powerful than the spawn had been.

"Not on my watch!"

Using "Blink," Liza slammed into the monster from the side, knocking it away from Mia.

But before Liza could regain her posture, the raging king burning bunny lashed out at her with its forelegs.

She managed to block the claws with her spear and jump away, but seeing the flames building in its throat, Liza put power into her Magic Spear with a do-or-die expression.

She was probably planning on an all-or-nothing attack, but that was way too reckless.

"Master, help us!"

"On it!"

Calling back to Arisa, I jumped into the battle.

Using "Warp," I teleported right in front of the areamaster's eyes, kicked it in the head before it could breathe fire, and used Dimension Cutter to slice right through its exposed neck, cutting its head off in one blow.

Fire started to spurt out of the top of its neck, but I put the corpse into Storage, fire and all, before it could burn my clothes.

Incidentally, I had learned the Space Magic spell Dimension Cutter from a scroll just recently.

"Is everyone all right?"

"Nana's okay!"

This report came from Lulu, who had run over to Nana when she was sent flying.

Tama and Pochi, who had also been knocked away, were getting to their feet while drinking recovery potions.

"Looks like it was a little too soon to attempt to fight an areamaster."

I healed everyone with Water Magic and handed out some bitter-sweet carbonated drinks.

With another five levels under their belt, they should be able to hold their own a little better.

"I didn't expect it to be such a beast," Arisa murmured into her drink.

"Agreed."

"Oui-oui!"

"We got our butts kicked, sir."

The other three younger kids nodded in agreement.

"What did the rest of you think?"

"It moved even more quickly than 'Blink.' I never had a chance to use my 'Triple Helix Spear Attack.'"

"It broke through my Flexible Shield and my physical shield, I report."

"I couldn't really keep up with my Fireburst Gun, either."

The older girls all voiced their assent.

Maybe this was a good time to make my suggestion.

"What do you think, everyone? Should we go back to Bolenan Forest for a while and get the teachers to train us again?"

"Training?!" Arisa turned to me in surprise. "A training montage! It's the training montage section!"

Her eyes sparkled with flames—she must have created some fire behind me.

You don't need to use Fire Magic just for effect. How dramatic can you get?

Arisa wasn't the only one who seemed enthused about my proposal.

"Yes, sir! An excellent suggestion."

"Retraining is a good idea; I agree."

"Mm. Spirit Magic. Stronger."

"I'd like to work on my aim, too."

Liza, Nana, Mia, and Lulu were all on board.

"Secret training under the waterfaaall?"

"We'll break falling logs with our heads, sir!"

Tama and Pochi seemed to be willing, too, though they were taking things in an odd direction.

"The elf village is great and all, but I'd love to train on a mountain with immortal wizards or in a giant library in a city-size academy, too."

Ignoring Arisa's nonsense, we decided to leave the labyrinth to start our retraining.

The time allotted for our stay wasn't quite up yet, so instead of going aboveground first, we went directly to Bolenan Forest using Return.

I had to use the spell a few times in succession, since we couldn't reach there in one go, but it was still a lot easier than traveling by boat.

Retraining

Satou here. I always loved ridiculous, over-the-top training scenes in anime and manga. Something about them really appeals to my inner child.

"Master Satou!"

When we stopped at the southern island on the way to Bolenan Forest, the first person to greet us was Yuuneia, a young girl whose black hair ended in red tips.

"Sister! Come quickly!"

After throwing her arms around me in a hug, she turned back to call her older sister, Rei.

A very small girl with blue-tipped white hair came running over as fast as her short legs could carry her.

At a glance, Rei looked younger than Yuuneia, but she was actually older than me or even Mia the elf.

She was a half-ghost—an extremely rare race—as well as the final surviving member of the ancient Lalakie dynasty. She had lived for more than two thousand years.

"Welcome back, Satou. Good to see you, everyone."

"You too, Rei."

Rei's tone was calm as usual, but it looked like she had been lonely on the island.

Further proof of this included how her little hand wrapped around mine and refused to let go.

Yuuneia, incidentally, was no longer clinging to me, having been dragged away by the iron-wall pair.

"Can you stay awhile this time?" she asked.

"No, we're on our way to Bolenan Forest, I'm afraid." When I saw

Rei's smile fade, I quickly continued, "Why don't you come with us? We stopped by to ask you to accompany us on a tour of the elves' forest."

"Are you sure the elves won't mind uninvited guests in their territory?"

"It'll be fine."

I had already gotten permission from Aaze—Aialize the high elf of Bolenan Forest—and the elf elders to invite the two along after the Lalakie incident.

"But…"

"Don't worry. Miss Aaze is in the elf village, and the World Tree's spirit light purifies miasma."

Rei was probably nervous because her body was very susceptible to the negative effects of miasma, which tended to gather in populated areas.

"Yuuneia, will you come, too?"

"I'd follow my big sister anywhere!"

Yuuneia was obsessed with her sister, so I knew that would be her answer.

The two sisters joined us, and we resumed our journey to Bolenan Forest with the help of multiple Return spells.

◆

"Okay, we're here."

Including the stop at the island, it took eight Return spells to arrive in Bolenan Forest.

Unlike the advanced Space Magic teleportation spells, my Return spell was limited to about two hundred miles per use, so it couldn't get to the forest in one shot.

Because having more people along also increased the amount of magic required, it ended up using almost the same amount as a single Meteor Shower.

When we arrived at our tree house in Bolenan Forest, someone else was already there.

"Hello, Miss Lua."

Lua froze, looking startled.

She was the elf priestess in charge of taking care of the high elf Miss Aaze.

"Welcome back, Mr. Satou. You've got quite a crowd with you this time."

She was accustomed to my teleporting in, though, and she returned my greeting calmly. From the look of things, she was airing out our rooms today.

"We were hoping to do some training, so we'll be staying for a while, if that's all right."

"Of course. You're always welcome."

"'This time'?" I heard the sharp-eared Arisa repeat behind me, but I ignored her, even when she went on. "Come to think of it, didn't Rei say 'can you stay awhile *this time*?' too?"

"Mm."

Nope, I'm not getting roped into this conversation. I'll just let it flow right past me like the wind.

"I'll contact Hiya and the others, then. Oh, and Nea was saying that she's managed to make vanilla extract."

"Yes, Miss Aaze told me that yesterday over Telephone."

Behind me, I heard Arisa and Lulu going over our schedule from the day before.

Their memory wasn't deceiving them. All through the previous day, they were fighting monsters in the labyrinth, and I was standing nearby researching golem magic.

"Stop! In the naaame of love!"

Why are you singing?

"Stoppp?"

"The naaaame of love, sir."

Tama and Pochi started imitating Arisa, as usual.

"What is it?"

"Question: Why did she say 'this time'?"

"Why, because Mr. Satou comes by every ten days or so."

Before I could come up with the best way to gloss things over, Miss Lua blew my cover.

I had been back here only maybe seven or eight times since we started out toward Labyrinth City.

"When in the world...?"

"Mrrr."

Arisa and Mia looked up at me accusingly.

"I just came back to share when I found some new ingredients or recipes."

That was the truth. The labyrinth was a treasure trove of rare ingredients, with monsters like moss crab bees, dungeon fungus, monster pumpkins, ancient land beasts, and bloodred turtles.

I had also visited Nea to discuss methods for extracting vanilla from monsters called "vanilla stalkers."

So I definitely wasn't coming back with the sole intention of seeing Miss Aaze.

"That doesn't add up...," I heard Rei and Yuuneia murmuring to each other.

Depending on how much time I had, I didn't always stop by the island on the way.

But why did I feel like a husband being accused of infidelity?

"Oh yeah? Question two: What's this about Telephone?"

"Huh? Didn't I tell you?"

I tilted my head, combing through my memories.

...Okay, maybe I never mentioned this.

"My Telephone and Miss Aaze's World Phone work well enough over the distance between Labyrinth City and Bolenan."

"Mrrr."

"We didn't know that!"

Mia and Arisa fumed at me. I had just assumed that they'd figured it out and were being nice enough to let it slide.

"Oh, that's right. Nea's prototype is cooling in the refrigerator. Take a look when you have the chance."

Possibly sensing the awkwardness, Lua generously changed the subject.

"She finished it already? Thank you very much. I'll definitely take a look."

"Prototype? You don't mean...!"

Heh-heh-heh. Yes, the thing I found on the sugar route.

Because Nea and her team were great cooks, I had them research ways to make it taste even better.

"You'll find out soon. We can have some after dinner tonight, so make sure you don't eat too much."

"At last! Ahhh, I wish dinnertime would come already. Don't you know the Song of Time, master?"

"Of course not."

I understood her excitement, but even if I knew how to do that, it wouldn't make time go any faster.

*   *   *

"Mr. Satou, I've contacted Lady Aaze as well as Mia's parents. They'll be here soon."

Lua was using Spirit Magic to send a magical messenger bird out the window as she spoke.

"Satou, is Lady Aaze the high elf you mentioned?" Rei asked in a small voice, tugging on my sleeve.

"That's right."

"Oh." Her expression held mixed emotions as she responded.

Uh-oh. Maybe my affection for Aaze came out in my voice.

Rei looked up at me.

"Satou, could I have some magic, please?" For whatever reason, she was wearing a forced smile. "I'd like to be in formal dress when I meet the high elf."

I nodded and used my hand to siphon some magic into her.

She grew as she received the magic, changing from an elementary school–age girl into a beautiful, well-proportioned woman, all in the blink of an eye.

This wasn't a spell. Because of Rei's unusual half-ghost nature, she normally stayed in little-girl mode to conserve magic, but this was her true form.

Rei's clothes also changed into the traditional garb of a Lalakie priestess.

Her clothes and accessories were made out of ghostly material, just like her body itself.

"Thank you, Satou."

Rei smiled bashfully.

Her priestess outfit was a bit revealing. I wasn't sure where to look.

Suddenly, Miss Aaze came flying into the tree-house room.

"Lua! What's this urgent business you—? Satou!"

As soon as she turned toward me, a smile bloomed on her face like a beautiful flower.

Yeah, she's gorgeous as usual.

"I'm back, Miss Aaze."

"Welcome b—"

Suddenly, she froze mid-sentence, and her smile faded.

…Huh?

"Welcome…back…Satou." Her speaking turned slow and stilted.

"Erm, is this girl…your lover? Have you come…to introduce…your wife to me?" she asked hesitantly.

…How do you figure?

"No," I responded plainly.

"B-but…!"

Miss Aaze looked at my right hand doubtfully.

Rei hadn't let go of my hand after I used it to provide her with magic. I tried to draw it away, but Rei hung on tightly.

"…Um, Rei?"

"Oh, I'm sorry, Satou."

Rei hurriedly withdrew her hand, then held it sorrowfully to her chest.

Um, if you keep looking at me like that, people will think you're in love with me.

"Miss Aaze, this is Rei. The girl behind her is Yuuneia."

"Oh, Rei and Yuuneia? The girls from Lalakie, right? I remember!"

I had told her about them before, but this was her first time meeting them in person.

"B-but I thought you said she was a much smaller child…"

Confused, Aaze looked at Rei's formidable bust with dismay, so I explained Rei's nature to her.

"It's an honor to meet you, O Holytree of Bolenan Forest. I am the last queen of the Lalakie dynasty, Reiaane Tuuwa Lalakie—or Rei, resident of Paradise Island."

Rei knelt in front of Aaze and introduced herself.

Following her sister's example, Yuuneia knelt as well.

Tama and Pochi tried to follow suit, but Pochi lost her balance and fell on her face, and the two of them rolled away to the far side of the room.

"Please raise your heads—there's no need to be so formal. The pleasure is all mine. I am Aialize, high elf of Bolenan Forest. Any friend of Satou's is a friend of mine, so please feel free to call me Aaze."

Miss Aaze introduced herself in a friendly tone, prompting the two of them to stand.

"Nice to meet you! I'm Yuuneia, a homunculus." She turned to Rei. "Sister, is this person Master Satou's lady friend?"

"…Yes, that's right."

When Rei confirmed this, Miss Aaze turned bright red and pressed her hands to her cheeks.

She was probably flustered by the use of the phrase *lady friend*. Frankly, it made me want to hug her tightly.

"Mrrr. Just friends."

"That's right! She totally rejected master already!"

OOF.

"So she's not his 'lady friend'!"

Mia and Arisa forcefully dissuaded Rei and Yuuneia from their choice of words.

Sometimes the truth cuts deeper than any knife.

I wouldn't have been surprised if my log said something like **Satou took 3,000 points of damage**.

"You don't like Master Satou, Lady Aaze?"

"Of course I do!!"

Aaze's emphatic response to Yuuneia's innocent question was a welcome salve for my emotional wounds.

Ah, I could live off those words alone for the next ten years.

It was rare to see Aaze's face look so frantic.

I snuck a photo with the Light Magic spell Picture Recorder and put it away in the Pictures folder of my Storage.

"You've all grown quite a bit."

After the initial chaos of Rei's and Yuuneia's introduction, things finally calmed down enough for some friendly catchup.

"Wait a minute, Lady Aaze." Miss Lua flapped her hand in front of her face. "This sudden growth isn't nearly so trivial, don't you think?"

"Really? Since they're with Satou, I think it's only to be expected that things might be a little out of the ordinary."

Miss Aaze, I appreciate that you trust me, but you're sort of talking like we are lovers.

Nearby, Mia's parents had arrived and were wasting no time in praising their daughter.

"Welcome back, Mia. You've grown ever so much! Why, that's terribly amazing! You must have worked very, very hard. You're a hard worker, you are! Did you hurt yourself at all? You're all right? You will stay awhile now, won't you?"

"Good job."

"Mm. Worked hard."

Mia looked pleased as her parents patted her head.

Her childhood friend Goya showed up, too, but once he heard about Mia's rapid growth, he ran off somewhere.

Hang in there, kid.

Technically, the boy was far older than I was, but I still sent him some silent encouragement.

"Yo! I heard Satou and friends are back!"

"It's master, sir!"

"Heya, Pochi! You've gotten awful strong since you've been away, haven'tcha?"

"Hee-hee, sir."

The elf teachers had arrived, led by Pochi's teacher, Miss Portomea.

In contrast to her brash manner of speaking, she was a beautiful girl with wavy shoulder-length hair and a doll-like face.

"Have you been well, Tama?"

"Aye-aye!"

Shishitouya, the elf samurai, patted Tama's head.

He was definitely male, but his long hair and soft features were very feminine.

"'Spellblade.'"

"Yes, Master Guya."

Gurgapoya, the helix-spear user, inspected Liza's "Spellblade" usage.

"Good."

"Thank you very much."

His short but sincere compliment put a proud expression on Liza's face.

"Excellent 'Spellblade' form. If you can just shorten the time it takes to invoke it and eliminate any magic leakage, it will be perfect."

"Agreed."

Liza's other teacher, the spriggan short-spear user Yusek, discussed the finer points of "Spellblade" with Guya.

"Praise."

"I am proud to receive my teacher's praise, I declare."

Miss Gimasarua, a Magic Swordsman, praised Nana with a single word, similar to Mia's speaking style.

Nana's other teacher, the dwarf shield user Mr. Keriul, didn't seem to be around at the moment.

"Hey, Satou. You've all grown quite a bit."

Finally, Hishirotoya, the wordy elf who was in charge of the teachers and had lots of connections, arrived to compliment us.

"Have you learned to do chants, too, Satou?"

"I'm sorry, not quite yet…"

"Ah-ha-ha. No need to apologize." Hishirotoya, or Hiya for short, smiled. "Are you practicing, though?"

"Yes, every morning and evening."

"Well, all right, then. Humans grow quickly. Keep it up for ten years or so, and you'll be able to do it in no time."

I didn't feel like I was getting anywhere with chants, but Arisa and Mia both said it was the kind of thing that just suddenly clicks one day. I put my trust in them and continued to practice.

"Miss Nea, I've learned lots of new dishes during our travels!"

"I can't wait. Let's make some later, shall we?"

"Yes, please!"

Nea taught self-defense to Lulu and the other rearguard girls. But she also loved to cook, so she and Lulu were always chatting about food.

"I want a teacher, too," Arisa grumbled.

"Mm. Aaze."

Mia pointed at Miss Aaze.

She was Mia's Spirit Magic instructor, but she was also capable in all the other kinds of magic, including Space Magic.

"Mm, I dunno. Miss Aaze seems like the type to ignore theories and stuff and just use magic based on *feelings* or whatever, don't you think?"

"How cruel!"

When Arisa's harsh assessment appeared to hurt Aaze's feelings, I pulled her toward me to comfort her. *Eeexcellent.*

"You are much too close."

Before the iron-wall pair could move, Lua the priestess pulled Aaze and me apart.

"You should speak to one of the elders about Space Magic. They love magic theory, so they'll talk to you about it for years if you let them."

Wow. I guess elves live so long that their lectures are on another level.

"Miss Lua, could you introduce me to a Fire Magic teacher, too?"

"Any one of the elders can use the four basic elemental magics well enough to teach others. You could have them help you with that along with Space Magic."

"Hooray!"

Arisa pumped her fist triumphantly when Lua agreed to introduce her to the elders.

"*Satou, candy!*"

"*Gimme candy!*"

Little winged fairies landed on Rei's and Yuuneia's head and shoulders.

I gave the sisters two small sacks of candy so they could hand them out.

"W-wait a second!"

"*Hurry it up!*"

"*I want candyyy!*"

Unwilling to wait for Rei, a few particularly rude fairies stuck their heads in the sack.

"S-Satou!" Rei called for help, and I assisted her in calming the fairies down.

One of the particularly lucky—erm, that is, disgraceful—fairies sat on Rei's chest, so I moved it to my shoulder.

"Wait your turn, or none of you gets any more."

"*I'll line up!*"

"*Yeah, me too!*"

"*Candy puh-leez!*"

The winged fairies quickly fell into line. My "Education" and "Animal Training" skills might have had something to do with that.

Although it could've just been their appetites.

"*Cut that out!*"

"Master Satou, are these little things people?"

"That's right. So be gentle with them, please."

Yuuneia was pulling on one of the fairies' legs until I quickly stopped her.

She was frighteningly innocent about it, like a child playing with a doll.

"Yuuneia! You must handle larvae with great delicacy, I advise."

Nana had also come running over when she saw how Yuuneia was handling the fairies.

"Delicacyyy?"

"It's like a food, sir."

Tama and Pochi repeated after Nana.

Their mixed-up vocabulary was nothing out of the ordinary, so I didn't bother correcting them.

"Yes, ma'am."

Looking forlorn, Yuuneia let go of the fairy.

Freed from danger, the winged fairy fluttered over to land on my shoulder.

"That one's crazy, mister."

I handed it some extra candy for its troubles.

"Dinner is ready, everyone!"

A group of house fairy brownies arrived carrying food, along with Nea's crew of elf chefs.

The long table was soon lined with seven kinds of curry, assorted vegetables and meat for toppings, and a wide array of side dishes.

It seemed that the curry craze I had started in the elf village was still going strong.

"Whoo-hoo! Chocolate parfaits!"

As soon as she saw the assortment of chocolate desserts that came out after dinner, Arisa's excitement shot off the charts.

"There's cake, too."

Nea smiled at Arisa as she placed a chocolate cake on the table.

There were also bite-size pieces of cut chocolate.

Unfortunately, the lava cake I had requested wasn't ready yet. Nea said they were getting close; hopefully they'd be able to make it while we were here for training.

"Hoo boy, I'm gonna gain weight..."

"Squishyyy?"

"So round, sir."

Looking at the buffet of chocolate desserts, Arisa slumped so that her gut deliberately stuck out. Tama and Pochi immediately lined up at her side and imitated the gesture.

"Excuse me! I'm not really that chunky!"

"Nyah-ha-ha..."

"Run for it, sir!"

"Run away!"

"She's gonna eat us!"

Arisa pretended to be furious, and Tama and Pochi ran away giggling, followed by the winged fairies.

"Go ahead and dig in."

At Miss Nea's prompting, everyone started reaching for the desserts.

"Bittersweeeet?"

"It's bitter but sweet and tasty, sir!"

Tama and Pochi appeared to have eaten the dark chocolate, which was for more mature taste buds. I pointed them toward the sweet milk chocolate, which earned even higher praise like "Yummyyy!" and "Delicious, sir!"

"It's very good."

Liza was chewing on a thick, uncut chunk of dark chocolate with a satisfied look on her face.

It was probably pretty hard, but she was crunching away at it instead of letting it melt on her tongue.

"Master, the chocolate cake is delicious, I report."

Nana was sharing pieces of her cake with the winged fairies as she ate. Judging by the unusual speed of her fork, she must have really been enjoying it.

"Sister! This is delicious! Almost as much as that strawberry cake."

"It really is. This is wonderful, Lady Nea."

"Hee-hee, thank you."

Yuuneia's eyes sparkled as she praised the chocolate cake, and her sister, Rei, thanked the baker Nea with her eyes equally round and shiny.

"It really is delicious. Can you show me how to make this later, Miss Nea?"

"Yes, of course."

Leave it to Lulu to already want to learn how to make it.

"Cake."

"The parfait is delicious, too. It has a nice, crispy texture on the inside."

"Gimme."

When Mia leaned over, Aaze fed her a bite of her parfait. I was a little jealous.

The "crispy texture" she had mentioned could be attributed to the cornflakes.

I took a bite myself, enjoying the delicate sweetness with a slightly bitter touch that melted in my mouth.

It was smooth and delicious, far better than it had been when I taste tested it last time. This easily compared to the high-quality chocolate that you could normally get only during Valentine's season.

Hmm?

A speck of chocolate had wound up on Aaze's cheek as she enjoyed the parfait.

"Excuse me, Miss Aaze."

I wiped the chocolate away with my finger, then cleaned her cheek with a handkerchief.

I almost brought the chocolate to my mouth, a habit from taking care of the younger kids in my party, but wiped it off with a handkerchief instead when I remembered the chicken rice incident.

"Guil—"

"Why, y—"

Mia and Arisa were all ready to scold me, but they stopped mid-sentence when they saw my course of action.

Heh-heh-heh. You won't catch me making the same mistake twice.

"Grrrr…"

That growl didn't come from Arisa.

"I've made a grave mistake."

"If we'd just held off on that last helping of curry…"

The elf teachers appeared to be too full to properly enjoy the chocolate dishes.

You guys eat way too much curry.

"So have you come back to relax for a while?"

"No, actually…"

Mr. Hiya asked about the nature of our visit, so I explained the situation.

"Hmm. Retraining, eh?"

"Would that be all right?"

"Of course."

The elf teachers agreed to my request right away.

◆

"First, could you show us the results of your training in the labyrinth?"

Lined up in front of Mr. Hiya and the other elf teachers, my group nodded.

We were in a wide-open wasteland outside Bolenan Forest thanks to the forest fairy Dryad's fairy ring teleportation. Miss Aaze and Lua had come along, too.

Once the girls gave their affirmation, Mr. Hiya turned to Aaze.

"Lady Aaze, produce a spirit for training, please."

"Is a behemoth all right?"

"No."

One of the taciturn elf teachers rejected Aaze's choice.

A behemoth was a pseudo-spirit that looked like a cross between an elephant and a hippopotamus, but it was level 50 and the size of a destroyer ship. It was probably a bit too strong for a practice battle for my party.

"If you'd prefer one with a physical body, perhaps a spirit of the wasteland or the sand?" Lua suggested.

"That sounds more like it." Hiya nodded. "Could you, Lady Aaze?"

"Of course! ■ ■ ■ ■ ■…"

Miss Aaze began the long Spirit Magic chant. When it was finished, rocks and dirt from the wasteland gathered together to form a giant golem-like monster.

It certainly looked more like a living creature than the golems I'd made with Create Earth Servant.

This spirit was level 40, so it should be about the same degree of strength as the areamaster.

"I've transferred command to you."

"Thank you."

Taking over the wasteland spirit from Aaze, Hiya tested out his control for a moment before having the spirit face my group.

"Are you ready?"

"But of course!"

Arisa responded on the others' behalf.

I stepped back with Aaze, Rei, and the other spectators to watch the fight with the elf teachers.

"A-amazing…"

"Were they always this strong?"

Rei and Yuuneia were surprised.

"They've been training hard in the labyrinth."

As I responded to the sisters, I peered over at the elf teachers.

Hmm?

For some reason, their expressions were a little strange.

At first, they looked as impressed as Aaze, Rei, and Yuuneia, but as the battle approached its final stages, they were beginning to frown a little.

Just as I was about to ask about it, my party's fight ended.

The wasteland spirit turned back into clumps of earth.

"Victoryyy?"

"Sir!"

The girls lined up in front of the teachers again, looking eager for praise.

"You've gotten a lot stronger…"

Pochi's teacher, Miss Poa, stepped out from among the teachers.

The girls began to smile at her complimentary words.

"…but it's a dangerous kind of strength."

At her strongly negative tone, my kids' faces froze.

"Do you understand why?"

"Because we're too focused on offense, perhaps?"

Liza ventured to answer the question from Mr. Shiya, Tama's teacher.

"No. Because you're depending too much on Satou."

"B-but we…"

Arisa started to protest but trailed off.

"If worse comes to worst, Satou will step in. You don't have to be too careful, because you know he'll protect you. That's what you're thinking, isn't it?"

The girls hung their heads at Shiya's accusation.

"Don't look away."

Poa started to scold them further, but Hiya stopped her and continued.

"Of course, it's not a bad thing to be able to fight calmly because you know Satou is behind you, but you shouldn't go into every fight assuming that. Do you understand?"

I see. So my overprotectiveness was the reason they'd been focusing on offense too much lately…

It made sense. Even if things weren't at their worst, I'd always stepped in if it looked like someone was about to get seriously hurt.

"That might be all right when Satou's around, but what if you had to face a challenge without him?"

"Then we'd—"

"Fight? Are you sure? Would you really be able to act with the assumption that he won't be there to rescue you?"

Hiya's tone was gentle as he interrupted Arisa.

"Well…"

"I don't think you could."

Arisa trailed off again, so Hiya answered for her.

To be honest, I thought he was right.

"It seems like you might need to distance yourselves from Satou a little."

"And the opposite is true, too."

Miss Gia followed up Miss Poa's statement, suggesting that I should fix my overprotective habits, too.

"So now that we know what the problem is, shall we begin training in earnest?"

"That's right, you lot! Think you've got what it takes to handle some *real* training?!"

Poa attempted to fire everyone up with a yell.

"Of course."

"Aye-aye!"

"I'll do it, sir!"

"I am ablaze, I declare."

"Mm. Retraining."

"All right, you guys! Let's do this thing!"

"Let's do our best, everyone."

The girls all cheered with eager expressions.

"That's what I like to hear, indeed."

"Lady Aaze, could you produce a spirit spider next?"

"Certainly!"

With that, the elf teachers began retraining the girls.

Confident that I could trust them and Miss Aaze to take it from there, I took Rei and Yuuneia away from the wasteland battlefield.

◆

"Welcome back, Lord Satou."

"Thank you, Gillil."

At the entrance of a white mansion amid a sea of trees, the house fairy brownie Mr. Gillil came to greet me.

I was here to borrow the house of Trazayuya the elf sage to develop some new armor for the girls as a reward for all the hard work they had been putting in with their training.

Rei and Yuuneia seemed to have been inspired by my group and were in the plaza outside our tree house, learning self-defense from Miss Nea.

"I hope our Lelillil isn't causing you too much trouble."

"No, she's a great help."

Gillil was Lelillil's grandfather. It was only natural he wanted to know how she was doing.

I guess even long-lived fairy races still doted on their grandchildren.

"Crystal sculptures? Are you making golems?"

"Just to serve as mannequins."

I made likenesses of my party members out of crystal and turned them into golems using Create Earth Servant.

I intended to put the new armor on them to test out their endurance and range of motion.

"So you'll be making armor, then?"

"Hmm, I think I might start with making tools to simplify the process first."

I stopped Gillil from preparing the magic equipment and described what I was thinking of making.

If I kept having to rely on Mia's Water Magic and Arisa's Space Magic to create magic tools and weapons, it would be imposing on them and make it difficult to create as many prototypes as I wanted.

Putting it all together at the end would probably still rely on them, but I wanted to make it so that I could do simple tests and prototypes on my own.

Running experiments in my imagination could only go so far, after all.

Using the ample equipment available in the mansion, I started making development tools one after another.

"Lord Satou, it is nearly sunset. If you wish to stay the night, shall I prepare dinner?"

"Oh, is it that late already? I didn't tell anyone I'd be away, so I'd better go back to eat at home."

I went to the tree house, telling Mr. Gillil that I'd return for dinner.

The girls were exhausted and their equipment was a wreck, but they looked determined as they scarfed down food.

After showering the hard-working girls with encouragement, I asked Miss Aaze and Mr. Hiya to introduce me to anyone who could use the magic I needed to create magic equipment, like elf elders and engineers.

From the next day on, I started making equipment with magic-circuit creation and transcription functions. And so I managed to complete the prototypes in just a few days with the help of the elves.

That was only the first step, but it still went faster than I thought it would. When it comes to magic, the wonders never cease.

"Gillil and Aea told me before, but I'm still surprised by how quickly you develop spells."

At the feast we had to celebrate finishing the equipment, one of the engineer elves came over to speak to me.

"Do you think so?"

"How many spells did you make during the development of this equipment alone?"

"Three or so, maybe?"

"No, you made eight."

Did I really make that many?

"Don't look so surprised. You made three brand-new spells and five revised versions."

Ahhh. Come to think of it, I did remember making offshoot spells five times or so.

Do those really count, though?

"Even we elves and the Holytrees cannot make them so quickly."

"Impressed."

"Agree."

Some of the other elf engineers and elders came over to praise me, too.

Why did this feel a little awkward, though?

"Still, to think that you could actually set coordinates and teleport after making a magic circuit..."

Gazing at the prototype magic equipment, one of the engineers murmured in what seemed like admiration.

"There have been some of us who thought of such a thing before, but none was ever able to complete it. Most of them gave up partway or were satisfied when they finished a single prototype and left it at that."

"This has far too many settings, though."

One of the other engineers let out a sigh.

Sorry, but it has to have a lot of different parameters.

"No sensible elf would ever attempt to make such a thing even if the idea crossed their mind."

That's rude.

Everyone was being quite blunt, maybe because they'd been drinking.

Besides, they were complaining about the amount of data, but it was still less than a gigabyte at best.

That's only a quarter the amount on a DVD. It shouldn't be too hard to input by hand if you put your mind to it.

I manually input some simple data, since this time was just a test. When I actually made the next prototype, though, I planned to use Menu-related linking spells, so they didn't have to worry so much, in my opinion.

I had used some of these linking spells to set it up to load data files from Storage, which meant manual input was required only the first time. And if I converted the functional modules into a library, then I could use those preexisting assets like activating a spell, lightening the workload even further.

Incidentally, I had gone to the scroll workshop in the old capital earlier that afternoon to get the scrolls of three linking spells I'd already requested from Viscount Siemmen. I was pleasantly surprised to find them completed sooner than expected.

I visited them in the guise of my merchant alias, Akindoh, but brought a letter with the Pendragon family seal, so it was fairly simple to earn their trust.

One afternoon, a few days after the prototype equipment was completed...

"So they're facing off against spiders today?"

I went to check in on my group's training and have them test out the prototype.

However, due to the prototype being capable of inscribing only cuboid magic circuits, it was less effective for weapons and armor.

Blue was difficult to keep stable. It was hard to use it to make overly large and complicated mechanisms, too. It would probably still be a while before I could implement functions to make God-given Holy Sword–class weapons.

"Hey, Satou. Welcome."

Mr. Hiya gave me a friendly greeting and beckoned me to his side.

The girls were fighting spider-shaped pseudo-spirits of various sizes, created by Aaze.

Fighting spirits didn't seem to grant much EXP, so they were all still level 42. The experience bar hadn't changed much since the training started.

As the elf teachers and I looked on, my group fought hard in a white arena made from the spiders' thread.

There were a lot of enemies, and they could attack from any direction using the thread hanging across the arena. Thanks to that, the vanguard and rear guard alike were struggling.

"That thread comes in a few different varieties. The elastic kind can be broken only by magic or 'Spellblade,' but if you use them too recklessly, the other thread will absorb your magic."

Hiya explained the difficulties of fighting the spiders.

The vanguard was indeed on the verge of running out of magic, and they were struggling to maintain "Spellblade."

"The small spiders move so quickly that it's difficult to defend the rear guard, and the large ones have thick hides that can be pierced only by magic or long-handled weapons. And since they're pseudo-spirits, there aren't any organs to aim for, either," Hiya added.

The only way to fight these enemies was with strategy and good use of support and de-buff magic.

"Electromagnetic Barrier!"

Arisa warded off a small approaching spider with a spherical Space Magic barrier.

It wasn't even remotely electromagnetic, but there wasn't any need to point that out.

"Take this!"

Lulu aimed her Fireburst Gun and shot down the small spider while it was still in midair.

"...■ *Create Snow Wolf Hyousetsu Shouryou Souzou.*"

Mia invoked Spirit Magic, creating four snow-covered ice wolves.

Their lower bodies were transparent, trailing swirls of fog as they ran through midair.

"Cut thread."

On Mia's order, the ice wolves attacked the spider thread that hung in the air, freezing them and breaking them to pieces.

"I'm going to restrengthen you!"

"Thank you."

Now that she'd fended off the small spider, Arisa used "Body Strengthening" on the vanguard instead of just attacking.

There was a considerable distance between her and the vanguard, so it cost a large amount of MP. Before the retraining started, Arisa probably would have jumped straight to attack magic for maximum effectiveness in this situation.

Maybe I should add staffs that improve the range of magic to my list of things to develop?

"Hi-yaaaa!"

A small spider flew on the wind to launch a surprise attack at Lulu, but she smacked it away with the stock of her Fireburst Gun.

"Shurikeeen?"

Tama finished the flying spider off with a throwing star.

She had been taught how to use these by the female samurai Ayaume in the old capital and was continuing to study under her at night in Labyrinth City now that they'd been reunited.

I'll have to make some kunai *that return to the user's hand for Tama, too.*

I couldn't make weapons that flew around in the air and attacked enemies on their own like the Holy Sword Claidheamh Soluis just yet, but a boomerang-like function shouldn't be so hard.

"Carefuuul?"

Then, instead of gloating about the spider she'd defeated, Tama used another throwing knife to stop a spider that was about to attack Nana from her blind spot.

Meanwhile, the giant spider Nana was fighting spat a glob of poison at her from a distance.

"Shield, activate! I declare."

Instead of using Flexible Shield, which consumed a lot of MP, Nana used the Foundation technique Shield to deflect the poison.

The Shield dissipated as soon as it blocked the poison, but since it was lower cost and a little faster to activate than Flexible Shield, it was probably the most effective choice.

The giant spider jumped at Nana, trying to wrap its four front legs around her.

"Flexible Shield, mobile defense mode, I announce."

Nana shouted with her "Taunt" skill while creating three Flexible Shields, blocking the spider's attack.

One of the legs got past them, but she blocked it using her real giant shield.

"Let's go, Pochi."

"Attack, sir!"

Liza and Pochi were darting around the giant spider, scattering smaller ones as they closed in.

"Thunder Rod rifle, activate!"

Nana used a Thunder Rod rifle hidden behind her large shield to attack the giant spider head-on.

According to my AR, it didn't do a huge amount of damage, but it was enough to hinder the spider's vision.

"'Blink'! Sir!"

Pochi had been approaching with a regular dash, but now she used the "Blink" skill to close the last few feet in an instant.

Right before the jump, she applied "Spellblade" to her Magic Sword and plunged it into the giant spider's torso as soon as she arrived in reach.

But the spider's HP gauge still didn't go down much.

Twisting around, it grabbed Pochi and tossed her aside.

She went flying with a good deal of momentum, but Arisa used Space Magic to slow her down, and she landed right in a giant spider-web, so she didn't seem to be too injured.

"O 'Spellblade,' fill this spear of mine!"

The red light gleaming from Liza's Magic Spear wrapped around her entire body as she ran forward.

In response, the giant spider shot some poison at her.

"'Blink'! 'Triple Helix Spear Attack'!"

The "Blink" skill activated with an earth-shattering boom, and she moved forward nearly thirty feet in an instant.

The blob of poison hit the empty ground where Liza had been just moments before.

All the light around Liza, not only her spear, swirled with the helix attack.

Liza attacked as if her body and Magic Spear were one, slamming her whole body into the giant spider as her spear pierced through it.

That's a pretty crazy move.

The helix "Spellblade" around Liza bore into the giant spider's body, tearing through its huge frame.

Coming out on the other side of the spider's body, Liza whirled around in case of a counterattack, but the giant spider dispersed into white snow and tiny spirit lights.

The smaller spiders must have been a part of it, too, since they disappeared as soon as the giant spider was destroyed.

From the looks of things, their battle styles were all starting to evolve.

I was glad I had come to observe.

"Amaziiing?"

"Well done as always, Miss Liza."

"Agreed. A splendid attack, I declare."

The other girls gathered around Liza, gushing praise.

Her last attack seemed a little dangerous to me, but it didn't look like the elf teachers were going to scold her for it, so she must be practicing a new special move.

"Liza, preserve strength."

"It's perfectly fine to test out a special move, but you shouldn't bet everything on one final attack unless you have no other choice. Make sure you still have some energy left for yourself and your comrades in case the attack fails."

Liza's teachers, Guya and Yusek, gave her some pointers.

The helix attack was powerful, but it spent a lot of magic power, too.

"The spiders' thread didn't disappear?"

"Mm."

Mia nodded at Lulu.

"Spirit spiders' thread is a good material for summer clothing."

"Breezy."

"But it is transparent even if dyed, so it must be weaved with other thread or worn on top of more clothing."

The elf teachers explained how to use the thread.

It might be good for making some transparent outerwear.

"Good job, Pochi."

After Pochi came trudging over covered in spiderwebs, I cleaned her off with Everyday Magic.

"Master, I want a bigger weapon, sir."

It was rare for Pochi to make a request like this.

When I asked why, she explained that in their fights against pseudo-spirits, her attacks with her one-handed Magic Sword often weren't able to pierce the target's hide even if it landed a direct hit.

"What kind of weapon would you like?"

"Something big and strong-looking, sir."

I took out some prototype weapons from Storage.

"Lottts?"

"So many big weapons, sir!"

Pochi's eyes sparkled as she sorted through the weapons and swung them experimentally. There was a longsword, a broadsword, a war hammer, a longspear, and a battle-ax.

She was able to lift them all easily enough, but since Pochi herself was so light, she had difficulty swinging them without the inertia affecting her balance.

"Masterrr? One more, pleeease..."

Tama hefted a war hammer and asked me to take out another one, so I complied.

They were light compared with the giant mithril alloy hammer I'd used in the dwarf village, but they were still much heavier than Tama herself.

"Looook... A top...?"

Holding one giant hammer in each hand, Tama swung them around and spun like a top.

It was easy to forget, since she didn't have as much physical strength as some of the other vanguard girls, but at level 42, Tama was still considerably strong.

Arisa and Lulu giggled uncontrollably, muttering things like "Tama-top!" They were getting a real kick out of it. They were at that age where kids seem to find everything funny, so I guess it wasn't too surprising.

"Oooof, I'm dizzy, sir."

Because Pochi wanted to use a big weapon like a halberd or a broadsword, I had her tie some heavy weights to herself to keep the inertia from knocking her off-balance. I figured I could give her some heavy full-body armor to wear in battle instead of stone weights.

"I'm not dizzy anymore, but I'm too heavy to move, sir."

I guess I added too many stones.

Despite her complaints, Pochi was still dragging the stones around and moving well enough.

She probably just didn't like that she couldn't move as quickly as usual.

"Looks like heavy armor and weapons aren't the right choice."

I crossed my arms in thought.

"Satou, why not use an alloy of adamantite and bluesilver?"

"What sort of alloy is that?"

Mr. Hiya's suggestion was a combination of two magical metals. If the alloy was supplied with magic, it could expand or shrink at will.

That alloy was probably the source of Claidheamh Soluis's size expansion feature.

I learned that the weapons with size-adjusting functions that occasionally turned up in labyrinth treasure chests were usually some variation of this alloy, too.

Leather and cloth products like the Flying Shoes were normally made with special materials that could be supplied with magic or weaved in a particular way.

I already knew about the latter thanks to Kea, an elf from the textile studio. The special weaving pattern could also be used for the bands of underwear and things like that, but it was easier to just use elastic cord.

"If you want to know more, ask Aea or her teacher," Hiya suggested.

He explained that Miss Aea the alchemist and her teacher, who was one of the elders, were both well versed in this alloy, so I decided to go ask them about it tomorrow.

According to Hiya, it was also possible to fuse orichalcum and dark stones to make a metal that got lighter when provided with magic.

I was embarrassed that I'd once thought I had mastered the art of magic metals by using orichalcum in alchemy. Clearly, there were still a lot of variations for me to learn about.

> **Title Acquired: Knower of the Unknown**
> **Title Acquired: Eternal Student**

"By the way, Satou, didn't you come here to show us something?"

"Oh right. I almost forgot."

Miss Aaze reminded me of my original purpose in coming here.

I produced some armor from my Item Box to show everyone.

"Wow, a Floating Shield!"

"It's just a prototype for now."

The girls' eyes sparkled as they gazed at my new prototype.

This one was cast with mithril, but I was planning to make the final product with alloys of orichalcum, adamantite, and so on.

It was able to float in midair using the same theories behind spells like Floating Board and Cube.

"Pochi and Tama, can you combine those prototypes with this Magic Sword?"

I had equipped these with a feature that leeched magic power from the opponent and supplied it to the wielder.

This was something I'd designed a while ago, but the runes were complicated and I would have to get Arisa and Mia to learn new spells for it, so I hadn't made a prototype yet.

It hadn't even succeeded until the fourth attempt. Even if I had asked those two to help me from the beginning, they would have gone through a lot of wasted effort in the process.

Using "Spellblade" consumes the wielder's magic; therefore, it would be impossible to leave the magic-absorbing function on all the time, but I thought it might be handy to strengthen the user through a long battle if it was used correctly.

I wanted to include a health-restoring function, too, but adding a function that stole health from the opponent required a miasma circuit like a cursed weapon. Needless to say, I decided against it.

According to the elves' documents, it was possible to make such a thing without a miasma circuit using bloodstones or bloodpearls, but those are rare ingredients made only in the Bloodsucker Labyrinth in the Saga Empire, so I was saving them for now.

"Lulu, here's your new equipment. There's a Magic Gun that fires real bullets and a laser gun made with Brightlight Pearls."

The former was meant for foes with a high resistance to magic, while the latter was for fast-moving enemies. Both were made with a simple wooden stock and had a long, rifle-like appearance.

For the real-bullet gun, I learned from my previous failures and added an Explosion Magic element to Shooter Version II, massively improving its initial acceleration.

I gave the former a red barrel and the latter a white barrel so they'd be easy to tell apart.

Maybe for the next upgrade, I can make laser sights and a sniping scope?

"Huh, what interesting weapons. Mind if I test one out?"

"Of course, go ahead."

Mr. Hiya tested out the sniper and real-bullet gun I'd made for Lulu.

"You might want to change the materials for the focus in this laser gun, no? You should ask Aea if she has any suggestions."

"I will, thank you."

I was already planning to stop by and see Miss Aea at the alchemy workshop, so I could ask her then.

"These weapons are for Lulu, yes? Then I'll teach her how to shoot. It would be best if she could use Wind Magic or Light Magic, but even Practical Magic can be helpful with aiming. She should study that, too."

"Yes, sir! I'll do my best!"

Lulu clenched her fist, agreeing to Mr. Hiya's unexpected offer.

I had already been thinking about asking him, but Hiya was always quick to pick up on these things.

"Were you able to study magic alloys?"

"Yes, I'm all finished."

Sitting in the tree house one morning, while eating a hearty breakfast to complement my group's training, I answered Mr. Hiya's question with a smile.

Miss Aea had taught me about the major effects and combinations and even loaned me a huge amount of data from the elves' experiments, so I figured I should be able to make a pretty wide range of magic metal alloys.

"A-already?"

"Well, I've only actually made five kinds so far."

This was my first day; I was still just getting started.

Tomorrow, I wanted to pick up the pace, prioritizing the order more.

"Five kinds?!"

"You learn at a remarkable pace."

"Aea was impressed, too."

The elf teachers were good at compliments.

It might have been mere lip service, but to me it sounded like they really were surprised.

"That's amazing, Satou."

"No, not at all. It's only because Miss Aea is such a good teacher."

Miss Aaze joined in on praising me when she overheard the teachers.

"Hey, master. While you're making equipment, could you maybe make a fridge for the orphanage, too?"

"Didn't we install a spare one there already?"

"Yeah, but that thing's way too small. It'd be best to have a fridge *and* a freezer, and the fridge should be able to hold around five tons."

I checked my ice-stone stock in Storage to see if Arisa's request was possible.

"Hmm. I'm a little low on ice stones, but maybe I can use wind and water stones?"

With my current supply, my only options were to freeze it directly with ice stones or use wind and water stones to vaporize the heat and keep things cool that way.

The circuit for the latter was complicated, meaning the process was more of a pain and required a lot of magic. I was really hoping to avoid it.

"Mr. Satou, if you have any wind stones to spare, would it be at all possible to lend us some?"

"Sure. How many do you need?"

According to the priestess Miss Lua, the finfolk—a mermaid-like race—who lived near Bolenan Forest were making a new undersea village, and they needed some wind stones to put on the site.

Unlike the gillfolk, who were more like traditional mermaids, finfolk didn't have gills, which resulted in their need for wind stones to create breathable areas in their villages.

I wasn't sure why mermaids who couldn't breathe underwater would make their villages in the ocean, but if I gave them all the wind stones I had, that should be more than enough.

I could just go get some more ice stones to create a refrigerator before my next round of crafting.

The snow-covered Black Dragon Mountains were right near Bolenan Forest, after all.

"Hei Long... Ah, he's sleeping, of course."

On a sunny peak in the Black Dragon Mountains, Hei Long the black dragon was snoozing contentedly, letting out enormous snores.

Even when I came closer, he didn't stir. It seemed dragons really were fond of sleeping, just like the landlady of the Gatefront Inn in Seiryuu City had told me once upon a time.

He was completely defenseless, though that was probably because there was no one around who could pose a threat to him.

It made me feel a little guilty, but I used various resistance skills and my high INT stat to stay calm.

"Guess I'll leave him a message..."

I left some casks of mayonnaise and mustard where he would be able to see them upon waking, along with a note saying that I would come back to visit soon.

I'd also brought a goat I bought as a gift for him from the Ougoch Duchy, so I left it on a plateau that he should be able to see below. No wyverns or other monsters would come up there for fear of Hei Long. I figured it should be fine.

Next, I used my map search to look for ice stones in the snowy east side of the Black Dragon Mountains.

"Ooh, there's a good amount. Looks like they're in a frozen caldera lake."

At the bottom of the lake was a sunken mass of valuable ice pearls, too.

I used "Warp" to quickly teleport to the eastern side of the enormous mountain range, then switched to regular "Skyrunning" as I got closer.

"Now, that's impressive. This tunnel could be one of the Seven Wonders of the World."

I entered an enormous wind tunnel that pierced through a vast mountain. It was so big that a jumbo jet could have probably flown straight through.

Somehow, I couldn't help but suspect that Hei Long had something to do with this.

Aha.

I found a few giant wind stones dotted throughout the tunnel.

"I wonder..."

Searching the area, I found that there were a few rare wind pearl crystals, too.

I had gotten some wind pearl crystals from the queen forest cancer hornet's wings, too, but they seemed useful as airship propellers, so I took half of these anyway. It was a simple task, since I was able to pop them into Storage with my Magic Hand.

Pleased with my bonus finds, I passed through the tunnel and arrived above my destination, the caldera lake.

"…Ooooh!"

The frozen lake was so beautiful that I couldn't help but gasp.

The lake itself was splendidly transparent, but it was made all the more gorgeous by the cloudless sky reflected in its surface.

I drank in the blue and white scenery as much as I could, then used the Light Magic spell Picture Recorder to save a few photos in Storage.

While I could always bring my group here to see it someday, Miss Aaze couldn't leave Bolenan Forest, so the only way I could share it with her was through recorded image data.

"Whew. Guess I'd better get down to business."

I turned off the Air-Conditioning spell, which I was using to ward off the cold, and put on some extra layers instead.

I didn't want the heat to have a negative effect on the ice stones or the lake itself, after all.

"…Oof, that's cold!"

Shivering, I stretched my Magic Hand through the thick ice of the caldera lake.

There were ice stones littered amid the snow on the banks of the lake, too, but they were all very small, so I decided to target the ice-stone clumps and ice pearls beneath the icy lake instead.

Since it was so cold, I quickly finished my task and used "Skyrunning" to run up into the air, where I gazed down at the beautiful caldera lake and the stunning wind tunnel before I used the Return spell to go back to Bolenan Forest.

"Okay, let's begin the test firing."

I sent an attack spell toward a golem, which was using the prototype umbrella-style shield I'd made for my companions' new equipment.

First, I tried using five Magic Arrows.

Transparent, spear-size Remote Arrows appeared and zoomed toward the target.

The surface of the umbrella buckled slightly, but it managed to withstand the attack.

"Oh-ho, so it can resist the advanced spell Dancing Javelin, eh?"

Miss Aea looked impressed.

No, sorry, that was just the lesser spell Remote Arrow.

"Next test."

Once the shield had been fixed up, I fired the next spell.

This time, I used an intermediate Light Magic spell, Laser.

"That got through. It did reduce the power, but I guess it couldn't completely block an advanced piercing spell like Photon Laser."

Aea's misunderstanding aside, the shield had to be able to hold up to attacks like this in order to do any good against an areamaster.

After resetting the umbrella shield and testing it out several more times, I realized piercing attacks didn't immediately break through, so I tried adding a function that would spin the umbrella and turn the attack aside.

"That's impressive. But won't it require too much magic?"

"True. It would probably be difficult for one person to use it multiple times."

It was originally intended for a defense wall to maintain position in battle anyway.

"Which is why I'm considering adding a small Holytree Stone kiln to the armor to supply more magic."

"To the *armor*?"

I showed the confused elf my design sketches.

"I see. So you would attach a subspace to the armor just for the Holytree Stone kiln."

"Yes, the engineers from the Magic Bag workshop helped me."

I couldn't make this with my equipment alone, so I had created only two so far: one for Nana's armor and one as a spare.

The Holytree Stone kiln could provide abundant magic, but it was too costly to use all the time, and I figured I would have them use it only against strong opponents like an areamaster.

"You certainly come up with some interesting ideas."

"There were many tomes in my homeland that provided inspiration."

Mostly manga and anime.

I had more ideas that I wanted to implement eventually, like strength-enhancing armor that could bust through the walls of a subspace like glass to come to the rescue or a magical girl–style transformation set.

But of course, I would have to perfect my chanting for those.

*   *   *

"Wow, so much equipment!"

"Satou, we brought you a box lunch."

As I was inspecting some finished equipment, Yuuneia and Rei came to visit.

"Ooh, so round... Is that armor?"

"Yes, for Pochi and Tama. If you do this..."

"Whoa, it got smaller!"

Pochi's and Tama's special armor, which I was developing with the code name Round Armor, was made with the shrinkable magical alloy I'd learned about before. It came with two different modes: a round form to deflect impact from attacks and a slim form for high-speed battle maneuvers.

This function wouldn't work as well for the taller girls like Liza and Nana; their armor didn't have the shrinking feature.

"Wow, these boots are fancy—and these ones are so cute! Look at this, Sister!"

"Are these for Arisa and Mia?"

"I made some for you two, as well."

The armor I made for the two sisters and the rear guard was just sturdy leather armor, but the long boots for Nana contained spikes for digging into the ground as the tank and even anchors for reinforcing the surface beneath her feet.

The beastfolk girls' boots were equipped with a speed-boost feature to increase the acceleration speed of "Blink" movement.

It should be helpful when they used "Blink" followed by a special attack, for example.

"S-Satou, is this white spear...a dragon's claw?!"

Rei exclaimed with surprise when she saw the Dragon Claw Spear I made for Liza.

It was made with the dragon claw spearhead I'd acquired a while back and a tough adamantite handle.

I had a fang from Hei Long the black dragon, too, but I was waiting to use that until I mastered more technology for creating a strong handle.

"Good eye, Rei. That's exactly right."

"I saw them a few times on Lalakie."

Rei explained that the life energy of dragon claws was different from those of other living things.

"Wow, so many guns!"

"Yes, those are for Lulu."

This included an improved laser gun with a scope that made it look like a futuristic rifle and a prototype for a new bullet-shooting gun with the unrefined appearance of a hunting rifle.

When I tried using an eye lens from a giant monster fish to make a new ray gun for Lulu, the power improved exponentially. From now on, I figured she could use the Fireburst Gun for regular battles and the high-magic-consumption laser gun for finishing moves.

The real-bullet gun had improved, too, but it wasn't as convenient as the Fireburst Gun or laser gun and was less powerful than the latter; it would probably be useful only against foes that were impervious to magic.

"This one's pretty."

"It's an automatic frost cannon I made with ice pearls."

It looked cool, but it was more for show than anything useful, so it would probably be stowed away in Storage indefinitely.

"Is this short thing a gun, too?"

"Yes, it's a pistol for self-defense. I made some for you two, as well."

I had made a few different varieties of pistols, smaller than the kind I'd acquired from the Valley of Dragons.

They looked like guns, but they were actually Thunder Rod rifles for stunning targets within a fifty-foot range—in other words, basically magical Tasers. They had one mode that would only shock the target slightly and one that could knock out a grown man.

"Is this a cannon?"

"It's a small Magic Cannon for golem soldiers."

Rei answered Yuuneia's question this time.

I was developing this for Lulu, since she had the least firepower of the rear guard. My long-term plan was to make a floating battery with a coaxial-mounted Magic Cannon, like the kind on airships.

"What are these? A short sword and...?"

"That's a knife called a *kunai* and a throwing star called a *shuriken*."

I'd made the *shuriken* for fun. I didn't bother giving it any special qualities, but the *kunai* employed a function similar to Magic Hand to return to a corresponding glove after it was thrown.

"Watch this…"

I put on the glove and threw the *kunai* at a target. Partway through, I flicked my wrist and the *kunai* returned to my gloved hand.

"Whoa, it came back!"

"Wanna try?"

"Yeah!"

I handed Yuuneia the glove and let her play around with it.

The glove was made with orichalcum thread, so it would protect the thrower's hand from being cut even if they messed up, and because it attracted the knife like a magnet, there was no risk of dropping it, either.

"Are those big swords just normal?"

"No, those have various features, too."

Tama's and Pochi's swords had the magic alloy that let them grow up to three times bigger with magic, and Nana's sword included electric- and shock-projection mechanisms.

I had made a few other prototypes when I was testing out blue and orichalcum, like a handful of orichalcum longsword-size Holy Swords, but they weren't very useful.

I already had plenty of extra mass-produced Holy Swords to use as magic power batteries, so I figured I could test these next time I was out and about as Nanashi the Hero.

"These, um…clothes? Armor? I'm not quite sure what to call them, but they're cute."

"That's equipment for Arisa and the rest of the rear guard."

When I saw Rei and Yuuneia taken with the cute designs, I decided to make them visually similar equipment as a gift sometime soon.

After showing them the new staffs I'd made for Arisa and Mia, we moved to the warehouse with the non-battle items I'd been working on.

"What is this, Master Satou?"

"It's an artificial leg."

While testing out the equipment, I had made this artificial limb for Mr. Kajiro. Its improved jump power and running strength were all well and good, but I shouldn't have given in to Arisa's requests to add a rocket that shoots out of the knee and even an emergency barrier. Giving this artificial leg as a gift to anyone would be a problem.

I decided I would do more research on what kinds of functions I could add before remaking a leg for him.

"The devices next to it are a mixer and a juicer. And the big ones are freezers and a vacuum freeze-drying machine."

"Juicer?"

"Freeze drying?"

The sisters basically had question marks floating above their heads, so I did my best to explain.

The freeze-drying machine was a prototype I'd made with the ice and wind stones I'd acquired, thinking it might be useful for preserving vegetables long-term or making powder for smoothies.

"We'd love to have cooking tools like these on Paradise Island, too. Right, Sister?"

"Yes, they do sound useful, but…"

"I made some for you as well, of course."

Rei didn't seem to want to impose, so I reassured her with a smile.

I was planning to make more of these cooking instruments for Miss Nea the elf chef and the brownies, too.

Once I'd shown them around, we left the warehouse.

"Ah, so that's where you've been hiding."

"Did you need something?"

When we stepped out of the building, we found Miss Aea looking for me.

"You've got guests, right? I can just come back after lunch or something."

"Um, excuse me. If you'd like…"

Aea started to leave, but Rei called out to stop her.

Apparently, they'd made more lunch than was really necessary for the three of us. We wound up inviting Miss Aea to join.

"Seafood today, huh? Very nice."

"Try the soy-boiled fish, Master Satou! Sister made it."

"Y-Yuuneia…"

Since the sisters had become friendly with Miss Nea while she taught them self-defense, she'd started teaching them cooking as well.

"Mm, it's delicious."

The sweet and salty boiled greenling was very tasty.

It went well with rice, but I would've liked to try it with some dry Japanese sake, too.

"Really?!"

"Yes, I mean it. It's really good."

I responded earnestly, which made Rei's cheeks turn pink as she smiled shyly.

"Master Satou, try a rice ball, too. I made those!"

"Oh? Let's see…"

…Why is it so heavy?

She must have squeezed it pretty tightly when she made it.

"It's got just the right amount of salt," I remarked.

"You like it? Go ahead—have another!"

"Don't mind if I do, thanks."

It was a little dense, but not nearly as hard as the rye bread and biscuits that were so common in this world, so I was happy to enjoy their homemade box lunch.

Miss Aea seemed to prefer the deep-fried crab and the salt-boiled shrimp rather than the intense flavor of the greenling.

For some reason, I was the only one eating the rice balls, but I wasn't going to complain about that.

Most of all, I was fairly relieved that Rei and Yuuneia, who hadn't been here long, seemed to be enjoying themselves in Bolenan Forest.

"So what brings you here today?"

After having some post-lunch tea, I asked Miss Aea what her original business was.

Rei and Yuuneia had left, smiling on their way to study herb-growing with the house fairy brownies.

"Oh right, I forgot. You were asking about magic potions that can restore a lost limb, right? We had an extra one in the workshop. I thought I'd bring it over for ya."

Miss Aea put a large vial of potion on the table.

This meant the artificial leg I'd made would go to waste, but I was sure Mr. Kajiro would prefer to grow his own limb back than get this artificial one with a bunch of weird gimmicks.

"Are you sure? This must be really valuable."

"Yeah, it's fine. We've got Holytree Stones thanks to you, so once they're done repairing the light ships and stuff, Lady Aaze can make plenty more."

Wow, really?

Judging by her tone, she seemed to be telling the truth.

"Well then, thank you very— Wait. A greater recovery potion?"

In the middle of giving thanks, I blurted out the information from my AR display in my surprise.

"Yeah, one large vial of that is enough to restore a lost limb."

No, it isn't… Is it? Shocked by her words, I searched through the documents I had on hand.

Just as I had remembered, it said a greater potion or a lesser elixir can't restore an entire lost limb.

"What's wrong, Satou?"

I produced the book in question from my Item Box and showed it to her, explaining my doubts.

"Oh, that's a misprint," she responded casually. "From when they first transcribed the book. I didn't know there were still copies out there with the error."

I see. So the person who was copying it by hand must have mixed up can *with* can't.

I used a pen to correct that part and made a note of the date and the name of the person who'd given me the information, Miss Aea.

"If you want to restore a human's lost limb, all you need is a large vial of a greater healing potion or a small vial of a lesser elixir or above."

Well, in that case, I could've healed Mr. Kajiro's leg a long time ago, as thanks for keeping the mansion secure, with the lesser elixir I'd found in that treasure chest— No, wait.

If it weren't for this mistake, I would've been able to fix Kajiro's leg already, but then I couldn't have healed Tifaleeza's eye when she was on the verge of death after that fire.

This potion would heal Mr. Kajiro's leg now, so maybe that misprint worked out for the best in the long run.

"Sorry, Satou. I didn't realize we gave you a book with a misprint."

"No, no, not at all."

I explained what I'd just been thinking and how it had all worked out for the best, and the two of us laughed together.

"Well, that's good. Now, restoring a lost limb takes a lot of magic and stamina, so if the person drinking the potion doesn't have much MP, you should make sure they eat tons of meat and bread with powdered bone. Otherwise, they'll be so exhausted that they'll end up bedridden for a while."

I thanked Miss Aea for the warning.

"Still, I'm surprised you didn't see through a misprint like that right away."

"You're giving me too much credit."

As I responded, I realized why it hadn't occurred to me to doubt that information.

I'd assumed that even greater magic potions couldn't restore a lost limb because when I met the elf Cyriltoa the Songstress in the old capital, she had an arm that had been replaced with an artificial limb.

That gave me the impression that even the elves had difficulty replacing limbs.

"Miss Aea, are you sure it's all right if I take this potion?"

"Yes, of course. Why, is there a problem?"

I asked her if it was okay that they weren't prioritizing the healing of Miss Cyriltoa's arm instead.

"Ah, you met Ciya, did you? …She's just stubborn. You've heard about the incident where many young elves died in Labyrinth City, right? She's one of the few survivors, along with Yuya."

Aea quietly told me about the past.

The "Yuya" she referred to was Yusaratoya, the manager of the general store in Seiryuu City.

"When the elves who had lost their children became emotional and exiled Traya, Ciya and Yuya felt like they should atone, too. So Ciya started using an artificial limb Traya created instead of restoring her arm and ran away. Yuya ran out after Traya and Ciya, too, and never came back."

She didn't clarify, but this "Traya" person who was exiled must be none other than Trazayuya, the elf sage who had made the Cradle.

There were similar events mentioned in the journals he left in the Cradle, so there was little doubt in my mind.

But still…"atone," huh?

Once I learned to make magic potions that could restore lost limbs, I thought I would offer her one, too, but if that was her reason, it might be unwanted meddling on my part.

I apologized to Miss Aea for making her discuss such a difficult story, then changed the subject.

"So earlier, you said that once there are Holytree Stones to spare again, Miss Aaze can make greater magic potions…?"

I was curious about this topic anyway.

"That's right. You would need at least four Ladies of the Holytree to create a Treespirit Pearl large enough and pure enough to make an elixir, but Lady Aaze can create the shards used to make a regular greater potion on her own."

And with these Treespirit Pearl shards, Miss Aea and her crew could alchemize greater potions.

I found it a little strange that this would be described as Aaze making the potions, but if Aea herself saw it that way, then there was no need to comment.

...Wait a second.

An elf village with four Ladies of the Holytree—in other words, high elves—could make elixirs?

Then if I asked the high elves from a village besides Bolenan, I should be able to get elixirs...

I imagined Aaze lamenting her lack of ability but then weighed that sadness against the possibility of having an emergency measure in case anything happened to one of my kids.

It was a little tough, but in the end, the latter was more important.

While I didn't want to hurt Miss Aaze's feelings, I should definitely ask one of the other village's high elves to make elixirs for me.

If anything, I was ashamed of myself as their guardian for not making that choice immediately.

"It might be possible with substitutes for the Treespirit Pearls and bloodpearls. But you can only get things like soul pearls and ghost pearls through mass murder, so I bet elixirs made with those would come out cursed."

Miss Aea sounded troubled.

Yeah, that doesn't appeal to me, either.

It seemed like the kind of choice a powerful ruler would make that would lead to their own destruction.

"...And you can use the dragon-strength stones and true-dragon pearls that ancient dragons and sky dragons create, but if you laid a hand on those, that would get your whole land set on fire."

Aea shrugged and smiled wryly.

Ancient dragons and sky dragons?

...No way... Right?

I was doubtful, but then I remembered the time I'd found those bluecoins to be used in place of Holytree Stones.

So just for kicks, I searched through the Valley of Dragons/Graveyard and Valley of Dragons/Spoils folders in my Storage.

...*Found some.*

Looking at the search results, I cautiously posed a question.

"Miss Aea, are dragon-strength stones and true-dragon pearls acquired by killing ancient dragons and sky dragons?"

"No, no. That's how you acquire dragonheart crystals, since they're crystallized from the hearts of lesser and full-grown dragons. But it's said that dragon-strength stones and true-dragon pearls are created by crystallizing both mana from a dragon's territory and the life energy of dragons themselves."

I see. In that case, I probably don't have to refrain like with the bluecoins, right?

I separated the dragon-strength stones and true-dragon pearls from the Valley of Dragons/Spoils folder into their own folder. It was a pretty large amount: tens of thousands of the former and hundreds of the latter.

I had dragon god pearls, too, but those sounded a little intimidating, so I decided to leave them alone for now.

"Miss Aea, do you know the recipe that uses dragon-strength stones?"

I produced the smallest dragon-strength stone I could find from Storage to show her. It was a transparent blue gem about the size of a beach ball.

Simply holding it felt like magic and energy were seeping into my hand.

Not that I really needed that, since I already used magic-charged Holy Swords as batteries.

"Wha—?!" Aea shrieked in surprise. "Where did you get that?! Have you been to a dragon nest or something?!"

I wished she would stop contorting her pretty face into such ridiculous expressions.

"You really are fearless, aren't you? ...Well, all right, then. The recipe is more or less the same, but I'll give you a few warnings."

With that, the exhausted-looking Aea taught me how to make greater potions and elixirs. This meant I wouldn't have to go to the high elves of another forest; I wouldn't have to hurt Miss Aaze's feelings. That was a relief.

*   *   *

"Even lesser elixirs are fairly difficult to make, aren't they?"

"Well, yes, but…"

Miss Aea kindly shared some already prepared ingredients with me, so it was fairly simple this time. But making it from scratch could easily take a month or more.

"…Most people don't make it without failing on the first try after hearing the recipe once."

She muttered this last part, but I heard it with my "Keen Hearing" skill.

I had proceeded with extra caution, since I didn't want to waste the ingredients she gave me.

"Looks like I made eighteen in total. I'll leave half of them in the village."

"No, no. Just two or three is fine, or even just the one."

Nine would be more than enough for my labyrinth-exploring party, plus a few to leave with Rei on the island, but Miss Aea refused to take any more than three.

"Goodness. I've lived a long life, but this is the first time I've ever seen a top-quality lesser elixir."

Appraising the vials I gave her, Aea let out a whistle of admiration.

"Really?"

"What kind of crazy training did you do to be this talented at your young age?"

Sorry. All I did was put skill points into things with my Unique Skill.

Miss Aea's praise stung a bit, to be honest.

"Will you be making regular elixirs next, I suppose?"

"Actually, I've already…"

"What? You made one already?"

Well, the basic recipe was the same as lesser elixirs.

I messed up the magic regulation a little, so it didn't come out at the highest quality, but I was confident that I'd gotten the hang of it enough to make top-quality elixirs from now on.

However, I was missing some of the ingredients and had only enough to make the one.

Once I got more ingredients, I was eager to give it another shot.

Incidentally, I left the creator's name field blank in case these potions went around.

I also used recognition-inhibiting techniques on the vials themselves, making it more difficult to analyze detailed information like the name of the creator.

"I'd like to mass-produce some greater potions next. Could I borrow a bigger transmutation set?"

"Go ahead. We don't use the big one in the workshop that much, so you're welcome to it."

I set my name to a blank space again as I started working.

I had plenty of the ingredients for this and was able to crank out lots of greater health and magic potions with ease. The extra-large Transmutation Tablet was very handy for this mass production.

"Honestly. He makes it look easier than making lesser potions… How does he even have enough magic for all this?"

As I kept making greater potions, I heard Aea grumbling with a mix of shock and admiration behind me.

I decided to donate around half these potions to the elves of Bolenan Forest, too.

◆

"It's like a monster movie."

Before my eyes, a behemoth and a sand giant were locked in close combat.

I would have liked to watch my kids fight them, but unfortunately, by the time I arrived on the training grounds by way of the fairy ring, the battle was already over.

Sitting on the sidelines, the girls were receiving instructions from their teachers.

"Don't forget that feeling, Liza."

"Yes, sir!"

Noticing my approach, Liza yelled "Master!" and came rushing over.

"You won't believe it, sir! I finally mastered it!"

Liza proudly informed me that she had succeeded at the Spellblade Shot, a manga-like technique in which the user fired the energy cloaked around their blade at a target.

"That's amazing, Liza! I'll make whatever kind of meat you want for dinner tonight."

"Thank you, sir!" Liza's face broke into a huge smile.

It was a rare expression, but it suited her well.

Hot on her heels, Tama and Pochi came trotting over next.

"Tama learned a dagger barrage...?"

"Pochi learned a secret move, sir!"

"Me too!"

Both of them demonstrated the form for their new moves. The random flailing didn't do much to explain anything, but no doubt they were excellent techniques.

"You must work hard to master them."

"Aye-aye!"

"You too, Pochi."

"Yes, sir!"

Tama's teacher, Mr. Shiya, and Pochi's teacher, Miss Poa, gave words of encouragement, to which the duo responded with their trademark salute.

Beyond them, I saw Arisa chatting with a Space Magic–using elf elder.

"Miss Arisa, you must never use the spell you learned today against other people, understand?"

"Of course! I'll only bust it out to beat really powerful monsters or demons!"

From the sound of things, Arisa had picked up a pretty ominous Space Magic technique.

Later, she told me it was a brutal spell that dismantled the target at a molecular level.

No wonder her teacher had told her not to use it on people.

"Satou."

Looking exhausted, Mia tottered over and threw her arms around me.

"Learned Behemoth."

"You still don't have enough magic power to use it on your own, though. Remember that, all right?"

Miss Aaze threw in a warning.

"Mm. I know."

Judging by this conversation, Aaze had passed down the Spirit Magic spell Create Behemoth that I'd once seen her use in space.

Mia couldn't use it on her own yet, but eventually she should gain enough MP by leveling up.

"Master, I would like you to increase the follow speed of the Floating Shield, I request."

Nana was next to return, her instructions finished.

"I thought I made it pretty fast. It's still too slow?"

"If I move quickly with 'Body Strengthening,' my movements are slightly hindered, I report."

I had her demonstrate for me and saw that there was a bit of stress on the item that served as a reference point for the Floating Shield, slowing Nana's movements slightly.

I was able to figure out the problem, but due to the nature of the Practical Magic mechanism the Floating Shield currently used, it was physically impossible to make it any faster.

If I wanted to improve it further, I would have to figure out a Space Magic mechanism instead.

"I can't fix it right away, but I'll take care of it as fast as I can."

"Yes, master."

For now, I gave the Floating Shield to the rear guard to use instead, and I resolved to start developing a new one for Nana tonight.

As for the equipment that proved problem-free in battle, I would have to have Mia and Arisa learn new magic tool–creating spells, as much as it pained me to do so.

But this was all for the sake of improving my kids' equipment, so I would simply have to come up with a good reward that would make it worth their trouble.

"Master! Miss Nea and I made some chocolate desserts like bon-bons! We'll have them after dinner tonight. Please don't eat too much, okay?"

"Sure. I'm looking forward to it."

She said they had omitted the alcohol from the bonbons, but I would have to double-check them with my "Analyze" skill before I let the girls eat them.

"Master Satou!"

As I was chatting with Lulu, Yuuneia ran up and latched on to me from the opposite side of Mia.

Behind her, I saw her sister, Rei, as well as Nea, who'd been teaching them self-defense again.

"Satou, we got our novice self-defense certificates from Lady Nea."

"That's great, Rei. Good job, both of you."

I patted the proud-looking sisters on their heads, and they closed their eyes like a pair of cats.

They weren't actually related by blood, but certain mannerisms like this showed their sisterly bond.

◆

After the battle with the sand giant, our ten days of training and crafting were coming to a close.

We had to update our estimated return date along the way, so I had gone back to Labyrinth City just once, but other than that, we'd all been working hard in Bolenan Forest.

Miss Aaze looked a little sad when we left the tree house, but once I promised to come back soon, she saw us off with a smile.

On our way out, Aaze asked Rei and Yuuneia if they'd like to live in Bolenan Forest, but they declined, saying that Paradise Island was their home.

"See you soon, Master Satou."

"Please come visit us again anytime."

"I will, of course."

With our arms full of sunflowers and tropical fruits that the two had given us, the rest of the group and I used the Return spell to go back to Celivera.

"Phew. Feels like we've been away for a while."

Arisa stretched.

"I wish to plant the sunflowers at the orphanage, I declare."

"An excellent idea…"

Liza nodded.

I agreed, too. They were easy to grow, and sunflowers go well with the smiles of children.

"…They can be an emergency food supply."

Okay, Liza's reason was a little different from mine.

"We still have some time left before our return date. Should we just head back to the mansion for now?"

The girls looked at one another. After a moment, Arisa stepped forward to speak for them.

"We want to fight! So we can really prove the results of our training!"

"All right, then. If you want to test out your new techniques, we can go to a place with a lot of fairly strong spawn enemies. Does that sound good?"

They nodded, and I checked my map for an appropriate site.

"How about beetles, like the kind Jelil was fighting? Or the butterfly and moth area? That area has a pretty decent spawn rate, but we'd need a way to deal with their powder."

The army ant area and soldier mantis area were good contenders, too, but both of their areamasters had annoying special abilities, so I didn't offer them as options.

"Hmm. Jelil's basically our rival. Let's pick the same place as him to compare our strength!"

"I agree. Beetles will be an excellent target for my spear."

"They're a good enemy, sir!"

The others all agreed with Arisa's suggestion.

The kin monsters there, like the storm stag beetle and thunder stag beetle, were a notch stronger than the kin in the other areas. And the areamaster, the elder lance beetle, had Lightning Magic and Wind Magic but no troublesome unique abilities. It wouldn't be a problem if the girls decided they wanted to try fighting that, too.

There was also an area near the elder lance beetle's lair populated by monsters called Evil Anemone, which were impervious to magic, and mud statues, which were strong against physical attacks, so it would be the perfect opportunity to really put their training to the test.

"Oh, that reminds me. Weren't Zakorin and his pals going after an areamaster when we first came into the labyrinth? Think they beat it already?"

"That would make sense, time-wise."

I opened my map and searched for Zarigon's name.

The areamaster they were fighting was a giant deer called a "lightning elder stag," and it looked like they hadn't beaten it yet.

Hmm.

"What? Another situation?"

"These guys just can't keep themselves out of trouble."

It looked like we wouldn't be able to conquer the beetle area until after a little bit of meddling.

Checking the location of the closest seal slate, I used Return to teleport our whole group there.

Monster Incense

I just wanted to get outta the sticks, where working from morning till night is barely enough to get by. So I ran away from my village and did everything in my power to become an explorer. But all I learned was that only a certain handful of people get to be heroes...

"What are we gonna do, Besso?"

"Shut up, Tahere. I'm trying to think."

I shoved the idiot's face away.

While we were hunting maze cockroaches, I risked life and limb to acquire some bewitching slime: an ingredient for making Monster Incense. But the new boss of the black market, Skopi of the Mud Scorpions, said they wouldn't buy bewitching slime.

He told me the plunderers who used to buy it at high prices were all gone, but I didn't believe that crap. His only goal was to give us a hard time.

All the old black-market guys got dragged away by the guards, and demonic potions were crazy expensive now. *This whole world's a load of garbage.*

"Mr. Koshin hates us by this point, and Troy and the other new guys are dead for sure. We managed to pay off this month's interest on the loan we owe Koshin, but next month we're gonna be screwed..."

"You think I don't know that?"

Our bad luck started when we picked up that noble's ant-nectar request.

Thanks to those cowardly beastfolk and useless women who couldn't even serve as bait, we almost got killed in the process, too.

Plus we got hit with a crazy fine for bringing a monster chain rampage to the labyrinth army's barracks.

At least the beastfolk and wenches got stuck with part of the fine, too, so we had to pay less than half, but there's still no good way for us to pay off that much money.

Should we refuse to pay it?

The idea crossed my mind, but I quickly shook my head to shoo the stupid thought away.

If we defaulted on that payment, we'd be wanted as robbers, and no town would have us anymore.

From what I've heard from explorers who were former robbers, that's no way to live.

"Hey, Besso."

I glared at Tahere, but he wasn't looking at me.

"Isn't that Zarigon?"

"They're lookin' pretty beat-up for a bunch of garnet-badge explorers. Maybe they tried to fight an areamaster to compete with Red Dragon's Roar?"

"So even beasts like those guys can't beat one, huh?"

I snorted at Tahere.

This idiot didn't understand a thing.

"If they were that easy to beat, other explorers would all fight areamasters for their treasure chest instead of going after mantises and frogs."

…Treasure chest, eh?

Hunkering down my shoulders, I furrowed my brow and started to form a plan.

Tahere was saying something, but I ignored him and kept plotting.

"Hey, Tahere. You didn't throw that thing away yet, did you?"

"No, of course not. It'd be suicide to take it out in the labyrinth, yeah?"

"Come with me."

"H-hey, Besso! At least tell me where we're going!"

Instead of wasting my breath trying to explain my plan to Tahere, I headed toward a rundown shack in a back alley where an unlicensed old alchemist lived.

I was going to have him make Monster Incense from the bewitching slime.

As payment, I offered the demonic potion I'd been saving as a last resort.

But because I couldn't have him running off with it, I stayed in the smelly old shack for the three days it took to complete.

"…So that's Monster Incense, huh?"

"Heh-heh, that's right. As long as it's in this tube, it's harmless. But once you pull this string, the smoke will come out. Make sure you throw away the string, though, 'cause monsters will be attracted to the incense that's soaked into it."

I took the tubes from the man: two small ones and three regular size in all.

"What are these small ones?"

"There was a little bit left over, so I put it in those. I'm sure you wanna test out the effect somewhere, right?"

"Yeah, I sure do."

Putting the small tubes in my pocket, I kicked Tahere, who was snoring away on the floor.

"Get up, Tahere. The stuff's ready. Put it in that warehouse of yours."

"Oh, it's done? 'Item Box,' open."

Tahere opened his warehouse and put the three tubes inside.

Usually it contained only food and water, but it was big enough to hold about four casks of water.

This skill was the whole reason I'd stuck with this idiot Tahere for so long.

"I'm gonna negotiate with Zarigon. You go recruit five or six speedy explorers."

"Gotcha. I'll check with the Runaway Arrow and Rabbitfoot parties."

Leaving the dirty work to Tahere, I did some all-important negotiating to get us into Zarigon's areamaster-fighting party.

Unfortunately, we were allowed in only as bag carriers and not proper fighters, but it wasn't like I wanted to fight monsters in the vicinity of an areamaster anyway.

All we really needed to do was have Zarigon and his guys protect us until we got to the areamaster's lair, then let them deal with it while we look for the treasure chest.

"Besso!"

Once I'd finished my work, I was gulping down some ale when Tahere came running over.

"How many'd you get?"

"None. There are some weird rumors floating around, and now neither party wants anything to do with us."

"It's your job to talk 'em into it anyway!"

The rumors were that exploring with me led to getting betrayed or
caught up in chain rampages.

"The veterans and even the newbies all knew about it, too." Tahere
spoke like this wasn't his problem. "What are we gonna do, Besso?"

"Can't you use yer head once in a while?"

As Tahere cowered in fear of my rage, I noticed some kids who
clearly seemed fresh from the boonies across the way.

Beastfolk kids. They looked just like the fleet-footed type we needed.

"Hey, brats! You rookie explorers or what?!"

"I'm not a brat! The name's Usasa!"

Beastfolk were always so damn hard to understand.

"You got guts, huh? I like that. You kids bronze badges?"

But they'd be perfect to use as bait.

"N-not yet."

"What, wood badges, then?"

"No."

"Oh, so you're only bag carriers?" Tahere stared at the kids, and they
hung their heads.

"L-look, if we had weapons…"

"Shut up, Tahere." At that, the brats looked up toward me. "I'll teach
ya how to earn money. I'll hook you up with explorer equipment, too."

"B-but why?"

"Not for free, idiot. You can pay me back once you're a full-fledged
explorer."

The little greenhorns fell for my candy-coated lie, hook, line and sinker.

I bought them some secondhand bone armor and goblin clubs,
helped them get their wooden badges, and then got them upgraded to
bronze by having them fight some goblins, which I gathered by testing
out a small tube of Monster Incense.

"Besso, this stuff really works."

"Yeah, it's better than I thought."

The Monster Incense was good stuff.

So many goblins and maze moths—which were usually rare in these
parts—had gathered around us. I actually thought we were gonna die.

We used it while that softhearted Dozon's group happened to be nearby, so they tackled any monsters we couldn't handle. Still, this was definitely not the kind of stuff you could use normally.

"Big Bro!"

Ever since I'd bought them some cheap bug meat to celebrate getting their bronze badges, the brats had started calling me "Big Bro." This plan was going even better than I thought.

"Some weird guys said they have business with you, Big Bro."

Three broke-looking men were standing behind the brats.

"Are you Mr. Besso? We heard you got into Zarigon's group."

"Only as bag carriers."

I'd seen these guys around in the black market before.

They were probably out of a job now that the old boss had gotten thrown in the brig.

"Can you take us with you?"

Somehow, they already had bronze badges. Their equipment was cheap, rusted iron, but...

"It'll be your lives on the line."

"We know."

"Then you're more than welcome."

...*As bait, of course.*

So with three new cronies working for us, we went into the labyrinth with Zarigon's group.

◆

"Big Bro, looks like some more fawns are nearby."

"Yeah, they move in herds."

Zarigon's group had chosen a huge deer monster called a "lightning elder stag," which lived in an area full of rocks and weeds.

Right now, the group was fighting monsters in a huge clearing to take on the areamaster.

The little deer who could make bolts of lightning were a huge pain.

"We want to fight deer, too."

"Yeah, we're sick of skinning and weeding."

The cronies were complaining.

They could learn a thing or two from the beastfolk brats, who always quietly followed orders.

"Pipe down. You're barely even good for weeding, let alone anything else."

"Weeding" referred to defeating wheel-shaped monsters called "rolling weeds."

They were no stronger than goblins, but since they were tough and moved quickly, fighting them was exhausting.

There were palm-size insect monsters, too, but these were small fries that dropped only core dust.

Hearing a *thunk*, I turned around to see an angry-looking Zarigon kicking a barrel open.

"Damn it, what idiot told us that deer were easy to beat?"

He was starting to take out his anger on others more often, probably because progress was so slow.

Maybe our chance was on the horizon?

"Mr. Zarigon, please calm down," I said, handing him a bottle of grape wine that I'd snuck into the labyrinth.

He took it without a word, drank it down, and muttered "cheap stuff" as he tossed the bottle aside.

What a bastard.

"I have a proposal. Hear me out."

I suggested to Zarigon that we use Monster Incense to gather all the monsters on one side of the room and have some scouts draw out the areamaster and get it alone.

"You're gonna use Monster Incense to attract all the monsters...? Are you serious?"

"Very. In exchange, just share some of the spoils with us."

Zarigon looked suspicious, but he gave permission to use my strategy. "Fine. But know this..." Still, he pulled out his sword and put the blade to my throat. "...If you try to lead the monsters in a chain rampage back toward us or anything like that, I'll cut you down before the monsters can reach you. So don't get any funny ideas."

"Of course not, sir."

Cold sweat ran down my back.

I managed to pull my neck away and escape unscathed.

"Now, that's a lot of monsters..."

One of the cronies looked down over the cliff and shuddered.

We were on a precipice overlooking the large cavern where the areamaster lived, on the opposite side of the room from Zarigon and his troops.

"You scared?"

"Am not!"

"Shut up! You wanna get eaten by monsters?"

I silenced the cronies and brats with a hiss.

After we got permission from Zarigon, we put on cloaks infused with monster repellent and used a map from one of Zarigon's scouts to make our way along a thin path across the wall.

The only ones here were Tahere, the beastfolk brats, the three cronies, and me.

Zarigon had sent a scout with us as a precaution, but he'd headed back once we crossed the halfway point of the room.

I had Tahere open his warehouse and take out the four tubes. Then I glanced at the strings, took the specially made dud, and had the beastfolk brats take the tubes with the Monster Incense.

"Listen. On my signal, pull the purple string on the tube and throw it down below. Make sure you don't touch the string until I give the signal. Got it?"

I explained how to use the tubes.

We'd be parting ways from here, so I made sure the three who were carrying the tubes understood how to use them.

"Once you've thrown the tube, start running. Don't throw away the string. If you bring it back to me, I'll give you a gold coin in exchange."

"G-gold?!"

"Damn!"

Of course, I had no intention of paying a gold coin to any of these idiots.

They were just bait to pull the strings and throw the tubes.

"Why the string, though?"

"To prove that you used the tubes properly. I'm not generous enough to give a gold coin to some idiot who threw the tube without pulling the string first."

One of the cronies asked a suspicious question, but he seemed satisfied by my explanation.

We split up in four directions and started moving.

Aside from Tahere and me, they were all in groups of three.

"Besso, looks like the farthest guys have gotten to their spot."

The monster repellent cloaks Zarigon lent us seemed to work quite nicely.

I'd be using mine a lot from now on.

"Tahere, give the signal."

"R-right."

On Tahere's indication, I pulled the string and kicked the tube off the cliff.

The four tubes belched white smoke as they fell.

"Besso! They're coming!"

Of course they were.

That was the whole point of the plan.

Drawn by the incense, the monsters gathered around the tubes and smoke.

The flying monsters rose up along with the smoke, swarming around the cronies and brats.

I saw the greed-driven cronies trying to steal the brats' purple strings and run away.

"Yikes. That bastard kicked the beastfolk kid down and ran."

The brat who'd been kicked disappeared under a swarm of insect monsters in seconds.

Survival of the fittest. That's what it means to be an explorer.

"Let 'em try and get away."

As long as they were carrying the Monster Incense–infused strings, monsters would chase them no matter how far they ran.

They wouldn't be making it back to Zarigon.

"Stay still."

Tahere looked restless, so I warned him in a low voice.

If he moved too soon, we'd just draw the attention of the monsters.

We held our breath and waited for the monsters to clear out from below us.

It shouldn't take long, since the tube I'd kicked contained not Monster Incense but monster repellent powder mixed in with a simple smoke screen.

"Let's go."

"Where?"

"To find the treasure, obviously."

I threw the purple string off the cliff, then pointed at the rocky hill in the center of the room so even the idiot Tahere would understand.

The areamaster wasn't there.

It was moving toward the three Monster Incense tubes along with the rest of the monsters.

Once the monsters beneath us were gone, we carefully made our way down the cliff and ran across the plain toward the hill.

As we were climbing the hill where the giant deer had been, we saw the lightning elder stag turn to run toward Zarigon's group, having been targeted by a scout's "Taunt" skill.

"Heh. Beat that guy for us, fellas."

So we can get away safely, of course.

On the other side of the hill, the route toward Zarigon's group was in the shape of a terraced field.

Getting back should be easy enough.

"Besso! Found it!"

I heard Tahere yell from behind a rock.

There was a treasure chest in a corner of the deer's roost—and a big one, at that.

"C-can you even open this, Besso?"

"Of course I can. Why else would I take all this risk?"

I'm good at opening locks, but this one was pretty tough.

"B-Besso, bad news!"

I glanced in the direction Tahere was pointing. The spawn of the areamaster were starting to come back this way.

"Wh-what are we gonna do, Besso? The Monster Incense must be wearing off."

"Keep it down. The monsters'll find us!" Snapping at Tahere, I struggled a little longer before finally managing to open the chest. "Heh-heh, looks like I win this bet."

I pulled out the most expensive-looking sword from the jewel-packed treasure chest, and when I removed it from its sheath, it glowed dark red.

A Magic Sword. Jackpot.

"Th-there's a short sword under the gems, too. And some potions."

Surprisingly, the short sword was a magic weapon, too.

We got lucky. The goddess of fortune must be on our side.

"This potion has gotta be the good kind, too, right?"

"Huh? Yeah, of course. Put it in the warehouse with the short sword."

"R-right. The potions alone can probably pay off our debt."

"Our debt? Buddy, if we sell these two swords, we're both gonna be set for life."

Tahere and I smacked each other on the backs and laughed heartily.

I hadn't laughed this hard in ages.

Maybe we should make a grave in Labyrinth City for the brats and cronies who'd died for us.

"Huh?"

Suddenly, a shadow loomed over us.

…Spawn.

"B-Besso…?"

"Don't provoke it. You run away while I buy us some time."

"B-but!"

"I'm not gonna get eaten by a monster here. You just run like your life depends on it; 'cause it does."

I pulled out the Magic Sword and motioned for Tahere to run.

"Y-you'd better make it back alive!"

With a brave parting line, Tahere ran away without looking back.

The spawn that was looking down at me turned to watch Tahere leave, ignoring my Magic Sword and me.

Then, moving slowly but surely, it turned and started to run after him instead.

"Like I'm the one who's gonna die, idiot."

I twirled the purple string in my hand as I watched Tahere flee.

A slim trail of white smoke was coming out of the bag on his back. It was the last small tube of Monster Incense.

"Heh. See ya, sucker. If you live long enough for us to meet again, that is."

I threw away the string in my hand, put the sword back in its sheath, and shoved it into my bag.

"Urgh!"

Just as I started to walk forward, one of my legs buckled, and I fell face-first to the ground.

"Tch. I guess even I'm a little nervous."

I quickly tried to get to my feet.

But my legs wouldn't move.

"Did I break a bone, or…? What the?!" My leg was starting to turn to stone. "Wh-what is this?!"

Something long and pink stirred in front of my widened eyes.

No way.

A rank wind hit my face.

Turning around, I saw the shape of an enormous gray snake.

The beast that could turn men into stone: a basilisk.

"S-stay away!"

I reached out to pull the Magic Sword from my bag, which had fallen to the floor. Something fell to the ground with a hard *clunk*.

My right hand.

The basilisk was devouring my right arm, which had turned to stone.

Don't eat that. That's my arm!

I heard the same crunching noise from below.

Smaller basilisks were eating my leg.

It didn't hurt, even though I was getting eaten.

I have to get out of here.

Desperately, I tried to drag myself away with my left hand.

But then it started to turn gray.

Powder fell from my eyelids.

My vision turned gray and then black.

The last thing I saw was the basilisk's drool, thick and with a rancid odor, coating my stone flesh.

The Areamaster

Satou here. Every battle comes with a price, but unlike in games, real battles mean a single mistake can lead to lifelong consequences. My rule of thumb is that life is precious.

"So what's the situation? Are Zakorin and friends in trouble?"

"I think so. There's something strange about the way their enemies are moving. Let me look into it a little more."

Once we'd teleported to the nearest area with Return, I opened my map while answering Arisa.

The areamaster, the lightning elder stag, was the only monster facing off against Zarigon's troops; the rest of the monsters in the large room were all gathered unnaturally on the opposite side.

"Another chain rampage? What? Are chain rampages a fad with the explorers in Labyrinth City right now?"

Sort of like that old chain letter fad?

I wonder if they have chain letters in this parallel world...

Okay, enough nonsense. I zoomed in on the part of the map where the monsters were gathering and checked the details.

"Uh-oh. This doesn't look great."

I hurried toward the cavern with my group in tow.

"Up aheeead?"

"Flying buggies, sir!"

Farther down the passage, someone was lying on the floor, covered in black bugs.

On the verge of death.

I frantically opened my magic menu and used Healing Magic on the whole area, insects and all.

There were monsters stuck on the man, too, so I used Paralyze Water Hold instead of Bug Wiper to knock them all out.

"Take care of him!"

"Yes, sir!"

I left Lulu and the others to heal the wounded and ran ahead to help the rest.

In the three passages, there were six beastfolk kids, all near death as well. There were three human men, too, but unfortunately, they were already dead. The beastfolk had probably survived because the bug-type monsters that had gathered around them were fairly weak.

Making sure no one was looking, I used "Flashrunning" and Magic Hand to zip around and rescue all the kids from the flying insects.

"Monster Incense…"

At the bottom of the cliff, enraged monsters like deer and rolling weeds were fighting one another to the death.

In the middle of the madness were tubes containing Monster Incense.

The three men must have died because of the incense-soaked strings they were desperately clutching.

On the other side of the room, Zarigon and his group were fighting the areamaster.

"So they used these nine people as sacrificial pawns…"

I knew Zarigon was a rude meathead, but I hadn't thought he would sink so low.

Even if he wound up having a brush with death, I wasn't going to save him.

"Master, the injured parties have awoken, I report."

I guess kids around the age of thirteen or so were no longer larvae to Nana.

Now that they weren't covered in insects, I could tell that there were four rabbitfolk, one dogfolk, and one bearfolk kid.

"Thank you for saving us. I'm Usasa, a rabbitfolk."

After the boy named Usasa introduced himself, the others volunteered their names: Rabibi, Tokaka, Gikeke, Gaugaru, and Kevea. I wasn't going to remember all of those and made no attempt to commit them to memory.

"Do you mind if I ask what happened?"

Usasa started to answer, but then he suddenly looked around frantically.

"Wait, where is he?! Where's Big Bro Besso?!"

His speech was a bit difficult to understand, so I mentally adjusted for it as we spoke.

"If you mean the three men who were with you, unfortunately..."

"No, not those bastards! I mean Big Bro Besso and Tahere!"

There were others, too?

Trying to calm the frantic boy, I searched the map for the name Besso. Unfortunately, he was already dead. For some reason, he was in the center of the room, not near the walls like the others.

Even so, they probably wouldn't believe me if I told them outright, and I agreed to try to find him.

"Tama, Pochi, could you use your longscopes to see if there's anyone else out there?"

"Aye-aye, sir..."

"Roger, sir."

In the meantime, I got more information from the beastfolk kids.

Led by the rabbit boy Usasa, they explained that Besso was a kind person who had helped them when they were out jobless on the streets, gave them equipment, and assisted them with getting their bronze badges.

"Besso is that criminal who keeps causing rampages, right?" Arisa murmured to me.

I nodded. He was the troublesome fellow we'd seen causing a maze ant chain rampage when we first entered the Celivera Labyrinth, and had recently done it again with maze cockroaches.

"He didn't seem that nice to me... He sacrificed some newbies to cause that whole cockroach situation, too. He probably just recruited these kids to use them as bait, don't you think?"

I agreed. The Besso these kids described was a far cry from the one I'd heard about from the Lovely Wings and the explorers at Koshin's party.

""""That's not true!"""""

"You don't even know Big Bro!"

Overhearing our conversation, the kids jumped to his defense.

I'm sure they really believed he was a kind man.

"We do, though. That's why we're saying it..."

The beastfolk kids started to charge toward Arisa, so I held them back and used the Space Magic spell Clairvoyance to look for Besso's corpse.

I figured seeing how he died might shed some light on the situation.

...Gray?

Besso's body was lying next to an open treasure chest atop the rocky hill in the middle of the room, turned to stone and being consumed by a basilisk.

His petrified hand grasped a Magic Sword and a piece of string with the effects of Monster Incense.

As far as I could tell, the Magic Sword was inscribed with the runes for Good Luck and Fortune—in mirror writing.

Which meant the sword really carried the effects of Bad Luck and Misfortune.

The man called Tahere was lying dead on the plains halfway between the rocky hill and the area where Zarigon's men were fighting. He had been trampled to death by giant hooves.

According to the kids, this man was Besso's partner.

It was hard to tell, since he'd been crushed, but there was a Monster Incense tube near the man's waist, and he seemed to have been running toward Zarigon.

I was starting to see what happened here.

Most likely, these two had used those men and the beastfolk kids as bait to try to steal the treasure from the chest and had failed miserably.

I guess Zarigon's innocent, then.

Glancing back at Zarigon and his men with Clairvoyance, I saw that they were still battling the areamaster. It looked like they were putting up a pretty good fight.

"So that's the areamaster? It's like something out of a *kaiju* movie." Arisa must have been using Clairvoyance to watch their battle, too. "Zakorin's not half-bad at this."

The lightning elder stag charged forward and batted shield users away with ease, but Zarigon and company used three enormous metal nets they had set up in advance to stop it in its tracks. One probably wouldn't have been enough.

Once the giant deer stopped moving, they peppered it with magic and catapult attacks.

Right on the front lines, Zarigon's attacks were particularly powerful. With "Spellblade" on his broadsword, he used a special attack to cut through the lightning elder stag's defenses, dealing some serious damage.

The ridges that ran along the stag's back and up to its head glowed all at once, its enormous antlers glowed white, and in the next instant, enormous lightning bolts struck the opposite side of the room with a clap of thunder.

"Geh!"

The lightning attack seemed to have broken Arisa's Space Magic spell.

"Did that take out Team Zarigon?"

"No, it looks like they had Thunder Rods ready."

My Clairvoyance was still working, so I relayed information to Arisa.

Maybe the poles that supported the metal net had just served as Thunder Rods by coincidence, but either way, they spared Zarigon and his men any major damage.

The lightning elder stag's defense power seemed to go down after using that move, as it was now taking more damage from their counterattacks than before.

Since its charges and lightning attacks had both been thwarted, the giant deer resorted to trying to trample the men with its hooves.

But Zarigon and company still had power to spare. At this rate, they would probably win the fight.

Mentally apologizing to Zarigon for blaming him for a crime he didn't commit, I silently prayed for their victory.

"No ooone?"

"There's nobody living or dead, sir."

Tama and Pochi reported in, lowering their longscopes.

"Big Bro Besso wouldn't die on us!"

"All right. Maybe he just went back to your base, then. Let's head over there."

Finding the route that was relatively safest, I took the kids along toward Zarigon and company.

◆

"Uh-oh."

"What is it, master?"

Liza looked at me with concern.

"Oh, it's just…"

According to my map information, Zarigon and the others were starting to evacuate their camp.

When I checked half an hour ago, they seemed to be reducing the lightning elder stag's health at a pretty decent pace, so some unexpected issue must have arisen.

We kept moving along our path and came to the remains of the camp, which monsters were prowling around.

The bags and tents left behind had been trampled, and the ground was damp with water from the broken barrels.

"Whoa, it's overrun with monsters!"

"What should we do, Usasa? Nobody's here."

"Does this mean we can't get back?"

Looking at the ruined campground, the beastfolk kids began to panic.

Still, most of the monsters were small fries with levels in the single digits.

"Don't worry. I'll get you back to Zarigon's group."

If it turned out that Zarigon saw them as disposable, then I would take them aboveground myself. But the group had brought even the most gravely injured bag carrier along in their retreat, so there was probably nothing to worry about.

"Just hide behind this rock for now, okay?"

I sent the kids to hide and started giving instructions to my group.

"Liza, clear a path for us, please."

"Understood."

Liza took Tama and Pochi to dispose of the monsters prowling the camp, since passing through it was the only way we could catch up with Zarigon.

"Hi-yaaa?"

"Whoosh, sir!"

Tama destroyed a basilisk's eye with a *kunai* knife, and Pochi ran up the wall, did a flying leap, and cut off its head with her sword lengthened by magic.

"■ *Fire Hi,* ■ *Wind Kaze.*"

Mia used the lowest grade of Spirit Magic to create fire and send it toward monsters on the wind.

The small insects went up in flames, and the rolling weeds started to flee.

"Take this!"

Aiming at the maze swallows and lesser cockatrices that were flying around near the ceiling, Lulu fired her new gun. I was surprised that the cockatrices could fly when they looked so much like chickens.

"Huntiiing?"

"Grilled meat skewers, sir!"

As the bird monsters fell, Tama and Pochi zipped over and cut off their heads.

Liza was using her longspear to silence the fawn monsters that charged at her. The fawns tried to shoot lightning from the bumps on their forehead, but Liza cut them down before they could.

Nana and Arisa were fighting monsters that rolled up like tires and resembled armadillos.

Once the monsters had all been defeated, I went over to check on everyone. I left the beastfolk kids to wait behind the rock.

"How's the new equipment?"

"Very niiice?"

"It's amazing, sir! I can even beat big monsters, like *slash*, sir!"

"The laser gun has great aim, even from long distances. But this physical rifle sends monsters flying when it hits, so it's really fun!"

Tama, Pochi, and Lulu were all smiles.

"Good."

"There is little negative impact when I block monsters, I report."

"I like the Floating Shields for our rearguard dress armor, too. When the thorn armadillos blocked shots, the shields moved on their own to protect us—although I sent those shots away with Space Magic before they reached us, of course."

Mia, Nana, and Arisa seemed to like the new equipment, too.

"Arisa, could you do me a favor?"

"Okey-dokey."

I had Arisa set up a Space Magic barrier on the border of the large room and stationed Nana there to guard her, just in case.

"Master, would it be all right if I used the Dragon Claw Spear as a backup weapon?"

"That's fine. Was it hard to use?"

"Not at all. It cut right through even the toughest of hides and channeled magic as well as before. It's just…"

Liza hesitated, looking away.

"My weapon of choice is still the Magic Cricket Spear," she said clearly at last.

She seemed to be very attached to her first spear. It wasn't quite as effective as the other vanguard weapons, but if she insisted, I would gladly let her keep using it.

Whenever the Cricket Spear got damaged in battle, she poured potion over it and wrapped cloth around it, which was apparently enough to fix it.

I told her that was fine as long as she used the Dragon Claw Spear on enemies that proved resistant to the Magic Cricket Spear.

"Okay, we shouldn't get any more unwelcome guests for a while."

"Thank you, Arisa."

Arisa came back with Nana from putting a Space Magic lid to block off the large room.

"The metal poles and nets they were using to hunt the lightning elder stag were all melted into puddles. Areamasters really are on another level, I guess." Arisa shivered. "Should we just leave this one be?"

I nodded. Zarigon and the others might want to come back for another shot.

"Aw, what a waste. This'd be the perfect chance to hit it with an advanced Space Magic surprise attack and take it down!"

"Arisa, monster or not, we ought to challenge the lord that reigns over an area head-on, not defeat it with such underhanded tactics."

"Geez, Liza, you're so cool! I guess that's true. I want to beat our first areamaster when it's at full power, not already wounded by someone else!"

Half listening to Arisa and Liza, I looked over the map information to double-check our best route.

"Master, should we retrieve the baggage? I inquire."

"No, let's leave it. They might come back for it later."

Zarigon and the others probably wouldn't be retrieving these, but I didn't want to get accused of stealing or anything like that.

Once we retrieved some cockatrice meat, we continued following Zarigon's party, defeating monsters along the way.

A few members of his group had the "Analyze" skill, so I had my group put on recognition-inhibiting cloaks shortly before we caught up.

◆

"…What is it, twerp?"

Once we caught up to Zarigon's party, who were all taking a short break in a safe zone, I asked to meet with their leader and was surprised by the way he greeted me.

To put it simply, he was horribly wounded.

"Ah, have I not introduced myself before? My name is Satou Pendragon, a knight of the Muno Barony."

He didn't seem to remember me, so I politely gave my name.

"I know that. You're the guildmaster's booze boy, right?"

I was glad I hadn't brought Arisa and the others to this meeting.

Ignoring his rude front, I carried on the conversation. "Those wounds look painful."

"Go ahead and laugh. This is what I get for trying to compete with Jelil and taking on a fight I couldn't win—petrified by an enemy I wasn't even expecting."

Zarigon scowled peevishly.

Indeed, his right arm and right leg had been turned to stone, and the latter had broken off at the knee. He was covered in plenty of fresh scars, too.

"It looked like most of the others were injured, too. You can't treat your wounds?"

"We healed the ones who were closest to death for now. The rest'll have to wait until our priests Tii and Asam recover their magic."

Zarigon's party's priests were from the Garleon and Heraluon temples.

Both of their levels were in the high 20s.

"Can Holy Magic fix petrification, too?"

"You got a lot of questions, twerp. That don't mean I gotta answer 'em all, though, see?"

No, I suppose it doesn't.

"Then perhaps I can offer you a potion in exchange."

I produced an intermediate MP recovery potion from my Garage Bag.

It was one that I'd made along with the greater magic potions in Bolenan Forest recently, with the creator's name listed as Trismegistus.

Zarigon had one of his comrades with the "Analyze Goods" skill inspect it.

"I-it's an intermediate magic recovery potion!"

The man reacted with overdramatic surprise.

I'd picked the intermediate kind so that they wouldn't get overdose effects like the guildmaster and the others had dealt with in the battle against Ludaman, but judging by his reaction, I guess I should have stuck with the lesser kind.

"Hmph. All right, then. I'll give you your answers."

Zarigon addressed my earlier question.

"Yes, Holy Magic can heal petrification. But Tii and Asam can't do it. A head priest from Labyrinth City or the royal capital could probably fix it, but that ain't gonna happen."

"Why, do you need a letter of recommendation or something?"

"It's a question of time. Asam's Holy Magic is keeping the petrification curse from spreading, but in a matter of days, these'll turn into stone for good. Then there'll be no fixing 'em."

Curse? Is petrification a curse?

I activated my "Miasma Vision."

It was a curse, all right. Instead of the rune shapes of the curses that were on Rei and Yuuneia, this one was a primitive, murky type.

I had a feeling I could probably fix it, but I didn't want to reveal my secret abilities to a stranger, so I refrained.

"Then couldn't you send someone to buy a cure-all or an anti-petrification potion or something?"

"What, and have them get killed on the way? Besides, I ain't a noble, so how would I get my hands on a cure-all? The guildmaster might be able to get an anti-petrification potion for me, but…by the time I make it out of the labyrinth, the curse will have gotten worse, and there'll be side effects."

An anti-petrification potion for the basilisk's curse… I had the recipe and the ingredients, but it wouldn't be easy to make it on the move.

"Just bad luck on our part. We brought plenty of lesser potions, but I've never even seen the greater kind—of course I didn't have any."

As Zarigon cursed his bad luck, I took out a cure-all and a greater health potion from my Garage Bag and placed them in front of him.

"All right, then. You owe me a favor."

I couldn't help smiling a little as I spoke.

Since it was Besso and not Zarigon who had tried to use the children as bait, and he was a friend of Princess Meetia's, I figured I ought to help him.

The princess was a friend of Mia and Arisa's, and when her guard was injured, Zarigon and his friend-slash-rival Jelil had protected her for free until her guard recovered.

So I figured I could just give him the potions as a favor.

Besides, I had lesser elixirs for my own kids now and could always make more.

"A c-cure-all?"

The man with the "Analyze Goods" skill looked like he might faint.

I didn't blame him. Even Baronet Dyukeli had been reluctant to use such an expensive item.

"...A-and this one is a greater health recovery potion!"

The latter seemed to take a while to analyze due to the technique I'd used on the vials, but he was eventually able to recognize it for a greater potion.

"Who the hell are you?"

"Oh, just the guildmaster's booze boy."

I smiled broadly, and Zarigon grimaced like he'd swallowed something sour, apologizing for his earlier rudeness.

"I've been looking for these for the viceroy and some other noble acquaintances, but it seems to be that your need is rather more urgent, so I'm sure they would understand."

With that, I prompted Zarigon to drink the potions.

I gave him the advanced healing potion to test out if it really would recover a lost limb before I tried to use one to heal Mr. Kajiro's leg.

Yeah, this is just an experiment.

I have no other motives, none at all.

"And you're sure all I owe you is a 'favor'?"

"Yes, you have my word." I nodded.

"All right, then."

As soon as Zarigon drank down the cure-all, he was covered in pale light, and several magic circles appeared around his body.

It was a pretty fantasy-gamelike effect.

The light slowly faded, and Zarigon's stonelike gray limbs turned back to the color of flesh.

As soon as the petrification was healed, his leg started gushing blood. His comrades hurriedly stanched the bleeding with cloth and cord.

Next, he drank the greater magic potion, and his leg went back to normal like a reverse-time-lapse movie.

I hate to say it, but it was pretty gross to watch.

I would have to remember to look away next time.

""""Zarigon!""""

For some reason, Zarigon turned pale and passed out. His friends gathered around him.

Oh, shoot.

Too late, I remembered what the elf alchemist Aea had told me.

Restoring a lost limb takes a lot of magic and stamina, so if the person drinking the potion doesn't have much MP, you should make sure they eat tons of meat and bread with powdered bone. Otherwise, they'll be so exhausted that they'll end up bedridden for a while.

Zarigon must have had little magic and stamina left after the fierce battle, which was probably why he fainted.

I handed one of his comrades a nutritional supplement potion and told them to have him drink it and get lots of rest.

Zarigon's party promised to bring the beastfolk kids back to Labyrinth City with them, so we decided to go ahead early.

"Thank you, mister! We swear we'll return the favor someday!"

The rabbitfolk boy called out to me from among the bag carriers as they prepared to depart.

"I'm looking forward to it," I replied.

But my smile faded when I heard a rumble that sounded like thunder.

"R-ruuuuun!"

An explorer shouted out hoarsely. Then a murmur of alarm spread from the back of the ranks, and people began to flee in a panic.

"The areamaster is chasing us!"

I opened my map to check.

Sure enough, the lightning elder stag was running in this direction.

I hadn't expected it to break through Arisa's Space Magic barrier so soon.

"Bring me my spare sword. I'll buy us some time."

"Zarigon! You can't!"

The haggard-looking Zarigon stretched and rose shakily to his feet.

"You're in no condition to fight! Leave it to us shield-men."

"But your damn shields are all broken!"

Ignoring Zarigon, I glanced over at my kids.

They were looking at me with what appeared to be hopeful expressions.

That's what I like to see.

"Please just go on ahead and leave this to us. We can buy time on our own."

Zarigon and the others all stared at us.

It was a moment befitting a *shonen* protagonist, if I do say so myself.

"What the hell are you—?"

I didn't have time to answer. I moved faster than the eye could follow to hit Zarigon in the jaw and knock him unconscious, then told his comrades to take him and flee.

"Don't die, okay?"

"Of course. We'll be right behind you once we've bought enough time."

Once Zarigon's party was on their way, we headed back into the main passage to meet the lightning elder stag head-on.

"It barely even fits in the passage! I'm surprised it tried to chase us."

The lightning elder stag came galloping around the twisting passage with a thunderous sound.

Although without my "Night Vision" skill, the others could probably see only its footprints and its three glowing eyes.

No, wait.

Its horns were also glowing in the dark with lightning.

It was level 50, with the inherent skills "Summon Lightning" and "Spawn Strengthening" and the regular skills "Charge," "Thrust," "Lightning Magic," and "Lightning Resistance," so as long as we could deal with the lightning, it should be easy enough to fight.

Flowing down from its antlers to the ground, a bolt of lightning illuminated the giant stag's outline.

"...I'm sorry, master. I should have killed this monster when I had the chance."

Arisa grimaced.

She must have also noticed what I saw during that flash of

lightning—something in the stag's teeth that looked like a human hand.

The mood was so dead serious that I couldn't bring myself to tell her it was just a demi-goblin's.

"Arisa, there is nothing to be gained by regretting what has already occurred."

"Master, forgive my insolence, but would you grant us permission to fight the lightning elder stag?"

Liza pulled the Dragon Claw Spear out of her Fairy Pack.

As she clenched it tightly, I could see her hand shaking with quiet rage.

Liza must have seen the hand, too.

Still, they were getting a little too worked up, I thought.

I should probably tell them the truth, even if it decreased their motivation.

"If you want to fight, I'll allow it, but—"

"Thank you, master."

"We are most grateful, master. I promise that we will avenge the fallen."

Arisa and Liza brandished their staff and spear respectively.

"...But are you that concerned with avenging a demi-goblin?"

"...Bwuh?"

"A...goblin?"

"If this is about the hand in the lightning elder stag's mouth, that is a demi-goblin's."

"O-oh, I see..."

"Whaaat? Why didn't you say so sooner, then? Geez!"

Liza's and Arisa's shoulders sagged.

"Geeeez?"

"Yeah, sir!"

Tama and Pochi, who were imitating Arisa, seemed to have noticed the hand's identity as well.

The kindhearted Liza and Arisa looked dispirited, so I patted their heads and looked around at everyone.

Even knowing the truth, they seemed as determined to fight as ever.

"Master!"

Hearing Liza's tense voice, I turned back and saw that the lightning elder stag was getting ready to charge at any moment.

Oops, better focus.

I used Create Earth Servant to make two basic golems between us and the areamaster.

Even the twenty-foot-tall golems looked small in front of the giant beast.

"Block its charge!"

"*MVA.*"

"*MVA.*"

The two golems stepped forward to engage with the lightning elder stag.

"Here it comes!"

As Arisa spoke, the creature destroyed the two giant golems in a single attack and started charging toward us.

"Activate Umbrella!"

A transparent magic barrier appeared in front of Nana's giant physical shield, like an umbrella opening.

The bits of golem that came flying toward us were knocked away by the magic barrier.

One particularly large piece looked like it might bust through the shield, so I used Magic Hand to catch it and put it in Storage just in case.

In the blink of an eye, the areamaster was right in front of us.

"Drill Bash, I declare!"

The umbrella-shaped barrier began to rotate, and it collided with the stag's antlers, sending sparks flying.

Provided with an enormous amount of magic by a Holytree Stone furnace, the magic barrier held firm even as it took the full brunt of the lightning elder stag's attack.

However, the stag was so large that it started to push Nana back, forming deep furrows in the ground as the spikes in her heels cracked.

"Activate Leg Anchor!"

The pile-bunker-like mechanism on her legs shot out adamantite spikes that drove into the ground.

This helped slow her down, but at this rate, Nana's legs might break.

"I'll help you out."

"Thank you, I respond."

I caught Nana from behind and used the maximum number of Flexible Shields to hold back the lightning elder stag's head.

"Maybe we should take this elsewhere."

If we kept fighting here, we might get driven back to where Zarigon and the others were.

Using Magic Hand to grab my group and the monster, I used Return to teleport to an area we'd previously cleared.

While the girls finished getting ready, I kept the lightning elder stag busy in the middle of the large cavern with an imitation of bullfighting.

I had to admit, using a red cape and everything might have been going a little overboard.

"Master! We're ready!"

Arisa waved at me in the distance.

She must have finished casting buffs on everyone and recovering her MP.

Next to Mia was a pseudo-spirit made with Spirit Magic—a plant-like creature called a "green servant."

...Hmm?

My "Trap Detection" skill went off for several places nearby.

It looked like the girls had set up six traps in various areas near their base for the lightning elder stag. They also had made trenches to hinder its charging and a protected area for the rear guard.

Impressed, I dodged the lightning elder stag's charge and used Return to go back to where they were standing.

"Looks like you've really thought this through."

The elf teachers had told me to stop being so overprotective, but considering how much stronger their opponent was this time, I decided to use some Body Strengthening spells on them just in case.

"Well, yeah. No normal methods would stop that giant thing."

As I complimented their traps while casting the spells, Arisa rubbed the space under her nose modestly.

"Master, I desire a new model of the Leg Anchor, I request."

"Yeah, I'll work on it."

It would probably have to use the Space Magic spell Deracinator instead of physical spikes.

"All right, everyone! Just like we planned!"

"Here I go!"

Arisa gave the signal, and Lulu started the battle with a shot from her laser gun.

"DWEEEEZRLYE."

The lightning elder stag roared, the third eye on its forehead burning.

Jumping around, it faced away from us, kicking up dirt behind it.

"Uh-oh! Deracinator!"

"Activate Umbrella, I declare."

Arisa's and Nana's barriers warded off the dirt and rocks the lightning elder stag kicked toward them. It was a bigger barrage than one from a wartime catapult.

"Watch ooout?"

"Mr. Meat is coming, sir!"

Tama and Pochi warned the others that the stag was about to charge.

"Mia!"

"Mm. Go."

"*MWOOOORYWEE.*"

On Mia's command, the green servant took up position behind the trap.

"You walking venison! Become the main dish of our barbecue, I declare!"

Nana used the "Taunt" skill and shouted from near the lightning elder stag's feet.

There were now four Flexible Shields floating around her, probably in case it charged again.

The areamaster charged.

"Now!"

"You got it! Dimension Snare!"

As soon as Liza shouted, Arisa activated her Space Magic, but it only caused the stag to stumble a little before it regained its footing.

"Damn, it resisted me."

"But that still slowed it down, I report."

Nana reassured the frustrated Arisa.

"Gotchaaa?"

"Neckmate, sir!"

Tama and Pochi pulled on a rope woven out of thick ivy that was set in front of one of the traps.

I'm guessing Pochi meant to say *checkmate.*

The poles that were lying on the ground were yanked upward, and chains blocked the lightning elder stag's path, dust crumbling off them.

"Oooops?"

"Ouchie, sir."

Just like Arisa's Dimension Snare, the stag shook it off easily, charging forward with the chains and pillars dangling off it.

Tama and Pochi were sent flying but used their new impact-resistant "round mode" armor to bounce away harmlessly.

"Get it."

"MWOOOOORYWEE."

The green servant held out its arms and stretched endless ivy toward the stag.

Seeing this, the areamaster slowed down.

It was probably planning to cut the ivy with its antlers, then trample the servant with its hooves.

But then its hooves suddenly sank.

"DWEEEEZRYLE."

The lightning elder stag tumbled into a pit my group had dug, crashing into the side of the hole.

"DWEEEEZRYLE."

As it howled, the ridges on its back started to glow, and its enormous antlers lit up.

"Lulu!"

"Got it!"

At Arisa's signal, Lulu pulled the trigger of her laser gun.

A powerful light struck the creature right in the face, damaging part of its giant horns.

"DWEEEEZRYLE."

The areamaster roared in pain, and its bumps and horns stopped glowing.

"Mia!"

"Mm. Cover."

"MWOOOORYWEE."

The green servant's humanoid form collapsed, and it wrapped around the lightning elder stag, covering the pit.

"One extra-large Dimension Snare, coming up!"

Arisa's Space Magic spell wrapped around the neck and limbs of the struggling stag.

"Foolish deer! You are dumber than a donkey, I declare!"

Nana shouted with her "Taunt" skill.

Immediately, Liza came running and delivered a barrage of attacks with her "Spellblade"-wreathed Dragon Claw Spear into the lightning elder stag's hind leg.

A dark-red magical barrier appeared around the stag but the Dragon Claw Spear pierced right through it.

Oh right. I made that spear with blue like a Holy Sword, but Liza is using it with "Spellblade."

I had tried to use "Spellblade" on a Holy Sword once before, but I experienced some strange resistance. Maybe it was because the sword I was using was a "God-given" Holy Sword?

I took out a handmade Holy Sword from Storage to test it out, and I found I could use "Spellblade" without a problem. I guess that rule applied only to Holy Swords given by the gods.

While I was fiddling with that, my group relentlessly whittled down the lightning elder stag's HP as it was trapped in the pit.

Liza and Lulu were dealing a particularly large amount of damage.

"DWEEEEZRYLE."

The struggling beast howled, and its antlers and the ridges on its back started glowing again.

Immediately, the vanguard used "Blink" to move away from their close range.

"Lulu!"

"Sorry, I'm out of magic."

The laser gun was powerful, but there was definitely room for improvement for long-term use.

Maybe I'll add a pulse laser mode or something.

"Okay, then—Blast Shot!"

Arisa's Fire Magic attack sped toward the stag's face.

But most of it was dispersed by the areamaster's magic barrier.

Lulu's laser gun was probably able to hit before the barrier could go up because it fired so quickly.

"Thunder Rod."

At Mia's command, the green servant coiled its ivy around the lightning elder stag's neck and antlers, pulling it sideways.

A loud boom and a flash of light filled the room.

Most of the lightning went through the green servant's ivy wrapped around the lightning elder stag and flowed into the ground, but judging by the destruction that caused, it must have sent some serious electricity flying around.

Fortunately...

"Bwah-ha-ha! You fool! Bow before Arisa's ultimate Reflection Defense!"

Arisa had used the Space Magic spell Reflection Defense to bounce some of the lightning right back at the lightning elder stag.

However, since it had "Lightning Resistance," this didn't seem to cause much damage.

"It feels like I can probably only use that two more times! Whittle it down now while we have the chance!" Arisa shouted to the others.

The red-skinned demon I'd fought underneath the old capital seemed to have unlimited uses of its Reflection Defense, but that was probably a difference in their Space Magic skill level.

"Ankle Cutterrr?"

"Shining Slash, sir!"

The lightning elder stag had put one of its legs up on the line of the pit, but Pochi and Tama ran over to slash at it with their adamantite alloy Magic Swords.

"*DWEEEZRYLE.*"

"Drill Bash, I declare!"

"'Triple Helix Spear Attack'!"

As the creature spurted blood, it was hit by Nana's shield attack and Liza's special move.

The areamaster seemed very tough, though—even these special attacks reduced its health by only about 10 percent.

"■ *Wind Kaze.*"

Mia sent a gust of wind toward the lightning elder stag, carrying some small seeds.

The whirlwind danced around the beast.

"■ ■ ■ *Green Vine Entangle Midori Tsuru Sokubaku.*"

When Mia's second spell activated, the seeds grew rapidly, turned into thick vines, and wrapped around the lightning elder stag.

This was probably to replace the green servant, whose HP ran out just as the new spell was finished.

There was no need to block the stag's charge attacks anymore, and the chants for pseudo-spirits took a long time, so I thought that was a good call.

"*DWEEEEZRYLE.*"

The ridges on the areamaster's back glowed again, signaling an oncoming lightning attack.

"…■ ■ **Mustard Mist** *Shigeki no Kiri.*"

Mia's Water Magic spell enveloped the lightning elder stag's face.

The stag didn't seem too bothered by the painful cloud of irritating mist, but if it used its lightning now, it would probably electrocute itself as well.

Its antlers glowed, and the stag unleashed a second lightning attack.

"Zzzap!"

"Tingly, sir."

Without the Thunder Rod to protect them this time, my group took a bit of electric damage, too.

The Reflection Defense was able to block only the lightning itself, not the tiny sparks of electricity that flew through the air afterward.

"Liza, aim for its ridges! Then it shouldn't be able to zap us anymore."

"Understood!"

As Arisa shouted orders, she used spells like Deracinator and Dimension Pile to keep the stag from coming out of the pit.

Mia supported her with Green Vine Entangle and Paralyze Water Hold.

"Arisa, I'm all recovered."

"Okey-dokey! If the things on its back glow, aim for its face."

"Okay, I will."

Lulu used her scope to keep an eye on the stag's back.

"*DWEEEEZRYLE.*"

The lightning elder stag howled, and the antlers on its head glowed, creating floating balls of lightning.

"Geh, I forgot it can use Lightning Magic, too!"

"■ ■ **Ice** *Koori,* ■ ■ **Wind** *Kaze.*"

Mia used Spirit Magic to create ice spirits in the air, then sent them toward the lightning balls with a fierce gale of wind.

This destroyed a few of the lightning balls, but the rest rained down over the beastfolk girls.

"Take this!"

Lulu, who had switched to her Fireburst Gun, shot down the first lightning ball.

"Here they come."

"Uh-ohhh."

"Emergency maneuvers, sir!"

The girls dodged the rest of the lightning balls with "Blink."

But it soon became apparent that the stag was using these lightning balls to cut through Mia's Green Vine Entangle.

"Urk, it got out!"

The lightning elder stag was crawling out onto the ground.

"Pochiii!"

"Tamaaaa, sir!"

Standing at the edge of the pit, Tama spread her arms wide and called for Pochi, who hopped onto her shoulders.

Then she tumbled to the ground and sent Pochi flying up into the air.

Pochi jumped at the same time, echoing the move they'd learned at the thank-you party.

"Aaaah, you're not gonna make it!" Arisa cried.

"Will toooo! Sir!"

Shouting back to Arisa, Pochi caught her footing in midair and sped up, landing on the lightning elder stag's back.

It was a double jump, which she'd first demonstrated at the plunderer battle.

"Pochi! Destroy those bumps!"

"Aye-aye, sir! 'Blink'—and Vanquish Strike!"

Pochi enlarged her sword to the length of a spear, activated "Spell-blade," and brought it down on the bumps with astonishing speed, destroying them completely.

This was the special move she'd been studying in Bolenan Forest, which she hadn't successfully pulled off until now. I guess this predicament had finally pushed her to complete it.

Its power was on par with Liza's "Triple Helix Spear Attack."

"Tama toooo?"

Next, Tama used Liza as a launchpad to leap up to the base of the lightning elder stag's leg and shimmy onto its back.

"Vorpal Faaang?"

Tama's twin Magic Swords were surrounded by an enormous "Spell-blade" in the shape of giant fangs.

Spinning around, she stabbed her two swords into the stag's neck, creating bite mark–like wounds.

Each individual attack had less power than Liza's "Triple Helix Spear Attack" or Pochi's Vanquish Strike, but the total damage was on par with them.

"Hi-yaaaa, sir!"

Pochi used the wounds the Vorpal Fang attack created to run up right behind Tama.

"Horn Slasherrr?"

"Antler Hunter, sir!"

Once they reached the top, the two attacked the lightning elder stag's antlers.

"Haaard?"

"Can't make a dent, sir."

Their blades were blocked by the magic barrier protecting the stag's antlers.

They tried to use their special attacks again, but the areamaster stopped them by shaking its head rapidly, sending them tumbling back to the ground.

"■ ■ ■ *Green Bed* Ouyo Futon."

Mia's Spirit Magic created a net out of ivy and leaves that caught the pair safely.

They bounced around gleefully for a moment, then remembered that they were in a battle and jumped down.

"Over here, I declare!"

Nana shouted another taunt from a distance, leading the lightning elder stag into another charge.

Since its lightning-producing bumps had been destroyed, this was probably its next best attack.

"Heat Haze!"

Arisa's Fire Magic covered the stag's face. It wasn't the kind of spell that did much damage, but the suddenly superheated air warped the creature's vision.

Still, it continued charging toward Nana.

"DWEEEEZRYLE."

"You fool, I gloat."

Without even a hint of a smile on her face, Nana looked on as the lightning elder stag fell straight into the second pit in front of her.

Arisa's Heat Haze must have been to prevent it from noticing the trap and changing course.

"Liza!"

"Understood!"

Tossing aside the vial of the magic recovery potion she was drinking, Liza jumped onto the stag's back and ran up to its head.

"Comiiiing?"

"Three Musketeers, sir!"

Tama and Pochi dropped empty magic potion vials of their own and ran after Liza.

"'Blink'! 'Triple Helix Spear Attack'!"

Liza struck one of the stag's antlers with her special skill.

The magic barrier appeared again to protect it, but Liza's Dragon Claw Spear smashed right through it, the swirling vortex of "Spellblade" breaking the antler clean off.

"Vanquish Strike, sir!"

"Vorpal Faaang?"

The pair's special moves struck the remaining antler, damaging the magic barrier.

Crack.

I heard a faint noise with my "Keen Hearing" skill.

The Magic Swords that I'd made with prototype equipment didn't seem strong enough to hold up to the pair's powerful special moves.

Hopefully they would at least last to the end of this battle.

"DWEEEEZRYLE."

The lightning elder stag thrashed, shaking off the beastfolk girls.

Entwined in ivy, it howled and struggled in the pit.

"DWEEEEEZRYLE."

Even larger lightning spheres appeared around the stag, but there were only half as many as before.

Probably because it had lost one of its antlers.

"Lulu, can you aim for the other antler?"

"I don't think so. Not unless it stops moving a little."

At that response, Arisa looked around.

"Nana!"

"Listen, deer! Venison stew is delicious, too, I announce!"

Nana's "Taunt" caught the stag's attention, hatred glinting in its eyes.

"...Got it!"

As it stopped thrashing for a moment to glare at Nana, Lulu's laser gun glittered.

The shot landed a direct hit on the hole Pochi and Tama had made in the barrier.

"Whoo-hoo!"

Arisa cheered, then looked around at everyone.

They were all low on magic, but they should be able to finish it off at this rate.

"Now we just have to defeat it without letting it run away!"

Arisa seemed to have reached the same conclusion, giving the group the go-ahead signal while chugging a magic recovery potion.

Now that its health was down to less than 30 percent, the lightning elder stag seemed to be in some kind of berserker mode, thrashing around and shooting off lightning from all over its body.

However, the chains used to stop its initial attack were absorbing the discharge, rendering these attacks fairly harmless.

"Liza! Finish it off!"

"Do you not wish to do it yourself, Arisa?"

"Nah, I'm going to save my magic just in case anything else happens."

Arisa had been largely on support and de-buff duty during this battle, so Liza must have wanted to offer her the final blow.

"…Understood. Tama, Pochi, we'll use the same formation as before."

"Aye-aye, sirrr?"

"Roger, sir!"

The beastfolk girls all dashed toward the lightning elder stag.

"■■ *Green Bridge Ryoku Chou Kyou*."

Mia's Spirit Magic created an ivy bridge from the edge of the pit toward the stag.

The monster tried to bring the bridge down, but Arisa stopped it with the Space Magic spell Deracinator.

"Vorpal Faaaang?"

"Vanquish Strike, sir!"

Tama spun like a top, slashing at the lightning elder stag's magic barrier and the fur around its neck, and Pochi made the wound wider with her enlarged Magic Sword.

Then finally:

"'Blink.' 'Triple Helix Spear Attack'!"

Liza dove in with "Blink," her spear piercing right through the stag's neck.

"*DWEEEEZRYLE.*"

The areamaster howled and shook them off again.

There was far less force behind its movements now, but its HP gauge still wasn't quite empty.

"Close Umbrella—lancer drill mode, I declare."

The magic barrier in front of her shield snapped shut like an umbrella, spinning rapidly with a shrill noise.

"This is the end, I declare."

The spear created from her closed magic barrier sent up sparks as it collided with the lightning elder stag's own barrier.

The clash was over in an instant—Nana's spear broke through the barrier and pierced the stag's throat from the side opposite the beast-folk girls.

"*DDDWEEERRRYEEEE.*"

The edge of the pit crumbled beneath it as the lightning elder stag's head crashed to the ground, sending tremors through the earth.

Then its hateful eyes grew white and dim, and it finally stopped moving.

"Oh em geeee?"

"Pochi's sword broke, sir."

The prototype Magic Swords I'd made for them had broken apart under all the duress.

"Master, my shield's umbrella mode will not reactivate, I report."

It seemed Nana's weapon had broken from overuse, too.

"The speed mechanism in my boots appears to be slowing as well."

Liza inspected the soles of her boots.

I guess the prototype machinery didn't produce very durable equipment.

"Mew!"

"Master!"

Straightening up suddenly, Tama twitched her ears.

At the same time, Lulu pointed at a hole in the wall that was glowing red on the other side of the large room.

"N-no way...," Arisa murmured.

"Spawnhole."

Mia grimaced.

Sure enough, a spawnhole had formed in the wall opposite us.

That in itself wasn't too strange.

It happened all the time.

"Is it just me, or is it getting a lot bigger?"

As Lulu observed, the newly opened spawnhole kept getting larger. It was already big enough that a large truck could easily pass through.

Arisa's voice trembled. "Wh-what's coming out?"

Then, before long...

"Black liiight?"

"Horn, sir."

...a glowing black horn emerged from the giant hole on the other side of the room.

It was the elder lance beetle, the areamaster of the neighboring area. It looked like a gigantic Hercules beetle.

"Oogh, a Hercules!"

"Oogh...?"

"Oogh-oogh, sir."

Arisa took a step back, and Tama and Pochi mimicked her.

That was all well and good, but we had to decide quickly whether to fight or retreat.

"Mrrr."

"What should we do, Arisa?"

"Retreat would be wise, I recommend."

Mia, Lulu, and Nana looked at Arisa.

"Honestly. Fine, then, I'll slow it down."

Arisa shrugged and readied her staff.

"Master, I request permission to use my Unique Skills. I'll slow down the Hercules with a fully boosted 'Labyrinth.'"

"No Unique Skills."

"Awww, c'mon..."

I had been warned not to let Arisa use her Unique Skills too much.

"A fitting opponent. I will buy time while you retreat, everyone."

Liza readied her Dragon Claw Spear and glared at the elder lance beetle.

"Same boooat?"

"We're always together, sir."

Tama and Pochi pulled out their old Magic Swords from their Fairy Packs and stood at Liza's side.

As we watched, the giant beetle's back opened up, and it spread its wings.

"Now, look. There's no slowing down an opponent who can fly."

Arisa scolded the brave beastfolk girls.

"So, master…"

I held up a hand, and Arisa lightly high-fived it.

"…we're counting on you."

"Got it."

I used "Skyrunning" to head up into the air.

The elder lance beetle spread its wings again and slowly took flight.

Its giant horn started to turn red. Most likely, it was about to use some big attack.

"Sorry, but…"

I took out a mass-produced magic lance from Storage and held it aloft.

"…this is checkmate for you, pal."

The lance flew faster than the wind, leaving a crimson trail of light as it pierced right through the beetle.

The wall behind the elder lance beetle was crushed, and even the wall on the other side of the spawnhole crumbled and vanished.

Oops, I may have gone a little overboard. That spear's going to be a pain to get back.

Glancing around, I saw that the dead elder lance beetle was starting to glide down toward the group below, so I used Magic Hand to catch it and put it in Storage.

"Looks like it'll be a while before we can fight at master's side for real."

"We'll have to work hard, Arisa."

"Let's get trainiiiing?"

"Practice makes *perfect*, sir."

"Mm. Training."

"I'll keep working on my aim, too!"

"I would like a special move as well, I request."

I heard the girls talking with my "Keen Hearing" skill.

At this rate, they might be fighting a floormaster sooner than expected. I would have to finish up their equipment properly so that it'd be ready in time.

Epilogue

Satou here. It's hard to find the right balance when it comes to saving people. It might be delusional to want everyone to have a fairy-tale ending, but is it so wrong to at least want all the people around me to be happy?

"We're taking half a month off from exploring."

After our back-to-back areamaster battles, we ended up going back to Labyrinth City with Zarigon and company, during which time Zarigon made that proclamation to me.

If he wanted to take a break, fine. Why did he feel the need to tell me?

"I see. Yes, I'm sure you need some rest."

"Hmph. But let me know if you need help. If any explorers give you trouble, I'll sort 'em out."

Zarigon snorted and left with a short nod.

He'd been fighting normally on the way out, so that greater health recovery potion must have really worked wonders.

"Hey, mister…"

The redheaded Neru waved at us from a distance, flashing a smile that showed a pointy fang.

Unlike before, the *takoyaki* stand had a proper line now.

"We're a huge hit, all 'cause of Miss Tama! We owe ya big-time!"

"Don't worry, be happyyyy?"

Tama fidgeted shyly at Neru's praise.

The new signboard Tama painted, TWIRLING TAKOYAKI, had the same kind of mysterious appeal as the other three signs, making it next to impossible to pass by without buying some.

"Sir Pendragon, are you teaming up with Sir Zarigon?"

This question came from Luram, a regular customer at the food stalls.

For some reason, he sounded very worked up.

"…No. I wasn't particularly planning on it?"

"Awww, I see…"

Luram looked disappointed by my response.

Was this sort of like wanting to be friends with the friend of a popular athlete?

"Good-bye for now, mister! We're gonna pay you back, I swear!"

Amid the line of the expedition's bag carriers, I heard the beastfolk kids call out to me. As usual, I adjusted for their unnatural-sounding speech in my mind.

"I'm looking forward to it."

My response put enormous grins on their faces, like some neighborhood kids.

"What do you think they're going to do now?"

Arisa looked worried.

"The expedition party will probably break up, but they've got their bronze explorer badges now, so I suppose they'll keep exploring?"

I had already recommended that they take the rookie explorers' class.

"I hope they don't get taken advantage of by another jerk like Besso…"

Arisa seemed to have a lot of sympathy for the young beastfolk kids.

To be honest, I thought there were probably plenty of candidates out there who might be fooled in the same way.

"There should be some kind of seminar for kids who want to be explorers or something."

"Yeah, that does seem like a good idea."

Arisa and I chatted about this as we headed back to the mansion.

"Welcome home, young master."

"Thank you, Miteruna."

I greeted the staff and the head maid, Miss Miteruna, then followed her into the study.

"Do you have any pressing news for me?"

"Yes."

Despite how casually I posed the question, she answered immediately. "We had no less than three nighttime burglary attempts."

"Was anyone hurt?"

"No."

I let out a sigh of relief at that.

"Sir Kajiro and Lady Ayaume apprehended them all."

What excellent guards.

But they would probably leave once I healed them, so I might have to set up some surveillance golems like we had in our labyrinth vacation home.

I could easily make an army of them with my Stone Object and Create Earth Servant spells now anyway.

Oh right. This is a perfect chance.

"Miteruna, would you mind calling Mr. Kajiro and Miss Ayaume here for me?"

"Of course, young master."

While Miss Miteruna went off to find the two samurai, I checked through the letters I'd received while we were in the labyrinth.

There was a package from the Muno Barony. Opening it, I found letters from the baron, Viscount Nina, and some of the baron's daughters like Miss Karina and Miss Soluna.

The baron and Soluna were reporting on the latest developments, while Miss Nina updated me on the progress of rebuilding the barony and thanked me for the support I'd gotten them from Ougoch Duchy nobles.

Miss Karina didn't seem to be too accustomed to writing letters; she used a template I'd learned in the new nobility lessons I attended in the Muno Barony. They were mostly to express sentiments like "I want to go to Labyrinth City" and "I want to eat your cooking again." Typical Miss Karina.

I also got a letter from the viceroy's son Rayleigh, who was away in the royal capital.

He reported that he had sold all the Heaven's Teardrops there and attached a summary of the profits. It was pretty impressive.

Rayleigh had already left the royal capital and should have arrived in the trade city Tartumina around this time.

I also had letters from nobles of Labyrinth City, the Ougoch Duchy, and so on, but none from Seiryuu City. Since it was so far away, I would probably have to wait a little longer for any response.

"Sir Knight, Kajiro at your service."

Knocking at the door, Mr. Kajiro and Miss Ayaume came inside.

"Miss Miteruna told me about your hard work."

"Sake would make an excellent reward."

"S-Sir Kajiro, don't be rude!"

Ayaume grew flustered at Kajiro's blunt request.

"Well, I did acquire some fine sake recently, so I'll share it with you later."

I responded with a smile, then asked about what had happened with the burglars.

The burglars in question were layabouts from the downtown area, as well as criminal guild members. But they all confessed that they had been hired by some unknown person.

They were after our extra Magic Swords and other magical equipment.

Perhaps this was connected to the rumors of war in the western part of the continent.

The viceroy's wife, who commanded the guard, probably knew about this already. I figured I would just mention it to the guildmaster later.

Once this conversation concluded, I produced the greater magic potion from my sleeve and placed it on the table.

"A magic potion, is it?" Kajiro asked.

"Yes, I acquired it with a little help." I nodded.

"Quite a large vial."

Ayaume peered at the potion with some confusion.

"It's a greater health recovery potion, you see."

"...Greater?"

"It can't be!"

Kajiro and Ayaume looked from the potion back to me, a mixture of hope and restraint on their faces.

"Please use this to restore your leg."

I affirmed my request with a nod.

"...Oh, Sir Kajiro!"

Overcome with emotion, Ayaume flung her arms around Mr. Kajiro.

Normally, the pair didn't have a whiff of romance about them, but at times like this, I thought they suited each other pretty well.

"W-wait, Sir Knight!"

Looking flustered at Ayaume's rare show of affection, Kajiro nevertheless held out a hand to stop me.

"Greater magic potions are so valuable that even nobles and royalty hesitate to use them. It is far too precious an item for a humble samurai such as myself."

"That's not true. I ordered this potion specifically to heal your leg."

I had actually made it, but that was a minor detail.

"But…"

"Are you concerned because it has no certificate of authenticity?" I asked.

"No! That is not my concern, of course. But if you were to offer this potion to the Shiga Kingdom royals or the old noble families, surely you would receive any title you desired. I have heard that the third prince of this kingdom is gravely ill, is he not?"

No, he just got turned into an old man.

"This potion would not cure His Highness's ailment."

There might be some noble or royal family with a person suffering from a lost limb or similar, but I would much rather help a friend first than some rich person I'd never met.

"Besides, I don't need any more titles. Being an honorary hereditary knight is more than enough."

As long as my rank allowed me to bring the beastfolk girls into inns, get in and out of cities more easily, and so on, that was good enough for me.

Mr. Kajiro continued to protest, so finally I prompted, "Or are you worried about paying off a greater magic potion?"

Of course, I was planning to give it to him for free, but still.

"If I can heal my leg, then I'll gladly earn as many hundreds or even thousands of gold coins as it takes!"

"That's the spirit."

Kajiro had seen through my challenge but accepted it anyway, so I smiled and pressed the potion toward him.

Of course, I warned him to wait until after dinner to actually drink the potion, lest we repeat the incident with Zarigon.

Finally, I should note that the lesser cockatrice meat was more delicious in stew than any chicken I'd ever had.

And then, that night…

"Arrrrgh!"

Kajiro's manly face twisted in pain.

Since Lelillil told me when I was healing Tifaleeza and Neru that *magic can't heal old wounds*, I was a little worried, but when I reopened the wound and had Kajiro drink the greater potion, the regrowth began without issue.

"Uuuurgh!"

"Almost there, Sir Kajiro."

Obviously, regrowing an entire limb at this rate must be considerably painful.

Miss Ayaume held Kajiro tightly, as if trying to take on some of his pain.

My group stood by, their fists clenched as they encouraged him.

Finally, the lost leg returned to normal, and the red flesh took on a normal color.

"My leg… It's really…"

Looking exhausted, Kajiro stared down at his own leg.

His usual politeness was gone, but this was no time to worry about such things.

"Yes, it's healed."

"Sir Kajiro! Congratulations, Kajiro!"

Tears streamed down Kajiro's face, while Ayaume wept openly and wore a glowing smile.

The rest of my group let up a cheer from behind me.

Once everyone had calmed down a little, I spoke to Kajiro and handed him a rehydrating concoction. "Well done. Here."

"Sir Knight. I cannot begin to express my gratitude…" Without even sipping the drink, he bowed deeply before me. "In order to repay this debt, I, Kajiro of the Zi-Gain style, swear on the name of my ancestor Simahzu that I shall live to serve you until my dying breath."

No, that's going a little too far.

More importantly, I wondered if his ancestor's name Simahzu came from the Japanese feudal lord Shimazu. Was this Zi-Gain style based on the martial arts style *Jigen-ryuu*?

"I, too, vow to serve Sir Knight's house forever along with Sir Kajiro."

Ayaume lined up next to Kajiro. To me, this sounded like she was proposing to Kajiro in a roundabout way, but neither of them seemed to have realized this. I decided to let it slide.

"Please raise your heads, both of you. I appreciate your show of gratitude, but there's really no need for all that. I will certainly need you to continue protecting this house until we find your successors, but my only wish is for Sir Kajiro to return to the path of a martial arts master."

"Sir Knight!"

The samurai pair exclaimed at my quiet proclamation and broke down crying.

I wasn't quite sure how to take this reaction, but evidently they were grateful that I wanted him to keep up his life's work.

For some reason, the girls all ended up crying along with them.

"I swear to you that my name will be echoed across the continent as a master swordsman someday."

Kajiro's face was still damp with tears as he made this vow.

Whew, I'm glad I managed to change the subject.

Having normal employees and servants was one thing, but taking on vassals seemed a little heavy for me.

◆

"Lord Kuro!"

"Lelillil, can you get Tifaleeza for me?"

"Right away, sir!"

After Mr. Kajiro's leg was healed, I transformed into Kuro and visited the Ivy Manor.

"You called for me, Lord Kuro?"

"Ah. Sorry to have disrupted your sleep."

Tifaleeza was wearing a skimpy nightgown, so I apologized and got right to business.

"It's about the financial deficit we were discussing the other day."

I produced a few different branding irons. Upon seeing them, Tifaleeza froze for a moment.

That may have been indelicate of me. I had forgotten that she'd been burned by her stepmother and branded by a feudal lord in the past.

"Sorry, sorry. These are for burning runes into bones for the purpose of making bone armor."

It was only 20 or 30 percent as effective as carving the runes properly, but they would be significantly easier to apply this way.

"This is for carving runes, too, but while it's more effective, it also takes more time and effort."

The second object was a bronze template and a chisel for carving runes of a specific depth.

With these, even a relatively unskilled worker could carve runes into bones and wood.

"If we'll be making armor, won't you need to join an armor-related guild to avoid any problems?" Tifaleeza asked.

"Even if we're just supplying bones to armorers and workshops as materials?"

"I imagine they would allow it at first, but if we started to earn money from it, I'm sure they would try to intervene." She sounded confident.

I suppose it did make sense. Guilds were originally created to protect the rights and interests of artisans, so this would naturally fall under their jurisdiction.

"Then ask Polina to get us signed up with a guild. In the meantime, you can sell these."

I produced a bag from my Item Box that contained a large amount of crystal rings.

I'd made them by using the Stone Object spell on some of the many crystals that I acquired in the moss crab bee area.

They were smooth rings without any fancy designs, but since they were made of crystal, I figured they should still fetch a good price.

I tried making a sort of Venetian glass by fusing several kinds of crystals, but they came out so nice that I worried it might attract the wrong kind of attention, so I didn't offer her those.

Maybe we could start selling them once we had a storefront in the royal capital.

"L-Lord Kuro, what are these?"

"Use them to make money."

"V-very well. I'll send someone to sell them who has acquaintances in the market. Does three silver coins apiece sound all right?"

"Three silver coins?"

According to my "Estimation" skill, the market price for these ranged anywhere from one copper coin to three silver coins.

"I'm terribly sorry, but if we wanted to sell them for a higher price than that, they would need some sort of additional value..."

"That's fine."

I had assumed we'd sell them for one copper coin.

At this price, that should be enough to raise money for the time being.

Once the alchemist and doctors could reliably make veria potion, we would probably be selling those to the guild wholesale.

Oh right...

"I have a request about the veria potions."

I took out a sample veria potion and a fragmented recipe from the Item Box.

"Tell Sumina to bring these to the guild."

"Understood."

I gave her a letter detailing the order in which to bring them to the guild and a story for how I'd found the sample and recipe.

I also proposed offering a reward for gathering the fragments of the recipe.

Big Sister Sumina and company could definitely handle this.

"That's all I needed. You may go."

For some reason, Tifaleeza seemed a little dissatisfied when I dismissed her.

Oh, I get it.

"Tifaleeza."

"Y-yes?!"

When I called out to stop her, she jumped and turned around.

Her voice sounded a little higher than usual.

"Eluterina and the others reached the royal capital safely. In a few days, I'll go over there myself to help them out."

"Erm, okay..."

I updated her on the situation because I thought she might be worried about her friends, but Tifaleeza's response sounded half-hearted.

"Is that all?" she asked.

"Yes, that's all."

"Then, if you'll excuse me."

Tifaleeza's voice was as cold as ice as she excused herself.

Girls that age can be so difficult.

"It might be a little early to go home and sleep..."

For a change of pace, I decided to build some defense golems to protect the house and the orphanage.

I used the underground lab's equipment to format a core, then engraved it with the lookout algorithms I'd made in the elf village for

the figurehead golem on our ship and some simple battle algorithms. I supposed I would use this core as the base to make a golem with Stone Object and Create Earth Servant.

I went to the trouble of engraving the core as a precaution because the book of Earth Magic spells that I found in the labyrinth included spells for taking over someone else's golem, overriding their orders, and so on.

First, I used the Stone Object spell to make a human-size dragon out of blue crystal with a wand-like spear and ten chubby cats out of stone. The latter were for the orphanage, hence the cute design.

Crystal would be fragile, so I carved some strengthening runes into the dragon, then set all of them up with some prototype equipment to give them magic-barrier-producing circuits, awareness-inhibiting devices so they wouldn't be recognized as golems, and so on.

Furthermore, because I didn't want the golems to spread miasma around, I also set them up with a magic circuit made out of magical blue.

Finally, I used the Create Earth Servant spell to turn them into golems.

Both ended up being level 30, but because of the magic circuits, they got the title Consecrated Golem, too.

I also made ten of the simple, round original golems, each about four heads tall.

These were all level 10 and didn't have algorithm-engraved cores.

The next morning, under the guise of the Pendragon family's merchant, Akindoh, I went to the house to deliver the golems.

I set the cat golems up as statues at the gates of the mansion and the orphanage and on all four sides of each building; the crystal golem I put in the entrance hall of the mansion.

The regular golems were positioned to guard both buildings as actual golems.

The former were for stopping intruders, while I was hoping the latter would deter criminals from trying to break in in the first place.

When I set up the golems, I also installed the extra-large refrigerator Arisa had requested for the orphanage.

"Hmm. What a fascinating magic tool."

In the parlor of Baronet Dyukeli's home, I presented him with the juicer and explained how to use it.

"Just open this lid, put fruits and vegetables inside according to the recipes, close the lid, and provide it with magic power."

The maid timidly followed my instructions.

But when she reached the last step—

"Eeeek!"

Startled by the noise and vibration of the juicer as it pulverized the contents, the maid shrieked and threw the juicer across the room.

"Oh dear."

I immediately caught it and held the lid in place, but it was only thanks to my high DEX and AGI stats that I was able to react so quickly.

"I'm sorry. I forgot to warn you about the noise and vibration." Apologizing, I completed the first test myself.

"Intriguing. It looks somewhat like a thick soup," Baronet Dyukeli said upon sipping it himself after the maid poison-tested the juice.

"It's tastier than I expected. The sweetness of the fruit hides the bitterness of the vegetables."

"Yes, that's one of the benefits of vegetable juice."

When combined with fruit juice anyway.

"Do you think your son will be willing to drink this?"

"Yes, I'm sure he will."

Just in case, I gave him some recipes with suggestions for adding honey or sugar and variations with different kinds of fruit.

"But will preparing them so violently not destroy the vitamin spirits?"

"Don't worry. The magic tool is engraved with a rune that keeps it from harming the vitamin spirits."

I reassured the baronet's fantasy-world worries.

I'd forgotten that he thought vitamins were *good spirits that hide in vegetables and livestock entrails.*

"Very well, then. I shall have this juice prepared for my son starting with tonight's dinner."

Baronet Dyukeli nodded, looking satisfied.

...Oh right.

I still had one other order of business here.

"Your Excellency, could I ask you to have this potion and piece of paper analyzed?"

"Analyzed, you say?"

Looking suspicious, the baronet called for his servant with the "Analyze Goods" skill.

"...I can't believe it."

"Don't beat around the bush. What are the results?"

"Th-this is a genuine veria potion. It appears to be around the same level of effectiveness as a lesser health recovery potion."

I was impressed that his "Analyze Goods" skill could appraise the type of potion as well as the effectiveness.

"Veria potion? And the paper?"

"This is the recipe for veria potion."

"What?!"

Baronet Dyukeli grabbed the recipe from the table.

"Th-this is the recipe...?"

"I believe it is likely a fragment of the recipe. I dabble in alchemy myself, and these instructions appear to be the preface and a list of necessary ingredients. The recipe itself is likely on a separate fragment."

I gave the confused baronet the answer I'd prepared.

I was planning to hide the other fragments of the recipe in treasure chests in some of the more easily accessible areas of the labyrinth, along with a completed veria potion, so that young explorers could go looking for them like treasure hunters.

The recipe was broken into eight parts; I figured I would hide a lot of copies of five of the sections and less copies of the final three.

I also wrote the preface such that people could figure out that the recipe was split into eight parts if they read it closely enough.

I was hoping that some greedy mid-level explorers would get so caught up in treasure hunting that they'd pioneer new hunting grounds, too.

"Sir Pendragon, you're giving this to me—that is, to the alchemists' guild?"

"Yes, that's why I brought it here. If this recipe can be completed, I'm hoping that the price of magic potions in Labyrinth City will decrease and the tension between the explorers and the alchemists' guild will be resolved."

Before he could name a price, I explained why I had brought it to the baronet instead of the explorers' guild.

"Grrr... Very well. I swear upon the great ancestral king Yamato and the Dyukeli family name that I shall do as you ask."

After crossing his arms and grumbling for a moment, Baronet Dyukeli promised to comply.

This way, the highly in-demand lesser health recovery potions should finally be widely available at a cheap price. That should resolve the explorers' resentment and could possibly increase their survival rate in the labyrinth.

Hopefully, that would also mean that explorers would stop hating Miss Mary-Ann because she was the daughter of Baronet Dyukeli. After all, she wanted to be an explorer herself someday.

As I took my leave, Mary-Ann saw me off with an imploring look in her eyes, but I ignored her in case it raised any weird flags.

Taking care of her was a job better suited to the viceroy's third son, Gerits, who had an obvious crush on her, besides.

"Is this about your previous request, Sir Pendragon? Just a moment, please."

On the way home from Baronet Dyukeli's house, I stopped off at the west guild to see how my request for scroll-collecting was coming along.

The receptionist looked over a list, then brought up a small box from the back of the room.

"We've received these three so far. Your initial deposit covered the reward for them, so there is no need for any further payment. Here are the details and your receipt."

Explaining quickly and smoothly, the receptionist took the scrolls out of the box.

The three scrolls were for the spells Sand Control, Desert Mirage, and Acceleration Gate.

The former were from the Sandstorm Labyrinth, like Stone Object and Create Earth Servant.

Sand Control did exactly what it described, but I couldn't find any description of Desert Mirage in my spell books. My guess was that it created spontaneous mirages, but I couldn't think of any use for that except getting people lost in a desert.

But I guess it's all right to find a useless spell every once in a while.

The Acceleration Gate spell was apparently found in a place called the Wilde Labyrinth.

I couldn't find a spell by this name in my books, either, but I assumed it was similar to the Wind Magic spell Quick, the Explosion Magic spell Boost, the Dark Magic spell Boost Gate, and so on.

When I casually analyzed the scroll, it did seem like a composite of the above three spells.

Well, I'd find out soon enough if I went to the labyrinth or the desert to the west to test these spells out.

"There were seven other submissions, but…"

The receptionist explained that three of these were just standard market scrolls dressed up to look special, and the other four were fake scrolls.

"We've already disposed of them—don't worry."

I thanked the receptionist and asked her to keep collecting scrolls.

"Yes, of course. However, scrolls are found rather infrequently, so please do understand."

She said these three had probably come from someone's personal collection.

I was happy to keep my request going continuously. If people knew they could make a profit, I might get submissions from neighboring cities or the royal capital.

Thanking the worker, I left the guild.

"Satou."

"Oh? Why, if it isn't master."

Mia and Arisa spotted me amid the crowd and came running over.

I saw Liza behind them, too.

"What's going on?"

"Some of the orphanage kids want to become explorers, so we came to ask if there's any kind of school for that."

Oh right. A few of the kids asked Mr. Kajiro to train them before.

"Since the kingdom collects cores from the labyrinth, that seems reasonable."

Being an explorer was a dangerous job, but I wanted the kids to be able to pursue their dreams.

After I asked the teller at the guild, who didn't know, I turned to the guildmaster's secretary, Miss Ushana, when I spotted her.

"I'm afraid not. There's only the rookie explorers' class for new bronze-badge explorers."

"Are there any that aren't run by the kingdom or the guild?"

"Some explorer parties take on apprentices or students to do errands while learning the job, but there isn't anything like a school."

The only available option was a sort of apprenticeship system.

"But although there isn't a school for explorers, there are plenty of dojos and private schools that teach combat techniques."

There were also dojos that taught self-defense specifically for women, since the city was so full of rough-and-tumble explorers.

"Would we be able to make something like that ourselves?" Arisa asked.

"As long as you get permission from the viceroy to open a school, I imagine it wouldn't be a problem. There are no restrictions about it in the guild rules," Ushana answered.

If I could just find some instructors, all I would have to do is ask the viceroy's wife for permission and this could probably work.

...No, hang on.

I was getting carried away by Arisa's idea.

Since this was about the orphanage kids, all I really needed to do was hire a teacher to come to the orphanage once in a while.

"Please! Just give us three more days!"

"I swear we'll pay up!"

I heard a familiar conversation from the reception counter on the first floor.

"It's those girls again."

"Déjà vu."

Sure enough, it was the Lovely Wings pair negotiating with a guild employee again.

This time, however, things sounded a little different.

"I told you last time you were late on a payment, didn't I? I said that if it happened again, you'd become slaves."

For real? This fantasy world sure is harsh.

That certainly explained why they had been sobbing with gratitude when I saved them last time, though.

"Th-then enslave me, and we'll pay Jena's part of the fee."

"W-wait a minute, Iruna! What are you saying?! Don't you dare try to sacrifice yourself for me!"

I couldn't just ignore their plight, so I thanked Ushana for her help and headed over to the counter.

"Hello, Miss Iruna, Miss Jena."

"Mister!"

The two looked at me tearfully, like their savior had appeared.

"Could I ask the total of their debt?"

"Eight gold coins and four silver coins."

Oh, that's not as bad as I thought.

"Then let me pay off all of it, please."

Considering how bad these two seemed to be at earning money, they were probably going to end up as slaves sooner or later at this rate, so I decided to just pay off their whole debt in one go.

"M-mister, we can't let you go that far for us..."

"Y-yeah! If you could lend us the interest, that would be more than—"

"There's no guarantee I'll happen to be around to bail you out a third time, understand?"

The two of them tried to protest, but when I pointed out the truth, they fell tearfully silent.

I guess even they couldn't deny that fact.

So I gave the clerk nine gold coins and received my change in silver coins.

"Thank you so much, mister! We'll repay you with our bodies!"

"Oh? I'll take you up on that, then."

Since they had made such a ridiculous offer, I agreed to it with a cheerful smile.

The Lovely Wings pair turned bright red and got flustered, but I heard bellows of rage from behind me.

"Mrrr, guilty!"

"Absolutely not!"

The iron-wall pair of Mia and Arisa shoved their way between the Lovely Wings and me.

Liza stepped in to stop the furious pair. "Calm down, you two. Do you really think our master is the sort of person who would ever use debt as an excuse to coerce women into such liaisons?"

"I guess not, buuut..."

"Mrrr."

Perhaps I'd taken the joke a little too far. "Sorry, sorry. I only meant to mess with them a little," I apologized, making my real intentions known. "See, we actually have some kids at our orphanage who want to become explorers. I was looking for someone who might teach them for us. Do you think I could ask you two to take on the job?"

"Y-yes, of course! If you'll have us!"

"We'll teach the crap outta those kids!"

Jena and Iruna agreed to my request immediately.

They had teaching experience from the rookie explorers' class, and they were both good-natured young women. They'd be the perfect instructors for the orphans.

If I had time down the line, maybe we could even start offering a course for kids who wanted to be explorers. That might reduce the amount of gullible kids like those beastfolk children being taken advantage of by guys like Besso.

I didn't want to get too ambitious, but if there was enough demand and we could secure more teachers, I wouldn't be opposed to opening an entire explorer training school like Arisa proposed.

If we made it into a proper school, we could even offer lessons to noble kids who wanted to be explorers, too, like Baronet Dyukeli's daughter Mary-Ann and the viceroy's third son, Gerits.

"While you're teaching, feel free to use an empty room in our servants' quarters."

They lived downtown near the barricade walls, which would probably make commuting a pain, so I decided to offer some employee benefits.

"Man, that kid really knows how to rope in mistresses."

"The crazy thing is, he doesn't seem to have any ulterior motives."

"I bet some country girls would fall for that in a second."

My "Keen Hearing" skill picked up on some tasteless comments from the explorers around us.

The girls didn't seem to have heard, but I didn't want to let weird rumors spread about them. I stepped over to clear things up.

But by then, those rumors had already vanished.

After all, some much more interesting news had arrived.

"Veria potions, you say?!"

"Yes, that's right! We found it in a treasure chest in the labyrinth! There's even a piece of the recipe!"

The first voice came from a clerk, while the next was Miss Sumina, speaking loudly.

She must have come to carry out my request.

"Did they say 'veria potions'?"

"What is this, another scam?"

None of the explorers seemed to believe it.

Still, I could tell that deep down they wanted it to be true.

"No, it's the real thing! Look, just analyze it!"

"I-it's true! We've got to report this to the guildmaster! Sumina, come with me to her office right away."

"No problem! What'd I tell you? It's a real veria potion!"

Once the word had spread, Sumina followed the clerk to the guildmaster's office.

"S-so it's true?"

"That clerk has the 'Analyze' skill. It's gotta be for real."

"Damn! So we'll be able to get cheap potions?"

"Of course! There's more veria outside the city than you could ever cut down!"

"And even if you did, they grow back in half a month as long as you leave the roots."

The explorers excitedly chatted among themselves, the Lovely Wings pair included.

Then a second information bomb dropped.

This time it was another set of girls from the tenements, who came separate from Sumina.

"Didn't she say she found a recipe fragment, too?"

"I wonder if there are others?"

"She said she found it in the labyrinth!"

"We'd better search all the labyrinths in the recipes for treasure chests, then."

Some of the girls really needed to work on their acting. That last one, especially, totally flubbed the line beyond comprehension.

Still, the explorers seemed to get the gist of it anyway. The ones who overheard the conversation and understood it ran off in a tizzy.

They were probably headed straight for the labyrinth to look for recipe fragments.

"Is this your doing, master?"

"That's a secret."

I responded to Arisa's whispered question with a wink.

Once I introduced the Lovely Wings to Miss Miteruna, I would have to go hide the veria potions and recipe fragments in some treasure chests.

"We've got to have a welcome party tonight!"

"Mm. Celebrate."

"I shall go hunt for meat in the labyrinth, then."

Once I stopped Liza from her overexcited endeavor, we headed back to the house to introduce the pair to their new workplace.

That night, the near-limitless quantities of meat and veggies put smiles on the faces of my kids and the Lovely Wings duo alike.

Nothing makes people happier than delicious food.

EX-1: Dreamcrystal Mausoleum

I always thought I could do anything all by myself. But when I got summoned to a parallel world without any special powers, I realized I was dead wrong. I'm just a powerless loser. But I...

"Wake up."

A foreign language tickled my eardrums.

After those gentle words, the next thing I experienced was the harsh taste of alcohol burning my tongue and throat.

I started coughing violently.

Alcohol is the enemy. I've vowed never to drink it again, especially after I got wasted in the town of Yorschka and nearly fell into slavery.

"I am Number 1. What is your name?"

Sounds like a code name.

Her voice was sweet yet cold, like a goddess of death.

"I... I, uh..."

I could barely speak properly. My tongue felt like it was on fire.

"I'm Sumi... Wait, no. My name is..."

Still in a daze, I almost gave my real name in Japanese but stopped just in time.

I'd given up that name when I was summoned to that kidnapping kingdom of Lumork.

...John Smith.

That's my name now.

It's what my precious few friends call me: Garohal, Hoze, and even my former lover.

Incoherent thoughts drifted in and out of my mind.

Lilio... I want to see your face again...

"If your consciousness has returned, we request a verbal response, I declare."

"Number 1, we should begin awakening sequence by way of physical force, I suggest."

Through the haze of my confusion, I heard women's voices talking in a strange manner.

There were probably five or six of them, though I couldn't tell for sure, since they were all chattering at once.

"…Ow!"

A painful pinch on my cheek made me jerk upright.

Surrounding me were seven beautiful women, all with the same face.

They each had a different hairstyle, but it was still difficult to tell them apart.

"Are you awake?"

"Y-yeah."

The one who appeared to be the leader handed me a water pouch.

After being lost in the mountains for three days, my instinct was to chug it all down at once, but it was dangerous to do something so vulnerable in this violent, lawless parallel world.

I forced myself to stop after a few sips and tried to figure out these girls' intentions.

Under their coats, they were wearing matching travel gear and leather breastplates, but they were each equipped with completely different weapons.

The woman who spoke to me first had a huge shield on her back and a rapier at her waist.

The one with the braided ponytail had a war hammer, the one with the woven side ponytail had a gun blade, the one with her hair tied in a bandanna had a broadsword, the one with barely shoulder-length hair had a nasty-looking poleax, the one with two side buns had a short spear, and the one with short pigtails had a scimitar.

They were like a bunch of recycled character designs in an online game.

"Explain why you were collapsed all the way out here, I request."

The one with the short pigtails questioned me with that same strange speech pattern.

While the rest of the women all had large busts, I realized that this one alone had reassuringly modest breasts.

I'm not saying big equals bad, but I find a smaller size more comforting.

"Are you lost? I inquire."

"No, I…"

"*PYWEEEEE.*"

As I formed my response to the short-haired one's question, a piercing sound—likely from the culprit behind my collapse—suddenly echoed around us.

The valley full of rocks and withered shrubs was full of mist, making it impossible to see the source of the shriek.

"All hands, red alert!"

"Number 1! Requesting 'Body Strengthening.'"

"Permission granted. All hands, activate 'Body Strengthening'!"

"""""Confirmed. 'Body Strengthening.'"""""

A red magic circle appeared on their foreheads, and their bodies glowed for a moment.

It seemed closer to a magic spell than a skill.

"But…with no chant?"

Maybe they had shortened it somehow, but either way, that was abnormal.

Mages in *this* world always have to use a chant.

A Saga Empire spy who once helped me out told me that there's a technique for shortening chants, but they didn't say anything about a skill that destroys chants entirely.

Instead, they told me a little bit about chant-less magic: that the only people who can use it are Heroes or reincarnations.

But there was no way there would be seven people who were all summoned by the Saga Empire's Hero Summoning, a technique passed down to them by a god, in a place like this.

"Are they regular reincarnations, then?"

Reincarnations tended to have purple hair, but these women were blond— But no, maybe they dyed their hair.

For now, I'll just assume they're reincarnations.

"*PYWEEEEYEEEE.*"

A shadow appeared above the rocks, accompanied by the sound of flapping wings.

It was a creature whose upper body was that of a woman with bird wings for arms and whose lower half was that of a bird of prey.

However, the woman's upper half wasn't what you're probably picturing.

It was more like if you took a feral mountain witch and made it about five times more horrifying, to give you some idea.

"Enemy identified!" the one with the braided ponytail called. "A harpy, I report."

"Even numbers, prepare your Arrows!"

""""Understood!""""

On the command of Number 1, who had a low braided bun, four of the women produced red magic circles on their foreheads.

Transparent arrows made of white light appeared right before their eyes. They were short arrows, like the kind you'd use with a crossbow.

They resembled the Practical Magic spell Magic Arrow, which I'd seen once before.

"PYWEEEYEEE."

"Fire!!"

The harpy swooped down like a hawk just as the four women's Arrows flew toward it at high speeds.

The harpy twisted in midair, dodging the arrows.

"Hideous bird! Come at us, if you do not fear our blades!"

Number 1 prepared her shield and shouted, and the harpy wheeled around to speed toward her instead.

She'd probably used the "Taunt" skill.

"Now, Number 3."

"Victory is ours, I declare."

As the harpy crashed into the shield, the women with the gun blade and the poleax cut off its wings.

"BYWEDZEEEE."

"Finish it!"

The harpy shrieked as Number 1's rapier plunged into its heart.

Even with this world's gamelike level system, the only living things that could survive having their heart pierced were very high-level monsters.

The light faded from the harpy's eyes, and its enormous body slumped to the ground.

Incredible. Normal people could only hope to fight that thing with a team of archers, but these girls took it down without a scratch.

"Number 1, I have retrieved the core, I report."

"Thank you, Number 8. There is blood on your face. Please wipe it off with this cloth."

"Wipe it off for me, I request."

Number 1 wiped the blood off the girl with the short pigtails.

It was like a scene out of a *yuri* romance, but since their expressions barely changed, it felt more like watching an old 3-D cutscene or a puppet show.

"I repeat the query. What is your name?"

"I am Number 2," the one with the braided ponytail added, and the other girls introduced themselves in turn.

Their code names ranged from Number 1 to Number 8, although Number 7 appeared to be missing.

"I'm John Smith. Just John Smith."

Once she finished wiping Number 8's face, Number 1 approached me.

"Do you know the way to the foot of the mountain?"

"We are lost, I report."

"We have been wandering these mountains for nearly half a month, and I am exhausted, I complain."

"Number 1 has no sense of direction, I grumble."

After Number 1's question, the rest all chimed in with complaints.

"Silence. The rest of you equally lack a sense of direction, do you not?"

I got that they were strong, but I was still surprised they managed to last half a month lost in the mountains.

"So you want me to get you to the main road, is that it?"

"No, I declare."

"We must carry out our mission of delivering our former master's mementos, I proclaim."

"We have our current master's permission, I add."

Considering their lack of expressions and strange way of speaking, they sure were chatty.

"And what's in it for me?"

They may have rescued me when I was passed out, but I had learned that this parallel world is all about give-and-take.

"Our travel budget is quite low…," one of them said.

"If you have no money, pay with your bodies," I said.

With their strength, they could help me get through the rough spot that I couldn't handle alone.

"Our breasts belong to master, I reject."

"No, no. See, I'm looking for ruins that are somewhere in this valley. Guard me until we find the entrance. In exchange, I'll take you where you need to go."

I'd heard a rumor in a bar in Lessau County that the Dreamcrystal Mausoleum, the grave of the ancestral king Yamato, was somewhere in this valley.

The other people in the bar didn't believe it, but I did.

Because in the song that described the location of the grave, there was a hint that only Japanese people would understand.

"Can you locate it, Number 2?"

"One moment please. I will investigate with Signal Echo."

Number 2, who hadn't spoken much until now, produced a glowing circle on her forehead.

From what I'd seen so far, she must be using a magic I wasn't familiar with.

"There is some kind of barrier here."

She must have been seeking the direction of the ruins with magic.

I was right: It was in the direction of the harpy's nest, which I'd given up on getting past before.

"Let us go."

Number 1 beckoned to me.

I was starting to understand why they were so bad with directions.

"Other way."

"Other way?"

"That's the right direction, but we can't get there by going that way. We'll have to take this roundabout path."

Unlike birds and other flying creatures, humans couldn't just proceed in a straight line.

"There are the ruins, I report."

Number 8, with the short pigtails, put a hand to her meager chest in salute.

"…Yeah, you're right."

That was exhausting.

These girls weren't kidding when they said they had no sense of direction.

All we had to do was proceed along a narrow path, but whenever something caught their attention, they would wander off elsewhere. And by the time I found the one who'd strayed first, a different one would be missing.

It was like leading a bunch of children in adult bodies.

If I didn't know they were so strong in battle, I probably would've given up on them and gone ahead on my own by now.

But we had already run into several kinds of monsters, and the women destroyed them just as easily as they had the harpy.

"So now what...?"

I let out a sigh to forget the frustrations of the journey and focused on the situation in front of me.

There were about three hundred feet between the exit of this passage and the entrance to the ruins. The space in between was a wasteland of withered trees and weeds.

It was all dyed a dull gray, as if ashes had been scattered everywhere.

The space was surrounded on all sides, including behind the ruins, with steep cliffs, all of which were dotted with harpy nests.

I could already hear their annoying shrieks echoing off the walls.

"That is a large amount of harpies. Shall we destroy them, Number 1?"

The one with the woven side ponytail, which I'm pretty sure was Number 3, addressed their leader, Number 1.

"I believe this is too high a number, even for us. Shall we retreat, John Smith?"

"No, just wait here," I responded. "I'll go the rest of the way myself."

Fortunately, there were lots of rocks and fallen trees to hide under on the way to the ruins.

"John Smith, do you wish to commit suicide? I inquire."

"John Smith is reckless, I declare."

"John Smith, if you die, we will no longer have a guide, I observe."

The one with the side buns, the one with short hair, and the one with short pigtails all protested in monotone voices.

"Relax, I have a plan. Just wait."

I pulled out the break-action gun from the bag on my back and loaded it with bullets.

It was an antique family heirloom given to me by Garohal, who had saved my life in Yorschka.

I didn't have many bullets left, but it should be enough to serve as a diversion.

I focused on my "Obscure" skill, then sank behind the rocks and fallen trees, moving from shadow to shadow.

The "Obscure" skill is rare, but it's not all that impressive.

It certainly doesn't compare with the Unique Skills that Heroes and reincarnations have.

But so far, the harpies didn't seem to have noticed me.

So that was good enough.

"*PYWEEEEYEEEE.*"

At the top of a cliff, one of the harpies let out a warning shriek.

The rest of them all spread their wings menacingly.

Damn it. How'd they spot me?

"*PYWEEEYEEE.*"

"*PYWEEEYEEE.*"

More and more of the harpies started shrieking.

"We had better act fast, I report."

"Slow and steady loses the race, I wisely impart."

The voices came from right behind me.

"What the hell are you doing here?!"

Inexplicably, Number 8 was right behind me.

And behind her, Number 6 peeked out her face as well.

"Everyone, 'Body Strengthening'! Number 6, Number 8, transport John Smith. Everyone else, activate Shield!"

Number 1 came running up to us, shouting orders.

"Run for the exit at full speed!!"

The women's Shields fended off the harpies' diving attacks, but since they were trying to protect me, the harpies' sharp claws were cutting into them.

"Are you all stupid or what?!"

As Number 6 and Number 8 carried me, I squeezed the muzzle of my gun between the shields.

"Eat this!!"

Still frustrated, I pulled the trigger.

There was a loud *boom* and some recoil.

Blood, feathers, and the shrieks of harpies filled the air.

I had managed to scare them off a little, but they didn't take much damage.

"Run while we have the chance!"

I shouted hoarsely, and every last one of us managed to tumble into the entrance of the ruins.

"…Phew."

Lying on the cold stone floor, I let out a sigh, trying to calm my anger.

"John Smith?"

Number 8 peeked down at me.

Her expression was earnest, as if she wanted to say something.

I guess even these weirdos could feel remorse.

"Don't worry about it…"

"Only a stupid person calls others stupid, I inform."

So *that's* what she wanted to say? Talk about childish.

"It appears to have been thoroughly picked over by robbers."

"Yeah, no kidding."

According to the old guy who told me about this place, investigation teams had been dispatched here at least seven times since it was discovered about three hundred years ago.

I kept mapping the place as we headed down to the bottom floor.

"A large labyrinth, I declare."

The passage, which seemed like an audience hall, was lined with waist-height stone pedestals.

"Where is our destination? I inquire."

There were rectangular outcroppings in the walls, too, but like the pedestals, they displayed nothing but dust.

"It is sad to be ignored, I entreat."

I glanced over at Number 8.

"Do you promise not to go off and do anything on your own?"

"Yes! I promise, I confirm." She nodded rapidly.

I didn't really believe her, but I decided to let it slide.

"Let's go—"

"John Smith, there is something written on the far wall, I report!"

"I told you not to go off on your own!!"

Number 8 pointed at the wall and started to run over, so I grabbed her by her collar and bopped her on the head with a fist.

"Corporal punishment is painful, I report."

"Yeah, it's supposed to be. You idiot!"

"Only an idiot calls others—"

Number 1 appeared behind Number 8 and grabbed her, pulling on her cheeks.

"Number 8, defective goods with no learning function will be punished."

"I—I am sorry, I repent. Please do not punish me, I entreat."

Number 8 trembled, apologizing desperately.

"Next time, I shall punish you without warning. Remember that."

"Y-yes, Number 1."

The tearful Number 8 clung to Number 6 and nuzzled her face into her.

I guess she learned her lesson this time.

"It looks like Shigan language, but I can't read it…"

I'd done my best to pick up basic reading skills, but I couldn't understand this gibberish at all.

I could, however, read the other, larger font that said, PLACE YOUR HAND ON THE SLATE AND PROVE THAT YOU ARE WORTHY.

The song I'd heard that had prompted me to come here contained the words *you who share my birthplace, come and find me* in Japanese, so I figured there would be some hint here for a Japanese person like me, but apparently, it wouldn't be so easy.

"Ya ka su to ma be ra shi to ro se ma…"

Number 8 started reciting some mysterious chant.

"Number 8, are your language nodes malfunctioning? I inquire."

"Number 5, I was reading these letters, I retort."

Reading the letters?

Ah, she was reading that random assortment of letters out loud— wait a minute.

"No way…"

I collapsed to the floor in disbelief.

Using diagonal writing as code in this other world… Maybe the ancestral king Yamato wasn't as ancient as I thought.

"What is the matter, John Smith?"

Without answering Number 1, I put my hand on the stone slate.

"…*Kawa.*"

I spoke a word in Japanese, and waves of light spread across the slate.

When read diagonally, the nonsense letters spelled out the riddle: "Mountains and what?"

In the Shiga Kingdom, *mountains* would be associated with *valleys*, unlike in Japan where they were associated with *rivers*, or *kawa*. So it was likely that no one had gotten the answer right before.

But any reincarnation or ancient Hero should be able to answer this question.

So there must be more mysteries beyond this point.

Suddenly, my hand on the stone slate started to sink.

"John Smith, what in the world—?"

Before Number 1 could finish her question, I was pulled inside the stone slate.

◆

"Ugh, I can't move…"

I used all my strength to try to shift my head and arms.

All I felt was cold flood under my hands.

"Mana Light."

A voice spoke, and everything around me brightened.

Number 1 and the others must have grabbed me to try to pull me out and got pulled through the stone slate along with me.

The reason I couldn't move was because they were piled on top of me.

"It appears we passed through the stone slate."

Standing up, Number 1 offered me a hand and pulled me to my feet.

"Yeah, I guess so."

I looked around the now-bright room.

It was full of strange objects that looked like they'd been made by a particularly abstract sculptor.

All of them were fixed to the floor, so they didn't look movable.

The floor seemed to be made out of large tiles, each about three feet across.

"<YOU WHO SHARE MY BIRTHPLACE, COME AND FIND ME.>"

The same lyrics I'd heard in the song at the bar were written on the wall.

At least one other person must have been here long ago, then.

"John Smith, it says, <I shall wake from my slumber when time brings about a great uprising> up there, I report."

Number 8 pointed at the ceiling.

Sure enough, there were hiragana letters carved in the ceiling.

"Tell me, Number 8."

"What is it? I inquire."

"How can you read writing that's in *Japanese*?"

Were they really reincarnations from Japan after all?

Number 8 tilted her head in confusion, then looked to Number 1 as if to ask for help.

"It was included in Language Set One."

"It was necessary to read our former master's documents, I declare."

"I enjoyed the 'classic ess-eff,' I proclaim."

"The *Joe Joe* manga was much more interesting, I insist."

The others all followed Number 1's response with comments of their own.

"Our former master who created us was a reincarnation."

The reincarnation part made sense.

But there was a more important piece of information in that statement.

"Created you?"

Was that why they all had the same face?

Did this reincarnated "former master" of theirs use magic or alchemy to make some kind of clones?

"Yes. We are homunculi. Trazayuya the elf sage neglected to finish our production, so it was our former master who took over and completed us."

"Are there others besides you?"

"Number 7 is traveling with our current master, I declare."

Oh, good.

At least there weren't huge amounts of them like in a light novel I read once.

If there were twenty thousand of these powerful fighters, they could easily topple a whole country.

"John Smith, there is a strange engraving here, I report."

The one with the bandanna—Number 4, I think—beckoned from behind one of the mystery objects.

I had almost forgotten what we were doing here.

Right now, investigating these ruins took priority over figuring out where these girls came from.

If I didn't find something of monetary value here, all the danger I'd faced to come this far would be for nothing.

"A clock face?"

Number 4 appeared to have found an object based on an old-fashioned clock.

Maybe it had something to do with the *time* mentioned on the ceiling.

"It has no hand, I declare."

Number 8 pounded on the clock.

"Hey, don't be rough with it."

I smacked the careless Number 8 on the head.

What if a guardian popped out to protect the grave or something?

"Why doesn't it have a hand, though?"

Murmuring to myself, I casually touched the clock face.

Suddenly...

A giant eyeball appeared on the clock and looked around at us so ominously, I could practically hear a *DUN-DUN-DUUUN!*

"John Smith!"

"Danger, I declare."

Number 4 and Number 8 stepped forward to protect me.

The eyeball stared at me, blinked a few times, and then suddenly changed into a mouth.

"<The time has come.>"

The enormous mouth spoke in Japanese.

The tiles on the floor whirled around, pushing us and the strange objects into the corners of the room. A black hole opened up in the center, and a faintly glowing crystal pillar emerged.

"The ancestral king Yamato—or not?"

Locked inside the crystal was a girl with long, flowing black hair.

Tch, her hair's covering all the important parts.

"She is naked, I report."

"Staring is forbidden, I proclaim."

Number 8 and Number 6 closed in on me.

"I—I wasn't staring!"

I have to admit, I regretted the words as they came out of my mouth.

It made me sound like an embarrassed virgin...although I guess that's not inaccurate.

Maybe I shouldn't have chickened out when Lilio was after me.

"John Smith!"

Just as Number 1 cried out, the panel beneath my feet started to move.

It zoomed back toward the center of the room, where the crystal pillar had finished rising.

"Whoa!"

I managed to keep my balance without falling, but when the panel stopped abruptly, I was flung forward and landed on the crystal.

As soon as I touched it, the crystal pillar faded into nothing, and the girl fell down on top of me.

As my heart pounded furiously, her lovely voice reached my ears.

"Is that you…Ichirou?"

She looked up at me with hazy eyes.

"Huh? What?"

I felt so flustered and guilty for having accidentally touched her bare skin that my head was spinning.

"You finally…found me…"

She smiled like a blooming flower, taking my breath away.

And then, without another word, the beautiful girl fainted.

Feeling a little jealous of whoever that smile was meant for, all I could do was sit there and gaze at her face until Number 8 violently took her away.

"Hey, John, buddy. Someone's over there."

Mito—the beauty who had emerged from the pillar in the Dream-crystal Mausoleum—pointed at the fog at the foot of the mountain.

She peered through the longscope that she'd produced from her Item Box.

"That flag… Is it the local army?"

"Those don't look like official military uniforms, though."

As I searched my memory, Number 1 pointed at what appeared to be soldiers.

"John, is this still the Shiga Kingdom around here?"

"Yeah. This is Lessau County."

"Are we fighting with someone?"

"Nope. Lessau County borders other Shiga Kingdom noble lands on three sides. The last side touches the Fujisan Mountains. There's no one they'd send out soldiers to fight."

I remembered the military map Lilio had shown me back in Seiryuu County as I answered Mito's question.

"John Smith, the other group has a flag of a different color, I observe."

Number 5 pointed at a separate corps that was encamped in the shadows of a forest.

"Isn't that the Seiryuu County flag?"

Seiryuu County was two territories away. Why would their army be here?

I've got a bad feeling about this.

"Let me see that."

I grabbed the longscope from Mito and pointed it at the Seiryuu County Army.

…It's her.

Short red hair.

Determined eyes that were currently trembling with anxiety.

It could be only one person…

"Lilio."

She should be in Seiryuu County. What was she doing here?

"Friend of yours?"

"Yeah, kinda. From Seiryuu City."

I answered Mito vaguely.

"Oh-ho-ho. Judging by that tone, I'm guessing you either had a crush on her, got rejected by her, or she's your ex-GF?"

I looked away from Mito's strangely excited gaze.

"…Yep. Gotta be an ex!"

Mito hit the nail on the head.

I tried to ignore her, but she just kept searching my face, so I finally admitted she was right and waved her off.

She kept pestering me, though, and I ended up giving her a quick summary of how we'd dated and broken up.

"Mito, what is a 'love confession'? I inquire."

"This 'GF' must be short for 'gravitational force,' I deduce."

Number 6 and Number 8 started peppering Mito with stupid questions.

That was fine with me, since it changed the subject and all.

"John, bad news!"

As Mito was explaining things to Number 6, she suddenly stopped and shouted at me.

Across the way, a horde of monsters came into view, tearing through the fog to attack the armies.

"It is a monster chain rampage, I report," said Number 5 as she looked through the longscope.

"Let's go, buddy!"

All eyes gathered on Mito.

"Are you serious, Mito?"

"Yeah, duh! I mean, your sweetheart is over there, right?" Mito responded without a hint of sarcasm. "So we have to go save her! You're her one and only hero, John!"

"Me, a hero? But I'm powerless."

All I've ever been able to do is obscure myself among a group so I don't have to clash with anyone. How could I be a hero?

"Look, being strong isn't what makes someone a hero. A hero is just someone who works up the courage to try and fight for the people they care about!"

Mito waved around a white staff that she appeared to have pulled out of nowhere.

"Of course, if you show me some courage, I'm willing to give you a teensy bit of help…"

Mito looked into my eyes as if to see if I was determined enough.

Time to show some guts, John Smith.

I slapped my cheeks with both hands to get myself worked up.

"Please lend me your strength, Mito."

There was more power in my voice than even I was expecting.

"You got it, buddy! I'll throw in some extra free of charge, to celebrate my awakening today!"

Mito nodded, looking satisfied with my courage.

Then she waved her wand, and particles of life showered over us.

I felt strength and courage well up in my body.

It was chant-less magic.

The secret technique that only Heroes and reincarnations could use.

But right now, I didn't care about Mito's identity.

I started running at three times my usual speed.

Wait for me, Lilio!

I'm on my way!

EX-2: Team Zena in Trouble

I knew I would be putting myself in danger when I applied to join the expedition to Labyrinth City, but I never imagined that we would encounter so many troubles along the way. And even all of that seems tame compared with what happened next...

"Zenacchi, there's a swarm of monsters coming. More than fifty fliers. On the ground there are three large ones, ten medium ones, and... more small ones than I can count. But they must be several times our unit's size. Most of them are bug types."

When Lilio returned from scouting, the numbers in her report sounded fairly hopeless.

Especially since that was only one small part of the enemy forces.

Our left flank unit consisted of twenty-four elite battle troops from Seiryuu City, along with about three hundred farmers and serfs from nearby lands who'd been conscripted as soldiers.

These new soldiers were all trembling uncontrollably.

I couldn't blame them. Monsters were probably a rare sight for them normally, and now they were being forced to fight some without any decent equipment.

"Listen, all of you, just stay alive! Don't try to be heroes by beating the enemy!"

Vice Captain Leelo shouted encouragement to our allies.

"You're lucky, all right? We've got elite soldiers here who have fought not only wyverns but real live full-grown dragons and greater demons and lived to tell the tale. A bunch of lowly monsters or an intermediate demon is nothing to be afraid of."

That seemed a little extreme to me, but it must have worked: The despair on the soldiers' faces faded, much to my relief.

I never could have imagined that I would get caught up in a battle like this when I left Seiryuu City.

◇◇◆◇A few days earlier◆◇◆◆

"We're finally going to Lessau County, Zenacchi."

"I know!"

"Lilio, do as you please on your own time, but you ought to call her Squad Leader Zena."

"Fiiine. You're so strict, Iona."

Iona scolded Lilio, as usual.

Being called Squad Leader Zena was still a little embarrassing.

It was a few months ago that we had finally managed to get chosen for the Labyrinth Elite—the nickname for Labyrinth City Celivera's Elite Training Corps.

We were to depart at the beginning of spring, but we wound up moving up the plan at the count's request.

The Elite Training Corps was made up of two knight squads with four knights and squires each; three magic squads with one magic soldier, two guards, and one scout; and one combat engineering squad. There were also two civil officials, who had a total of four servants, making for a considerably large party all told.

Before we left, Captain Delio and Vice Captain Leelo were talking about the seasons, so perhaps we left early because snow would be coming late this year.

But as if to laugh in the face of our caution, this entire journey had been a series of misfortunes.

The bandits hiding in the hills didn't attack us, perhaps because we had eight knights to our five horse-drawn carriages. The trip went well enough when we first left Seiryuu City, but as soon as we crossed the border, the world bared its fangs at us.

"I just hope we can get through here without a problem."

Judging by Lou's murmur, she was remembering the same thing.

"I know they said an injured hydra was blocking the main road, but I still think it was a mistake to take this roundabout path through the mountains instead."

Lilio sighed wearily.

"There's no helping that we were trapped in that mountain village for more than a month because of the blizzards and avalanches, but that other thing was the worst."

"You mean the summoner who was controlling the lesser demon?"

"Nah, Captain Delio took care of that no problem. She must mean the incident where the necromancer turned a whole village into zombies, right?"

"Both of those sure took up a lot of time."

Iona and Lilio debated over what Lou meant by "that other thing."

"Ah, those were both tough, too, but I was talking about that stupidly huge slime that lived in a ravine and was eating anyone who tried to cross the rope bridge."

"Oh yeah. That was awful."

"Well, our fire mage Rodril seemed to enjoy that one."

Remembering how we had nearly gotten swallowed by the spreading fire and how I had to use Wind Magic to try to stomp it out, my mood sank a little.

As I gazed at the little flowers growing along the side of the road to pacify my heart, Lilio peeked over at me.

"By the way, Zenacchi…"

"What is it?"

I was cautious as I answered. When Lilio started edging toward me like this, she never wanted to ask me anything good.

"Considering how long this is taking, aren't you worried he'll get tired of waiting?"

I tried to stay calm, but I couldn't help twitching a little in response.

What should I do? If I said, *Who'll get tired of waiting?* then she would tease me even more. But I didn't want to say, *Nobody's waiting for me*, either.

"Who do you mean will get tired of waiting?"

As I hesitated, Lou ended up asking instead.

Darn that Lou. At least Iona was kind enough to stay quiet.

Just as I feared, Lilio started smirking evilly.

"Isn't it obvious? The boy!"

Lilio refers to Mr. Satou as "the boy."

He certainly looks younger than he is, which is still younger than we are, but I don't think it's such a big difference that a baby face like Lilio should be calling him that.

It's almost like a special nickname, which bothers me for some reason.

…Maybe I'm jealous?

"What boy?"

"She's referring to Zena's sweetheart."

Iona is a big fan of gossiping about romance, so she couldn't resist answering Lou.

"Ooh, is that true, Zena?"

"No, we're not sweethearts yet."

It took everything I had to respond to Lou.

"'Not yet,' huh?"

"'Not yet,' she says."

Ooh, Lilio and Iona are so mean!

I wished they would stop teasing me about this. It was so embarrassing and painful that I felt like I might lose my mind.

Little did I know that the peaceful atmosphere of this journey would soon come to a sudden end.

◆◆◇◆In the present◇◆◇◇

"We'll strike down the foes in the air while their land troops are slowed by our traps. We don't have many archers, so we'll need Zena and Norina to knock them flat with Wind Magic. Then the knight squads will trample them immediately. The rest of you are with Vice Captain Leelo. Attack with all your might and take out as many as you can."

Captain Delio went over our battle strategy.

"Zena and Norina, once you've used your spells, focus on recovering your magic right away. Your squads are there to protect you. No matter what, don't get lured in to fighting on the front lines… Ah, it's begun."

The captain's sharp eyes glared into the morning mist.

Positioned in the center, a baron from Lessau County and his unit had engaged in battle. We could see clouds of dust rising in the mist.

"Start the chants."

Captain Delio's knight squad set out to join the fight, so Vice Captain Leelo gave us the order in a strong, masculine voice.

Norina and I started our Wind Magic chants.

I was using Fallen Hammer, and Norina was preparing Turbulence.

It was a reliable combination we often used against wyverns: Turbulence prevented them from flying, and Fallen Hammer knocked them to the ground.

The problem was that this time, there were far more flying opponents than usual.

Turbulence would probably still be effective, but Fallen Hammer had a fairly narrow range.

I had to carefully aim my staff so that the spell would strike in the center of the flock.

"......■ *Turbulence Rankiryuu!*"

"...■ ■ ■ ■ ■ ■ *Fallen Hammer Rakkitsui!*"

My magic activated right after Norina's.

Perfect, right on target.

I managed to bring most of the forty fang horseflies crashing to the ground.

Right away, the captain's squad charged in to finish off the fang horseflies in a dense wedge formation. Quick as they were in the air, the monsters moved slowly on the ground, at the mercy of the knights' spears and horses' hooves.

"Everyone, charge!"

"""*Raaaah!*"""

On Vice Captain Leelo's order, all the squads except mine and Norina's charged forward.

We had to restore our magic, so we started meditating on the spot. Using the special breathing techniques we'd learned in the army, we could restore our magic faster than usual.

This left us totally defenseless, however, hence the need for the guards.

A few fang horseflies and stray glutton dragonflies tried to attack, but Lilio's crossbow and Iona's broadsword must have kept them at bay.

I was focusing on recovering my magic behind Lou's shield. There was no way for me to really see what was going on.

But evidently, we were the only squad whose battle was going relatively well.

The right flank was first to collapse, with the center beginning to fall soon after.

We were so focused on repelling the enemy right in front of our eyes that we had no time to take stock of our allies' condition. Which meant that we started the retreat too late.

And so we were stuck at the back of the fleeing ranks.

Unconsciously, my hand went to my chest, pressing against my leather armor.

The scarf was folded up underneath.

My precious good-luck charm.

"...■ ■ ■ *Air Hammer* Kitsui."

As the monsters started to close in behind us, I mowed them down with my Wind Magic.

But no matter how many monsters I defeated, more of them came right behind.

And soon enough, I would be out of magic.

Short of a miracle occurring, it didn't seem like we would get out of this predicament alive.

But I believed that every second we kept fighting could save our comrades' lives, so I started another chant.

"...■ ■ ■ ■ *Air Cushion* Kiheki!"

I used the final dregs of my magic to cast one last spell.

It barely slowed the monsters down at all—they just scattered around it.

Even Lou's shield and Iona's broadsword couldn't stop the endless stream of monsters.

One of the creatures knocked Lilio's sword aside with its fangs and closed in on me.

Just then—

I felt a floating sensation, and we were surrounded by a flash of light and a sudden shock.

◇◇◆◇A few days earlier, in the evening◆◇◆◆

"Did something happen?"

It wasn't time for a rest yet, but for some reason, the carriage had stopped. Lilio, who had gone up ahead to see what was going on, came back with information.

"I guess we ran into a Lessau County army."

"Well, we're in Lessau County, so isn't it only natural that their armies would be around?"

"Yeah, but apparently, they've got a young boy claiming to be the count."

"I thought the count was a grown man."

"Plus, it looks like they've recently suffered a defeat..."

As we were chatting, the captain called for us.

The captain explained that Lessau City, the capital of the county, had been destroyed. Furthermore, the destruction had been wrought at the hands of a demon commanding an army of monsters.

"The culprit is an intermediate demon that's at least level 40. He's commanding an army of two hundred flying monsters and no less than twelve hundred monsters on land."

"How strong are they?"

"There were a few powerful ones among them, but most of the monsters are just slightly stronger than the average soldier at best. We don't know the details about the demon, but he seems to have a horse's head and specializes in Fire Magic. The count's entire army was destroyed by a surprise attack from the demon alone."

Everyone's expressions clouded as Captain Delio spoke.

We could probably at least hold our own against a lesser demon, but against an intermediate demon, this army didn't really stand a chance.

All of us were between levels 10 and 19, except for Captain Delio and Vice Captain Leelo, who were in the late 20s.

If we had Sir Kigouri, the strongest fighter in Seiryuu County, or one of the imperial court mages, it might've been a different story... But that would be too much to hope for. Still, I wished we at least had some mages who specialized in long-distance magic attacks or a team of archers...

But all we had were three magic soldiers, myself included, and fighters like Lilio with crossbows, poorly suited to rapid-fire attacks.

And we didn't have much magic-power capacity, so we couldn't carry on a shoot-out for long.

In short, we didn't have the right lineup to take on a big army.

"The new Count Lessau is using the Azure Pact to request that we join in the fight against the demon. We cannot renege on our agreement. We'll evacuate all noncombatants to a nearby village. It should be safer than the city area now."

The "Azure Pact" the captain mentioned was the oldest agreement in our laws, exchanged among nobles when the Shiga Kingdom was first founded.

It stated that when there was a demon to fight, all the territories would provide martial support for one another.

This pact was very rarely invoked; we learned in school that the last time it was used was in the Muno Marquisate, before I was born.

Thus, we had no choice but to join up with the army that was hurriedly put together in Lessau County's second city.

Our forces consisted of eight hundred soldiers and two thousand militia men. Though we technically outnumbered the monsters, the militia men would provide little strength in battle. It was sure to be a difficult fight.

If the demon attacked us directly, it was all over, but if we used the city walls for a siege battle, we might stand a chance.

Fortunately, this city had a magic tool for emergency communication, so we were able to send word to the royal capital and neighboring territories.

All we could do now was wait for reinforcements to come.

I was sure sure we were all banking our hopes on that.

The young Count Lessau engaged in a field battle with the monsters the next day.

Our captains tried to talk him out of it to no avail.

Satou…

I might not be able to keep my promise to meet you in Labyrinth City after all.

◆◆◇◆In the present◇◆◇◇

"Still alive, Zenacchi?"

"Yes, somehow…"

I didn't remember exactly what happened.

We were fending off monsters at the rear while the party retreated…

"Looks like Lou protected you."

"Wait a second, Lilio. You're only worried about Zena, aren't you?"

"Well, you've got the heaviest armor, Lou. Besides, it's not like Iona would ever die."

"Glad to hear you have so much faith in me."

Iona returned from the other side of the wreckage.

"It looks like that flash was a greater attack spell fired by the monsters. Without Zena's defense magic, we would have wound up joining the ranks of the dead."

Everyone was covered in dust from head to toe.

We'd managed to hang on to our lives, but just barely.

I heard the monsters getting closer. And if we moved from our position, the demon overhead would undoubtedly swoop down to attack us without mercy.

The swarms of fang horseflies and glutton dragonflies around the demon formed into three groups.

"Iona, if those come after us, we can't hold them all off."

"R-right. Miss Zena, are you able to use defense magic?"

"I should be able to use Air Cushion, at least."

I had recovered a bit of magic while I was passed out, but a single Air Cushion would be the best I could do.

But I had no time to meditate and try to recover more magic.

The monsters swarming in the sky might swoop down on us at any moment.

"Shit, they're coming on the ground, too!"

A number of large jaw crickets appeared from the shadows of the rubble.

"...■ ■■■ *Air Cushion Kiheki!*"

My Wind Magic wasn't going to be enough to fend off the flood of large jaw crickets.

"Lou, time to show them what we're made of."

"Right!"

Just as the giant crickets broke through my Air Cushion, Lou's shield pushed them back, and Iona's broadsword whirled through them like a storm.

But that still wasn't enough to stop them all.

A few large jaw crickets managed to slip past them and charge toward us.

"I won't let you near Zenacchi!"

Lilio thrust her short sword into one of the large jaw crickets.

I drew my sword, too, barely able to fend them off.

Then another large jaw cricket charged toward Lilio's blind spot, gnashing its teeth.

"Lilio!!"

My cry drew her attention to the monster at the moment it was clos-ing in, and her face froze.

"Lilioooooo!"

Shouting suddenly, someone bathed in white light jumped in between her and the creature.

A young man with black hair.

...Satou?

No, he had similar facial features, but it wasn't him.

Satou would never make such a wild, frantic expression.

"John?"

"Don't let your guard down, damn it."

So close their lips were almost touching, Lilio and the boy exchanged breathless words.

At that moment, another monster closed in on them.

"On your right, you two!"

Just as I shouted, more than ten arrows came flying out of nowhere, transparent as glass.

In the blink of an eye, the arrows turned the monsters on the ground into corpses.

"Please save your flirting for later."

"We are in the midst of battle, I declare."

"I'm not flirting, okay?"

Seven magic soldiers in overcoats appeared, laying waste to the sur-rounding monsters with weapons that glowed with a mystical light.

Slashing monsters in half with a speed that belied their weapons' weight, they moved far faster than Captain Delio or Vice Captain Leelo, maybe even rivaling the powerful Sir Kigouri.

The black-haired boy who had saved Lilio didn't move with nearly as much grace, but the shining sword in his hand still sliced up monsters with ease in a single stroke.

"Mito's support magic is impressive, I praise."

"Yeah, no kidding... Wait, where did she go?"

"Above, I report."

"Above?"

Following the black-haired boy's gaze to the sky, I saw a black-haired young woman standing in midair.

She was dressed like a lesser noble, holding a long, straight staff that looked like just an ordinary pole.

And though she was facing off against a demon in midair, her expression looked entirely unruffled.

In fact, something about her reminded me of Satou.

"Hey, where'd the monsters in the sky go?"

"That black-haired woman defeated them all."

I overheard Lou and Iona talking.

I was so entranced by the woman that I hadn't noticed. But they were right: That enormous swarm of fang horseflies and glutton dragonflies had disappeared.

"*FWOONWYOOOO.*"

"Yeah, right! Break Magic!!"

The intermediate demon unleashed a giant Fire Magic spell that seemed to scorch the sky, but the black-haired woman made it vanish with a wave of her staff.

Almost like *the ancestral king in the legends.*

"Multiple Javelins…"

At least fifteen short, transparent javelins shot forth from around the girl.

The intermediate demon flailed desperately to avoid the shots.

"…with a bonus Divine Lance!"

Three enormous lances the size of barrier posts appeared around the black-haired woman.

"*Gooooooo!*"

Her long black hair fluttered, and one of the giant lances flew toward the demon at an incredible speed.

The intermediate demon managed to dodge the giant lance with a birdlike swoop, but in his distraction, he was hit by several of the Multiple Javelins from behind, piercing his body.

The second giant lance smashed right through the intermediate demon's upper body, and the third scattered the demon's remains as they blackened and turned to ash, disappearing into the sky.

"…Shoot!"

The black-haired boy looked up at the sky and clicked his tongue.

Above us, the black-haired woman was staggering in midair.

"That idiot, pushing herself when she just woke up!"

"All hands, destroy remaining enemies while rescuing Miss Mito!"

""""Understood, we report."""""

The blond magic soldiers ran toward the falling black-haired woman.

"Wait!"

The black-haired boy started to run after them, but Lilio grabbed him and held him back.

"Hold on! It is you, isn't it, John Smith?"

Oh right—that boy was Lilio's former sweetheart!

"Sorry, Lilio. I'll have to explain next time."

The black-haired boy—John Smith—stroked Lilio's hair gently.

"Don't do anything crazy until then, got it?"

He gave a small smile, then let go of Lilio's hand and ran after the magic soldiers.

"Anyone who's still alive, speak up! We're going to rescue our comrades trapped under the gravel!"

I heard Vice Captain Leelo shouting from the other side of the rubble.

One after another, men and women I couldn't see called out in response.

From the looks of things, we were saved.

Without this miraculous stroke of luck, we would surely have met our deaths on this battlefield like all the others.

…I have to get stronger.

At least strong enough to fight a demon.

We will get stronger, in memory of the comrades we lost.

Next time, we'll be the ones who bring forth a miracle!

Afterword

Hello, this is Hiro Ainana.

Thank you for picking up *Death March to the Parallel World Rhapsody*, Volume 12!

I'm very short on pages this time around, so I'll keep observations about this volume brief.

After putting a stop to a demon's plot in the previous volume, Satou and friends finally get to go back to training and prepare to eventually fight a floormaster.

During these preparations, they'll be reunited with some old friends, get some new equipment and techniques, and fight powerful enemies...

Of course, there are plenty of heartwarming moments and daring rescues, as usual. I've used the web novels as a basis while adding new episodes and rearranging some things, and at the end of the volume, there are two brand-new short stories where we get to see some familiar faces.

Also, the anime will start airing next month, so please check it out!

Finally, the usual thank-yous! To my editors A and I, the illustrator shri, and everyone else who was involved in the production, sales, marketing, and multimedia aspects of this book: Thank you all so much!

And of course, to all you readers. Thank you very much for reading all the way to the end!

Let's meet again in the EX volume, which will be a collection of various short stories as well as a brand-new novella!

Hiro Ainana

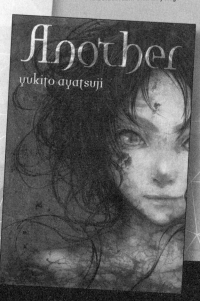

US $14.00 CAN $18.50

ISBN 978-1-9753-0165-1

EAN

9 781975 301651

51400 >

WITH FRIENDS LIKE THESE...

With the demon threat neutralized, relative peace has returned to Labyrinth City, allowing the residents to shift their focus back to the labyrinth itself. Between the mysterious chain rampages and the untimely appearances of several areamasters, though, the deeper levels prove more of a challenge than anyone bargained for! Looks like it's time for Satou and the others to head back to Bolenan Forest for some specialized training with the elves!